FRACTURED PROMISES

ALI PIERCE

♡ Ali Pierce

Fractured Promises

Copyright © 2019 by Ali Pierce

ISBN: 978-1-7337879-0-1

Editing: Jenn Wood

Editing/proofreading: Karen Gill

Cover Design: Sarah Hansen, *Okay Creations*

For my husband,
My heart is yours
today, tomorrow & always

PROLOGUE

PATIENCE.

It bought me perfection.

Perfection threatened by a few cheap, ink-stained papers belonging to an unworthy opponent.

Conquer and destroy, my game of choice. Win at all costs.

I finger the photo, turning my attention to the smiling face. I study it, looking for flaws. A laughing smile, one I know well, sits on a younger face.

I look at the papers, their existence mocking me. Impulse tells me to tear them up. Light them on fire. Burn this secret and let the ashes scatter in the wind. But I know better than to burn artifacts. I enjoy possessing expensive things, and this information is priceless.

When the time is right, I will share my treasures and revel in the devastation they create.

I gather the papers, carefully placing them into the folder from which they came. I meticulously avoid the photo as it slides away.

I am an opportunist, and what's the old saying?

Finders keepers...

1

KATE

NINE. NINE BOXES OF TAMPONS. FIVE DIFFERENT BRANDS. Super, super plus, regular. Crushed boxes, unopened boxes, a box housing one meager occupant.

"If anything, I'm prepared, though a little neurotic in my hoarding of tampons."

Amy, my best friend, isn't fazed by my neurosis. "When the Land Shark apocalypse hits, I'm staying with you. You'll be the only woman on Earth not waving the proverbial red flag."

I throw the remaining feminine hygiene products in a box, write "Bathroom" in big black letters on top, and add it to the pile near the front door.

"Moving stinks. Deciding what possessions to keep, recycle, or trash is *soooo* not my strength. I'd rather write a manual called *How to Bring Yourself to Orgasm in Thirty Seconds*, publish it in my own name, and display it on the bulletin board at the local church."

"When you finally get around to publishing that unicorn, let me know. I'm one-clicking it—in more ways than one if you know what I mean."

Amy raises a perfectly sculpted auburn eyebrow as if to say,

Remember Dick Quick, Tinder fail? Dick had crossed the "finish line" before Amy's second shoe hit the floor. Her review, if Tinder had them, would have screamed, "Clam Jammed by a Shoe."

"If you're only here for my top-secret book titles, you'll need to buy me dinner, not lurk in my bathroom, directing me how to pack feminine hygiene products."

"I think we deserve a break." Amy's willowy frame sinks into the oversized cushions of my leather couch.

I take a seat, ending up on top of her as the cushions engulf me.

She squints at me and chuckles. "I love you, Kate, but that's not the type of break I was suggesting."

We sit in comfortable silence as I look at bare walls that have heard my fears, felt my pain, and seen my tears. In a relatively quiet neighborhood, the converted townhouse, in the heart of Milwaukee, has been perfect for me. I will miss its comfort and familiarity.

Until sixty-four days ago, this had been my haven. Walking away from the contentment this place represents will be harder than I anticipated. Not for the first time, my gut tells me this move is going to change me.

"I didn't think I would ever consider moving to Chicago. It terrifies me, but also makes me feel energized and free. Is that stupid?"

Amy is the only soul who knows my history. She understands how a move has the potential to upset the fragile balance of my carefully cultivated happiness.

"What? Don't tell me you're scared of shacking up with your best friend."

I shoot Amy the stink-eye. "More like scared to see *who* my best friend likes to invite into her *shack*."

"Honey, a few weeks living with me and *my shack* won't be the only one giving out the invitations." Chuckling, Amy grabs my hand. "All kidding aside. You are my person. I will never let anything or *anyone* hurt you."

My eyes burn as I run a finger over the couch. "When I met you, I was broken and lost. You, my friend, were a gift to my soul. You will always be *my* person."

Amy wipes wetness from her eyes. "All this seriousness is making me hungry. How about Chinese carryout?"

"My treat. Consider it payment for your FPO—feminine product organization."

Amy uses her teeth to crack a fortune cookie and pull out the paper words of wisdom.

Revulsion contorts my face. "Is that sanitary? You know the paper is probably recycled from gum wrappers peeled from the shoes of Times Square tourists, right?"

"Hush. You're killing my fun. This right here is the best part of the night." She grabs her stomach and wrinkles her nose. "We both know it isn't the shrimp fried rice. Seriously. Yung Kong's messes it up. Every. Single. Time."

"I tried to remind you their shrimp and your stomach don't mix. It's not my fault you insisted on ordering it."

Amy looks at the paper, taking a moment before jumping into character. "Words pave the path to truth. Choose wisely." Her voice a spot-on impression of Master Yoda in both delivery and execution.

"Wow. That's deep."

I throw a napkin at her face, which completely misses the mark and flutters to her feet. Picking up my iced tea, I toy with the straw, while similar words creep from the corner of my mind.

I choose you. I want you. I love you.

Amy pops the remaining half of the cookie in her mouth

and jumps to her feet. "My butt better get on the road. My car isn't going to drive itself, even though that would be pretty cool."

I clear the dinner mess before meeting Amy at the door as she slips gloves over her fingers.

She shoots me a grin as she rocks on her toes. "Are you sure you want to give up my awesome packing and organizational skills? I can stay through tomorrow."

"Nope. Your help has been awesome. I'll be Chicago-bound in three, maybe four days tops." I lean in and give her a quick hug. "Thank you for being my person."

"Ditto. I'm excited to have you with me again!" Amy's squeal is so childlike, it pulls a smile from my lips.

"Do you need anything for the drive? Bottle of water? Stick of gum?"

Amy gives me a playful wink. "What I need, no *woman* can provide. See you later, sister."

I watch as she steps out the door and disappears down my front steps.

I love that girl.

As I pad to my bathroom, I send up a silent prayer of thanks for meeting my best friend the last year of college. Even though we were opposites, our friendship was instant, and our differences fueled an unconditional bond. Together, we've endured life-altering trials and found the strength to deal with our pasts and move forward.

As I wash my face and brush my teeth, my mind ponders the twisted path my life has taken. Truly in awe of the positive turns, I'm painfully aware of how easily my life could splinter. If I become too comfortable or someone manages to slip past my meticulously crafted public persona, my world could crumble.

Events in my past obliterated my dreams, leaving me jaded and mistrustful. What started as a therapeutic escape turned into a lucrative career. I wrote my golden ticket to a new life. For fourteen years, the public has known me as enigmatic Kennedy Willow, *New York Times* best-selling author.

An ironclad non-disclosure agreement, backed by a stipend larger than most house payments, works to maintain my privacy while giving Jennifer Slater, a Wisconsin housewife, notoriety and financial freedom. Few people know the stunning beauty on my book jackets is not me, but a carefully chosen substitute.

For the past five years, I reveled in the comfort of my life. Writing and living with a watchful eye, with little fear of discovery. Until sixty-three days ago. One newspaper headline threw me directly into the past, stirring up memories I had methodically repressed. My perfectly constructed, quaint Milwaukee life had threatened to crumble.

The day after my newspaper sighting, I planned and launched *Project: Relocation Kate.* Like cogs in an expensive time-piece, I executed my plan with precision. Housing secured. Current lease paid. Movers hired.

Amy had been skeptical when I explained I needed a change. I suspect intuition allowed her to see the hidden meaning in my explanation. She could have questioned my motives, but out of respect, she chose not to ask.

I was moving because of *him.*

Keeper of my past and swindler of my dreams.

I pull my favorite shorts and threadbare Northwestern swim team T-shirt from my drawer, then shed my clothes. I slide the cotton over my head indulging in the softness as it skims my skin. The shirt, a tangible extravagance I allow from my past.

I slide between my sheets, pulling my pillow to my chest.

Releasing the lock on my heart, I give myself over to jagged memories as I slowly drift to sleep.

2

KATE

"Yes, I'll have it to you in fourteen days."

"Perfect, that's what I like to hear. Now, there's a magazine that would like—"

"Absolutely not, Janet!" I cut off my publisher. "You know better than to ask."

I impatiently drum my fingers on the steering wheel of my Range Rover Velar, one of my only splurge purchases outside of designer purses. If I can carry a small toddler in it, it's mine. Don't ask me why. Big purses are my kryptonite.

"But, Kennedy…"

"I don't do interviews, *ever*! Don't ask again."

When did Janet lose her ever-loving mind?

I hit the "End" button on the steering wheel with such force, my nail breaks. *Great.* Pissed doesn't describe my current mood. If she doesn't get her crap together, our business relationship will be finished. Interviews have always been *off-limits*.

My move to Chicago had gone off without a hitch. A month of living together, and Amy and I hadn't killed our friendship or each other. A huge plus in the "win" column.

The only downside has been her frequent travel, a byproduct of owning her own public relations firm.

Currently in Los Angeles, she's pulling a newbie athlete out of the fire for posting pictures of his new Ferrari, *and* its license plate, on social media. Little does he know, she'll be raking him over the coals herself for his stupidity. It's like an athlete's common sense flows right out the end of his pen when he endorses his first paycheck.

"Come *on!*" I honk my horn, wondering why I'm moving at a snail's pace.

Friday afternoon traffic is a bear as it is, but to top it off, I'm dealing with a major block in outlining my new project, and my mind is unsettled.

I hadn't volunteered since leaving Milwaukee, and my mental state was starting to teeter. A basic web search retrieved two local places that looked promising. Too antsy to wait until Monday, I had taken off in search of a place where I could help kids and get my mind back on track.

When was the last time I took time like this for me? Note to self: More Kate time.

Hope blooms in my chest as excitement rolls through me. The weather is unseasonably warm for early March. I roll down my window, relishing the crisp air as it gently raises the hairs on my arm.

I slow my car as I approach my destination, surveying the nondescript metal building. According to the website, Beacon is a center specializing in providing teens an inviting, safe place for fun and recreation. The pictures on the website were impressive, and I'm surprised such a facility is available for Chicago's youth. Full athletic facilities, a swimming pool, a smoothie-slash-coffee bar, and a media lab were all available and free of charge for any local teen. This place would have been my haven during my teenage years.

I take a left into the parking lot, then pull into the first open spot. As first impressions go, the building is boring and doesn't live up to the shiny website pictures. The excitement previously generated dims as I look at the outside of the building. I have a feeling my next volunteer gig may not be with Beacon. This place is the antithesis of a fun, hip youth center.

I step out of my car, narrowly avoiding the puddle outside my driver door. It seems I found the reason for the parking spot's vacancy.

I check my scrap of paper. Looks like I need to find a guy named Jon Logan. According to the website, he's been the director since Beacon opened a little over two years ago.

I walk through the front door, and my jaw drops. Guiltily, I rescind my thoughts I had moments ago in the parking lot. This place is stunning. The large common area looks more suited to a tech company in Silicon Valley than a rec center for teens.

"Excuse me. May I help you?"

Startled, I turn in the direction of a throaty, masculine voice, and come face-to-face with deep chocolate eyes attached to a perfect specimen of male beauty. I am rarely at a loss for words, but my vocal cords are struck silent by the man before me.

Recovering quickly, I give him a tentative smile, then extend my hand. "Hi. I'm Kate Waters. I'd like to find out how to become a volunteer. I'm looking for Mr. Jon Logan? Could you point me in his direction?"

"I could." His full lips give a sexy twitch.

"OK?"

"I could, but then I'd lose your attention." The gorgeous man flashes me a wide, inviting smile. "Might I propose a deal? Let me give you a behind-the-scenes tour of our facility. It'll be fifteen minutes, max. When we're done, I'll deposit you at the door of Mr. Logan's office. Sound like a plan you can live with?"

Thrown off and feeling unsure of his intentions, I search his face, starting at his artfully styled, dirty blond hair and ending at his blinding white teeth.

"Fifteen minutes? We'll be in plain sight of others the entire time? And you'll introduce me to Mr. Logan at the end of the tour?"

Adonis, in the flesh, nods.

He's a stranger...but we won't leave the premises. Others will see us. Fifteen minutes. I can, and will, do this.

I give him a forced smile hoping it doesn't look as awkward as it feels on my face. "OK, stranger, let's see what this place has to offer."

Less than five minutes into the tour, I'm in awe. Adonis speaks animatedly of the facility and greets each teen we pass. It's obvious he genuinely enjoys being here.

My excitement builds. This place is nothing like I expected, given the look of the building's exterior.

During the tour, I see a full basketball court, an Olympic-sized swimming pool with adjoining locker rooms, and a media lounge equipped with every gaming system known to man. Large, oversized couches and a huge TV that could show an Avengers movie in full scale complete the space.

The ultimate, drool-worthy area for me is, by far, the technology lab, which is tricked out with top-of-the-line iMacs *and* PCs. I could volunteer *and* write here, if Mr. Logan agrees.

I imagine all the positive vibes Beacon brings to the neighborhood youth. I may ugly cry if this place isn't looking for volunteers.

As the tour comes to a close, we stop at an open doorway leading into a large office with a group of comfortable-looking chairs, a large drafting table, and a huge TV mounted on one wall. Next to the door is a plaque, which reads "Jon Logan, Director." It seems Adonis is a man of his word.

"I strung it out as long as possible. Unless I can interest you in seeing rooms housing the furnace, pool pumps, and cleaning supplies?"

I give him a small smile and scan the empty office. "It looks like Mr. Logan is out. Do you know when I'll be able to speak with him?"

"Two, maybe three seconds."

Adonis gives a playful wink and walks into the office. Turning to face me, he folds his arms across his wide chest as he leans against the drafting table.

"Now, Ms. Waters, I heard you were looking for me?"

3

SHAW

I GLANCE AROUND THE CONFERENCE ROOM AS MY CFO, STUART Johnson, gives his quarterly report. Normally, concentration is not a problem for me. On any given day, I eat, sleep, and drink work. Today is not one of those days.

My mindfuck of a dream last night resulted in a five-mile run and a grueling fifty laps in the pool, all before five a.m. It's only nine in the morning, and my sleep-deprived brain is wreaking havoc on my concentration.

The second Stuart finishes his projection report, I flip my computer closed and stand up. "Looks like you're still earning your six-figure salary. Your employment is safe for at least another week."

Stuart gives a hearty laugh.

My employees are familiar with my quick wit and sometimes off-color humor. They know I expect perfection, but I can infuse humor when a situation needs levity.

"Late night?" Stuart questions as he closes his laptop and waits for my response.

"Something like that." Giving him a forced nod, I walk out and head for my office, praying I avoid any employees who could potentially slow my progress. I sense today isn't going to get any better.

The couch in my office beckons me. I am looking forward to locking my door and taking a fifteen-minute power nap before my next round of meetings.

One foot through my office door and my plan dies a quick death. My already somber mood darkens to the color of midnight. My ex-wife, Elizabeth, perches on the edge of the couch, like a queen awaiting her subjects. Elizabeth showing up unexpectedly, while infrequent, is never a good thing. My fatigued brain needs to be in top form when verbally sparring with the woman I had been chained to for ten years of my life.

"What? No smile? No kiss for your wife?" Thinly veiled sarcasm hides behind a saccharine smile.

Pity how I never recognized the woman for the conniving, controlling witch she is before we got married. In truth, I know why I overlooked her flaws. She was sex in a skirt. Knockout body, blonde hair, green eyes. With her coloring and personality, she was a polar opposite of the woman I desperately wanted to forget.

Except, I didn't forget her. Not once in the past sixteen years. I hadn't been ready to be a father and didn't expect to become one at the time I did. Circumstance didn't care and hadn't given me a choice. Elizabeth had been willing to make things work. She gave me the impression she would be a great mom, and she had been damn good at fulfilling my physical needs in the bedroom. Always available for a fast, dirty fuck.

Deep down, I knew time would breed regret for our relationship. Yet, I powered ahead, believing it would ultimately close the door on my past.

As much as I didn't mind drowning in regret, my number one consideration had been for my little girl. She became my everything. From the first time I held Sarah's small body, I loved her.

Elizabeth had proven to be an Oscar-caliber actress, abandoning any pretense of loving Sarah after we married. Her irrational jealousy grew exponentially, eventually draining my interest, both in and out of the bedroom.

Elizabeth spent her energy wasting my money while trying to mold Sarah into a prim, spoiled society darling. Luckily, Sarah's strong will and stubbornness foiled Elizabeth's plans.

Too late, I realized Elizabeth was neither a child whisperer nor a satisfying bed partner. It had taken me years, but I eventually became wise to her calculated manipulations. Sarah had been Elizabeth's meal ticket, and I'd been too jaded and emotionally detached to see it. Divorcing Elizabeth and obtaining full custody was a choice I made a little over two years ago.

"Earth to Shaw. Have you heard a word I've said since you walked in here?"

Mentally preparing for the conversation that was guaranteed to incite a migraine, I turned to Elizabeth. "What are you doing in my office?"

"I want to talk about Sarah."

That had my attention. Elizabeth rarely made an effort to consult me about Sarah, and I didn't willingly provide information. My attorney had strongly advised me to send all communications through him, following a heated phone exchange I had with Elizabeth three months ago. Her attorney had served me with documents petitioning to re-open custody proceedings. I had been livid and let my anger overrule my common sense.

Nothing Elizabeth said could convince me of her sincerity toward Sarah. My desire to eliminate emotional disruptions from Sarah's life is the only reason I will entertain this conversation.

"Considering Sarah is a topic we rarely discuss, can you narrow the scope of your statement? Clue me in as to why you suddenly give a shit? You've seen her, what, four times in the past three months? You don't even have custody of her."

Elizabeth's eyes narrow. "No, I don't have custody right now, but it's still anyone's game."

My teeth threaten to crack as I clench my jaw. "That's the problem. Sarah and her living arrangements are *not a game*."

She rolls her eyes and re-adjusts her slim skirt. "You know what I mean. Don't be so dramatic."

I narrowly keep my anger in check while Elizabeth launches into an over-the-top, rehearsed speech, sounding more like a political pitch for thousands than a conversation with her ex-husband. "She's a strong-willed young woman, who has no desire to fit in with our circle of friends and their kids. She cares more about her 'volunteerism' than cultivating important friendships with the right type of kids. She hasn't attended one fundraiser I've organized. People are noticing, and they are starting to talk."

She brushes an imaginary piece of lint from her sleeve before she continues. "I think it best to cut off any gossip before it becomes problematic. Immediate enrollment in Easton Prep would be a good way to show she's serious about blending in with her peers. To achieve that goal, I'm willing to have her live with me during the week and visit you on the weekends."

My head throbs as my heart beats so wildly I can feel it at the side of my temple. I walk over to Elizabeth and lean into her space. A subtle reminder she can't manipulate me like she did in the past.

"Let me see if I have this straight." My voice is a calm breeze that belies my festering rage. She sits, clueless, in front of me. Ignorant of the storm her little speech has brought.

"Sarah has no interest in being around the spoiled, pampered peers in your 'circle.' *People* have started to talk? Translation: People have begun to talk about *you*."

A smoldering fire shines from Elizabeth's eyes as her smile falters, but I keep going. "You want to *help* Sarah by throwing her into a corrupt private school that has more kids on Xanax than a mental institution?"

Elizabeth's body grows rigid with anger.

"Speaking of Xanax, are you high? You openly admitted she's not the type of daughter you wished to have." I pin her with an icy stare. "The day I agree to your insane recommendations for Sarah is the day my body is lowered into a cold, dark grave. *Get. The. Hell. Out.*"

Elizabeth stands tall, shoulders back, as she walks to my office door. I follow a good distance behind so I won't be tempted to reach forward and choke the life out of her.

At the door, Elizabeth makes a last-ditch effort to sway me. "You think she'll be accepted within our social circle as an adult? No man of any worth will touch her if he thinks she doesn't have the training and discipline to be a society wife."

"If I can save her from a loveless, empty marriage like ours, I will consider my job, as her dad, a success."

Elizabeth's cheeks turn red, yet she holds her tongue, knowing my anger has reached the boiling point.

"Consider this a warning. The next time you think about stopping by my office unannounced, consider what your *circle* of friends will say as security escorts you out the front door."

I barely restrain myself from slamming the door in her face. She is still Sarah's mother, even if she *was* the biggest mistake of my life.

"I've always prided myself on keeping my disdain for Elizabeth in check. I must admit it's a feat equal to holding back a lion on the way to a kill, but I can't keep this to myself. What a *biznotty*!"

I clench my teeth and manage a choked swallow, saving Vet from being sprayed by the gulp of beer I'd just pulled from my bottle. "Excuse me? Come again?"

"You know, a *bitch!*"

I smirk and tip my bottle toward him. "Why didn't you say that in the first place?"

He lifts his shoulder. "What? I'm keeping it real. That's the word on the street."

"You live in a brownstone, dumbass, not on the street. I swear, a few more years, and I'll need an urban dictionary to translate a conversation with you."

My best friend, Vet—V, to me—chuckles as I scan the bar. A bit trendy for my taste, but it has a comfortable vibe and isn't far from my office, making it the ideal place for drinks after work.

"How is our place doing?"

Vet smirks. "Other than the occasional visit from an overbearing silent partner, it's doing great."

"As *the* silent partner, I feel it necessary to say you may need to find a new director. Last time I was there, he was messing around and joking with the members. Very unprofessional. I feel it's my duty to report him."

Scratching his eyebrow with his middle finger, Vet uses his other hand to pick up his beer. "All joking aside, the place is doing better than projected. New donations have put improvements ahead of schedule. Volunteerism is increasing, which, as you know, is a necessity for our success. In fact, I met with a promising new volunteer prospect this week."

His excitement for Beacon is contagious. After thirteen years, my best friend and business partner remains a passionate visionary, with Beacon being our most recent business venture.

I feel the increased stares from women the longer we sit shooting the shit at our high top. Two good-looking, professional men are like sitting ducks to women looking for a Friday night hookup. V's charisma is like a homing beacon. While my confidence and natural authority make me less approachable, I'm still recognized as a viable challenge.

The brown eyes of an attractive blonde meet mine from across the room. I return her smile and look away before she takes my politeness as an invitation. While I've been divorced for two years, I'm still not willing to jump into the fire of another relationship. Not even for brown-eyed, red-lipped, Busty Blondie.

I peruse the bar and hide a smirk behind my second bottle of beer. "It looks like the lionesses are out for the hunt. For your sake, I should get my cock-blocking, uninterested ass out of here. If we sit together much longer, your female prospects may mistake us for a couple."

Vet smirks. "I love you, man, but you had five more minutes to get lost before I escorted you out myself. The object of tonight's affections should be walking through the door soon."

I raise an eyebrow. "Not a desperate clinger from one of your dating apps, I hope?"

"Damn, I hope not. Jack set it up. Says she's a feisty redhead who seems fun but is a ballbuster when it comes to keeping his public image clean."

"She must be good. I've never heard anything remotely dirty touch his name, on or off the United Center's ice."

V's eyebrows dance as a devious smirk crosses his full lips. "Let's hope she saves the dirty bits for her own personal life, shall we?"

With a low chuckle, I take a final pull from my beer, throw three ten-dollar bills on the table, and head for the exit. I'm nearly to the door when a redheaded beauty stumbles through. She'd been looking down, texting on her phone, when the heel of her impossibly high stilettos caught on the doormat. As she rights herself, she looks up, and I'm eye level with piercing green eyes that challenge me to laugh at her clumsy entry.

I smile and give her a quick nod as I walk out of the bar. Looks like V's night of fun is just beginning.

Lucky bastard.

4

SHAW

I STARE STRAIGHT AHEAD AS THE TREADMILL WHIRLS BENEATH my feet. The large screen mounted on the gym's wall does nothing to hold my interest. After the nightmare I had last week, I need to get my thoughts back on track. Otherwise, my treadmill distances will rival that of an Olympic marathon runner.

I hadn't had the dream in a good six months. *Why now?* My mind rolls through the events of my dream. After sixteen years, I know it like the back of my hand.

"I don't want the summer to end." Her voice was a whisper as her naked body snuggled into my side beneath our blanket on the dock.

I stared out at the blue water. Since childhood, the water held a magic calming effect for me. I remember staring at it, for hours, from my window at the lake house.

I remained quiet, trying to puzzle out my dilemma. What was I going to do? I was supposed to report to work at Pierce Graham, my family's yacht building company, in four days. My next twelve months guaranteed rigorous domestic and international training, and no time for Kate.

I never realized the ability to fall in love resided within me. With Kate, my desire to love her, and be loved by her, had happened overnight.

Seeing her rushing through the dining room at White Eagle Inn, in her conservative skirt and button-down blouse had instantly piqued my interest. Her petite frame, wavy dark hair, and full lips caught me like flypaper. But what truly captivated me was the calming intensity of her piercing blue eyes, which reminded me of the Caribbean waters I had seen on a family trip to Aruba. Just like the water, staring at her eyes calmed my mind.

Intending to decompress after graduation, I planned a week-long visit to our family cottage. By day three, I met Kate, the beautiful, shy girl who derailed every one of my summer plans. That one week turned into two and a half months.

Her innocent shyness, mistaken for aloof indifference to my dogged advances, lit a fire within me. It took every trick in my well-used arsenal to convince her to have dinner with me. One dinner. That's all it took for me to see the life I had planned would be a pale substitute to the one I could have with her by my side.

Kate was a hard worker, determined to make her mark on the world. A junior studying business at Marquette University, she was already making plans for her life. The first being independence and space from her mom's depression. Kate worked a summer job at White Eagle Inn in Fish Creek, Wisconsin, taking advantage of the provided employee housing. An added bonus? Her cottage was less than a mile from my lake house. A convenience I utilized often. Kate kissed me as she climbed over me, straddling my lap.

"I'd say, 'A penny for your thoughts,' but judging by your emotional distance, I'm afraid you'd laugh and charge me a hundred bucks."

"Just thinking about the future. Looking for the best solution to our distance. You'll be in Milwaukee. I'll be who knows where in the world. My dad will be tough, but I know it's his way of preparing me for when I take his place."

She smirked at me. "I'm absolutely positive you will exceed his expectations, but only if you're up for the challenge." She already understood me better than anyone, and knew teasing me with a challenge was my weakness. Case in point, the swimming debacle that ended with me naked in Lake Michigan and Kate holding every stitch of my clothing as she laughed hysterically from the shore.

I nuzzled her neck, inhaling the smell of coconut. A scent I would forever associate with our first summer together. "You'll hear from me so often, you'll be sick of me."

I gripped her hips and looked directly into her deep blues. "We have three more days. You and me. Let's enjoy the time we have." I leaned in, placing soft kisses along her neck as I whispered across her skin, "You're it for me. You hold my heart. Every. Single. Piece. Hold it safe. Hold it steady. And we'll never be apart."

Kate placed her hands on my cheeks and tilted forward, gently brushing her lips across mine. "This summer has been the best time of my life. Going without my next breath would be easier than letting you go. I may hold your heart, but yours makes mine beat."

The incessant buzzing of my heart monitor pulls me from the memories. Blinking a few times, I look at the treadmill screen. I've clocked almost fifteen miles in the past two hours. Excessive, even for me.

I hit the button and start my cool down, willing my brain to lock away the memories my heart is unwilling to forget.

I walk into my condo, throwing my keys and mail on the credenza just inside the door. Today has been another long day. I hope my date with the treadmill bought me a full night's sleep.

Sarah should be home, but I don't hear her musical soundtrack filtering from her bedroom.

Walking down the hallway, I hear Sarah's voice. While it's impossible, it sounds like she's talking to someone. She knows my rule for visitors—no dad, no visitors. I don't intend to eavesdrop, but my anger at her disregard for my rules glues my feet to the floor. As I listen, my ears buzz.

"I hate that he's like that. I wish I could help him be happy.

I believe he thinks he'll give me the wrong idea. I wish he'd realize I'm not going to be around forever."

Who is she talking to? Is she being pressured by a hormone-ridden boy? My fists clench. Sounds like I need to pay a visit to some little bastard. I knock and push the door wide open. Sarah sits on her bed, alone, cell phone pressed to her ear.

"Gotta go, my dad just got home." Sarah ends the call and stares at her phone, refusing to look at me. She's embarrassed. My skin prickles. Maybe my brain's colossal jump wasn't far off. If some guy is pressuring my daughter, I'll cut off his balls with a butter knife.

I school my face into a forced, but neutral expression. "I'm going to order a pizza. Ham and pineapple good for you?"

"Yeah. Thanks."

Just as I turn to go, Sarah's quiet voice hits my ears. "Dad? How do you know if a guy is really happy?"

Uh, where the hell did that come from?

Taking a deep breath, I turn to face her, praying I don't screw this up. Like a soldier in a minefield, I wade into the conversation, hoping to avoid epic failure. I have no idea how to answer her question, so I opt for humor. "Happy with his dinner choice? Cellular plan? The number of likes on his recent social media post?"

"Dad, stop! I need you to be serious."

"Um. I would say if he laughs often. Has a couple close friends. Those could be a few checks in life's happy column." Sarah picks at her jeans, still unwilling to make eye contact. Taking a breath, I continue. "Ultimately, happiness is a perception. A perception that hinges on circumstance. One man's happiness could be anguish for another."

Where did that philosophical crap come from? And why didn't I bite my tongue before all of it flew from my lips? I sincerely hope my half-assed attempt answers her question.

She raises her eyes to mine and gives me a small smile. "Ok. Thanks."

I turn and walk to the kitchen on lead feet. In this circumstance, Elizabeth would be no help, nor would I ask her for one piece of advice about Sarah.

In times like this, I wish my sister was available. She'd research this shit, scan blog posts, and survey friends before giving the best advice in this situation.

Sadly, tonight, I feel like a poor man's substitute.

SHAW

ENGULFED BY THE LEATHER COUCH IN MY OFFICE, SARAH'S fingers fly across her phone screen as she shoots off texts with the precision of a seasoned firing squad. Her hair, the color of melted chocolate, falls across her cheek, hiding her small, pert nose.

Her preoccupation gives me a chance to study her. My daughter has transformed into a beautiful young woman. Her teenage frame hides the skinny arms and knobby knees of her youth.

Belatedly realizing Sarah's fingers are frozen over her phone, I glance away as I walk in and sit behind my desk.

She looks at me as a small half-grin ghosts over her lips. "Haven't you heard a picture lasts longer?"

Her crystal, robin's egg blue eyes steal my attention. Almost too large for her adolescent face, they shine with amusement for catching me in the act of staring. My brain remembers the first time those eyes locked with mine. Her small, trusting face and calm gaze had instantly stolen my heart.

"You have become a beautiful young woman. Realization

just bulldozed your old dad. I guess you're not an eight-year-old playing with Barbies in the corner of my office anymore."

Sarah gives an exaggerated head shake. "Nope. I haven't played Barbies in some time."

"You'll always be my little girl. Doesn't matter how old you are."

She rolls her eyes like a typical teen. "Um, thanks."

"Now that you have my undivided attention, what's up?"

My eyes catch the nervousness hidden just below her wavering smile. "I just came from Beacon."

"Uh-huh. And?"

"You know the new volunteer I told you about?"

"Wizard of words? Keeper of awesomeness? The amazing volunteer who helped you with your creative writing assignment? Nope, never heard of her."

"Dad, cut it out. She's awesome and an amazing writer. And...she asked me to help her with a new writing project." She jumps up with a scream and starts to pace in front of my desk. "Can you believe it? She said she would pay me! But... I need your permission."

"Sounds interesting and right up your alley. When would you do this?"

She stops and braces her hands on my desk as she moves in for the kill. She is a master negotiator, a trait I've been proud to see her develop over the years. She is amazing, but not so much when she turns her skills on me. "She said we could work at Beacon outside of our volunteer hours. She was adamant, I get your permission."

"You already spend a number of hours there. How much extra time do you think it'll be?" My mind returns to the argument I had with Elizabeth.

"I'm not sure. An extra five hours, maybe? Dad, I want to do this, and you know I love to write. Ms. Waters is patient, and her skills rock. This could be great for my high school transcript."

"How do you figure?"

"I get the impression working with her will be a once-in-a-lifetime opportunity."

If Sarah has a "job," she'll have a valid excuse for avoiding Elizabeth. Anything I can do to minimize Elizabeth's poisonous personality infiltrating Sarah's sweet nature is a win in my book.

"Why don't we try this? Tell her your dad agrees to a two-week trial period. If your grades don't slip, and she needs you beyond two weeks, you can keep the job."

Sarah circles the desk and throws her arms around me, snuggling her face into my neck. "You're the best dad a girl could ask for. Thank you."

I run a hand over her hair, which falls halfway down her back. My daughter is spreading her wings, so to speak. I am more than willing to be the air that lifts her as high as she aims to fly.

If Ms. Waters does anything to clip Sarah's wings, I will professionally crush her without a second thought. Then again, maybe this woman will prove to be the positive female influence Sarah needs at this time in her life.

My curiosity stirs. I need to meet this woman.

KATE

I INCH THROUGH RUSH HOUR TRAFFIC, MAKING MY WAY TO Beacon. Jon and I had agreed to catch a ride from there to Bangers and Lace, a trendy, local pub with a laid-back atmosphere and chill vibe.

Jon and I had become fast friends. A friendship anomaly for me, but one for which I was thankful.

I pull my Land Rover into my spot behind Beacon. Jon, being a gem, had given me my own parking space.

Beacon.

Promise.

Opportunity.

Hope.

Beacon overflows with opportunities wrapped in untarnished hope.

Grant and Tyler, two high school boys who are here as much as Jon, greet me with a "Sup" and obligatory head nod. As a volunteer, I feel charmed to be accepted by the boys. As an author, their grammatically incorrect greeting is like nails on a chalkboard.

"Hi, guys. Have either of you seen Mr. Logan?"

"Pretty sure he's back at the pool with Big Man."

"Um, thanks."

I'm completely baffled by a teenager's need to attach a nickname to everyone. It's strange but endearing.

I strip off my jacket as I walk around the facility. I'll definitely need it later, as I'm coming to understand the strange and inconsistent Windy City weather.

As I walk through the lobby toward the pool, my phone rings. Knowing I have time to spare, with Jon still in a meeting, I answer.

"Wanda Ring Iffu Masta Bait & Tackle, this is Mitch?"

A smile pierces my lips as I wait for Amy's reply. Our goofy phone game is still the same after fifteen years. The holy grail of the game is stunning the caller silent. Not wearing a bra for an entire day is the loser's consequence. I'm pretty sure that's why I got a Starbucks latte and a *thank you* fist bump from Amy's last blind date, Jack.

"Nope, not today, Mitch. Put Kate on."

"It's six p.m. on a Thursday night. Aren't you getting ready for your next Tinder victim...I mean, date?"

"Where are you?" Amy's demand is short and out of character.

"I just walked into Beacon. Jon and I are going for drinks."

"Is Jon there?"

"Yes, but I haven't seen him yet. Why?"

"Kate, he's not living in Milwaukee."

What?

No.

He's in Milwaukee. The newspaper article said so.

The blood drains from my face as my legs go numb. My breath is shallow and choppy. My body is on fire like someone ripped off a full body Band-Aid.

"I'm sorry. I wasn't sure how to tell you, so I went with fast and blunt."

I have no idea how I make it to the nearest couch. My legs give out, and my body crumples into the fabric.

"Say something. Please?" Amy's voice rises in panic.

Fear grips me. Afraid to voice my question and terrified of the answer, I choke out a stuttered whisper. "W-where is he?"

"Chicago."

One word has sucked the oxygen from my body. I feel sick. I feel like I'm drowning.

"Kate." Silence.

"Kate." More silence.

"Kate!" Amy's scream is quiet and muffled like she's standing at the end of a wind tunnel.

Gasping for air, I look down, confused why my phone is laying in my lap. I pick it up and press it to my ear.

"Kate? Kate? Are you all right? Do you need me to come get you?"

"I'm OK. Everything will be OK. I'm hanging up now."

I turn off my phone and throw it to the end of the couch like it's a grenade.

What am I going to do?

Eight weeks. The number of weeks I've been in Chicago.

Four weeks. The number of weeks I've volunteered at Beacon.

One week. The last time I had a nightmare.

One day. The last time I thought about him.

One minute. The time it takes for my heart to crumble into a million jagged pieces.

KATE

Jon sits across from me as I nurse the house specialty, "Be a Better Person," in a corner booth. I currently wish to be a *different person,* but apparently the bartender doesn't know how to make me one of those.

I feel Jon's hesitant gaze as it bounces around the bar. He raises his beer to his full lips. My personal observations tell me he is a gorgeous man on the outside, and even more stunning on the inside.

We have really connected since I started volunteering at Beacon, and he is only the second man I've ever called a friend. This experience is new. And, amazingly, I'm enjoying it. He gives me perspective and advice that Amy cannot, no matter how energetically she tries.

The boys at Beacon respect Jon and treat him with hero worship. The girls are just as enthralled with him, but probably for entirely different reasons. I doubt many females under the age of dead can pass him on the street without taking a second or third glance as they wipe drool from their chins.

"So...I'm not very good at this, but I can sense you're upset. Anything I can do to help?"

I push my glass to the side and pick at a cocktail napkin as I hide a smirk. "Just to clarify. Are you not good at talking to a woman? Or are you not good at talking about feelings?"

He tilts his head and purses his lips. "If you asked my last girlfriend, she would say 'yes' to both questions. I may be shit at this, but I'm willing to make an effort for you, my friend."

He is a gift to maintaining my sanity tonight. While I hate to divulge details of my personal life, I feel a strong pull to relieve the burden on my mind. Jon seems like a willing and empathetic participant. I figure I'll test the waters by starting slow.

"I grew up in Wisconsin, a suburb of Milwaukee. My dad was a successful cardiologist. My mom was an administrator for an exclusive private school. As irony would have it, my dad died of a heart attack when I was a senior in high school."

I raise my gaze from the table and peek at Jon. He is watching me and nodding, so I continue. "My mom and dad had the perfect relationship. Their marriage rivaled a sappy romance novel. We were all so annoyingly happy. When he died, my mom was devastated. She spiraled into a depression. Some days, I don't even think she knew, or cared, I lived with her."

"Did you have any siblings or family that helped?"

I shake my head, my eyes trained on the table in front of me. "Unfortunately, it was just my mom and me. It killed me to see her like that. But at the same time, I was angry, you know? She still had me. I needed my mom, but she didn't want me. I was a product of the love between her and my dad. She couldn't look at me, live with me, or love me because he was gone." My voice resonates woodenly in my ears. *Why was I never enough?*

Jon reaches across the table, placing both of his hands on top of mine. He encourages me to continue until I've successfully purged all of the pain.

"Luckily, my dad's life insurance policy was significant and allowed my mom to retire early, and me to go to college. I moved to school six months after my dad's death, and I never lived at home again. I was fortunate to find housing and employment for the summers."

It had been so long since I had talked about my dad's death. It was like the floodgates lifted, and I needed to get it all out before they slammed down again.

"Between my sophomore and junior year of college, my mom decided living was too difficult. She swallowed an entire bottle of her sleeping pills and just went to sleep. She never woke up. She never said goodbye." A single tear slides down my face. "She had been too blinded by her own pain to see I was falling apart too."

My mind drifts as unanswered questions swirl through my mind. A tornado, picking up speed, obliterating my happy memories and leaving a path of destruction in its wake.

Did she ever love me? Did she think of me before she did it? Did she want my help? So many questions, and never any answers.

"I've been on my own since I was twenty. Luckily, I met my best friend, Amy, not long after my mother's death. Amy was my beacon in the hurricane that was my life. She helped me navigate through the murkiness. It was messy, dark, and so damn painful. I owe her way more than I'll ever be able to repay."

Jon's jaw hangs open, his eyes wide and searching. His face is a mask of unmistakable shock spurred by my admissions. "Jeez, Kate. I'm sorry you had to go through something so horrible. First, losing your dad, then losing your mom. I can't imagine how you must have felt."

My lips turn up slightly. Little does he know, my emotional word vomit is not even close to what is bothering me. I didn't know it at the time, but my dad's death had set my life on a path that brought me both my greatest joy and my deepest regret.

I'd pushed my past to the furthest corners of my mind. Yet, random reminders managed to pull fragments from those corners, like a dog finding a buried bone. Forgotten in time, remembered in a second.

"Thanks for listening. It's not easy for me to just let go of my words like that. Oddly enough, this really helped."

Jon licks his lips. "Something tells me our conversation only grazed the tip of the iceberg that is Kate's life."

Was Jon a mind reader?

"Single, perceptive, and gorgeous. You are the holy grail. The trifecta to women across the globe."

He dips his head. "What can I say? It must be all the time I've been spending with the new volunteer at Beacon. She brings out the best in me." He shoots me a goofy exaggerated wink.

This guy. His playfulness paired with his looks makes him dangerous. Conversation detour needed stat.

"How is the new lifeguarding class going? I think the kids are really enjoying it."

If Jon is offended by my brush off, he doesn't comment.

Single, perceptive, gorgeous...smart guy.

KATE

I wake to the warmth of the springtime sun as it shines through curtains I forgot to draw before heading to bed. As annoyed as I want to remain, I accept getting a start on my Saturday morning a little earlier than originally planned. Stretching my hands over my head and pointing my toes, I stare at the ceiling while replaying last night's conversation with Jon. Talking to him had removed a level of stress I didn't realize I was carrying.

My mind drifts to the man I've lived in fear of seeing while walking the streets of Chicago. I abandoned my comfortable life in Milwaukee in an attempt to avoid him, only to find he lives in the very city to which I fled. Fate has served me a heaping plate of irony. As luck would have it, I've fallen in love with my little piece of Chicago, and I am not ready to give it up.

Apprehension runs through my body as I think about Sarah, the teenage girl from Beacon who I've taken on as my writing intern. Needing one for years, but never reaching a comfort level to hire one, I decided to give it a go.

We had taken an instant liking to each other. She'd allowed

me to read some of her short stories, and even asked my opinion about her ideas. Bonding over our shared interest in writing, I can already tell Sarah is a natural storyteller, blending words and eliciting emotions that practically leap from the page.

Looking to foster Sarah's writing while working through some ideas for my next project, I impulsively offered her a job as my intern. Only after extending my offer did panic set in. Hoping to provide an excuse to retract my impulsive suggestion, I required Sarah to get her parents' permission before starting. Unfortunately, I'd underestimated Sarah's eagerness and her ability to convince her parents, which makes today our first "official" day.

She has no idea I am Kennedy Willow. I'm not sure how this arrangement is going to work, but for Sarah, I am willing to try.

As I make a mental list for my day, I pull a short-sleeved sweater dress, chunky necklace, and a pair of flats from my walk-in closet, then head to my en suite bathroom. The cool tiles tickle my feet as I pad across the floor to turn on the shower, letting the ice-cold pipes warm the water to scalding before I jump in. *Is there any other way to take a shower?*

One of the advantages of moving to Chicago has been my living arrangement. Amy's house is a two-bedroom, two bathroom, fully updated house located in Lincoln Park. Within walking distance of entertainment, trendy wine bars, quaint pubs, and ethnic restaurants, it is the perfect blend of luxurious, yet casual living. Amy's home has amenities I'm not willing to sacrifice—namely my best friend—so I've been in no hurry to find another place.

Showered and ready for my day, I walk to the kitchen to make breakfast. As I return the carton of milk to the fridge, Amy saunters through the front door.

"Well, well, well. Whoever he was, he must have been outstanding. You never stay the night at a guy's place."

Amy walks behind me, flipping a piece of hair off my shoulder. "When he's so good that your legs go numb, a girl makes an exception."

"Better you than me. If it were that good, I'd probably suffer a leg cramp. It would totally put a kink in my night. Pun intended."

"Miss Kate, your day will come. I feel it. Chin up, tits out."

My friend is blunt, a bit crude, and totally inappropriate, but I love her more than anyone.

"I'm off to run some errands, then I'll be at Beacon for the rest of the day. My new intern starts today."

"I have a trip to San Diego coming up at the end of the week. Maybe we could grab dinner one night before I leave?"

"Absolutely. I thought living together would mean seeing more of you. An early morning kitchen rendezvous does not count."

"So true. I'm off to shower and catch a couple hours of pillow time."

Taking a bite of my soggy Cheerios, I glance out the window while mulling over Amy's words. Maybe I *am* due for a bit of no-strings fun.

As I walk across Beacon's common area, I allow the atmosphere to blanket me with contentment. It's the feeling I always encounter when volunteering with children and youth.

I stand in the doorway of the media lab, my eyes falling on Sarah as she sits, poised and ready for our first day. On a chair in the corner, one foot rests on the seat, leg bent in front of her chest. Her head is bowed, thick brown hair draping in front of her shoulders, partially shielding her face from view. I watch as her fingers fly across her phone's screen, pausing just long enough for her eyes to read responses before racing across the screen again.

She is a beautiful, inquisitive, innocent dreamer.

Fear simmers just below my skin. A prickly reminder that unpredictable, emotional reactions to Sarah could float to the surface. By no fault of her own, my mind is filled with questions. *Do both of her parents love her? Does she enjoy mom-daughter lunch dates? Do she and her dad share a common hobby?*

Giving myself a mental shake, I call her name, alerting her to my presence as I walk into the room.

"Wow. I thought I was doing well, getting here fifteen minutes early, but you managed to beat your new boss to work. How long have you been here?"

No longer texting, but continuing to look at her phone's screen, Sarah gives a small shrug of her shoulders. "I was at my mom's this morning. She offered to drop me here, as long as she could do it before her spa appointment at one o'clock."

Looking at my watch, I frown. "You've been waiting for me for over two hours?"

"It's not a big deal. I like it here." Finally looking up at me, I see a defiance masking hurt in Sarah's eyes. She is upset, but she has no desire to elaborate.

"How about I give you my phone number, so you can text me if this happens again? If I'm free, I don't mind rescheduling to get here earlier in the future."

A small, relieved grin appears on Sarah's face as she taps her phone twice, then looks at me, presumably waiting for me to recite my number.

Glancing at my watch, I do a double take. Sarah and I have been working for three hours without a break. I'm amazed by the way Sarah's mind looks at problems. Top down, she devises a variety of different angles at one time. I've only seen that type of problem-solving one other time. Refusing to revisit the jagged details of a time best left alone, I shut down my thoughts.

"It's almost six thirty. Time to call it a day."

Sarah looks at her phone, her eyes straying to me. "I can stay longer if you need me."

"We went three hours without a break. I don't want your parents pulling permission to work with me after your first day."

Sarah quickly diverts her eyes. "My dad would only notice if he's not working. I don't know if my mom would ever notice."

I look at Sarah, hoping my surprise isn't plastered across my face. After her comment, I know she has a story, but I don't know her well enough to push her to share it.

"I've already completed two character descriptions and a location description. They are rough, but exactly where I usually start. What we did today has taken me over two weeks for other projects. You are phenomenal at this."

Her face lights with pleasure. "I am? With practice, do you think I could ever be as good as Kennedy Willow? Her work is epic."

Her words cause my heart to flutter. For the past decade, I have received praise from both critics and readers. While not intentionally directed at me, Sarah's words are a warm balm settling across my chest. Her praise makes me elated and giddy and humbled.

I am the author Sarah aspires to be. She has no clue. I need to take the window she opened.

My chest tightens. Skin prickling. Heart racing. I can do this. Truth bubbles, my words ready to spring free. I have clung to Kennedy Willow so fiercely, she has splintered. She has become pieces. *My* pieces, with rough edges, no longer fitting together. Trapped between who I was, and who I want to be.

Worried my secrets could destroy me, I have let them suffocate me.

"Sar—"

"Don't answer that. Just wishful thinking on my part. I should get going."

My resolve fades with each word from Sarah's mouth. She gathers her notes, placing them in her backpack, before slinging it over her shoulder as she walks out of the room.

I should call out to her. Stop her. Share my truth before locking it away. Saliva gathers in my throat, coating my tongue like glue, trapping my admissions behind my lips. I promise myself to do it soon. I'll tell her the truth, hoping I don't break her trust in the process.

9

SHAW

Today has been one hell of a day. First, the CFO fiasco. Second, the paperwork from my attorney outlining Elizabeth's new demands for child support, in addition to a new shared custody request. Utter lunacy, considering she sees Sarah less than once a month. As soon as I saw the document, my vision went red. I wanted to wrap my hands around her neck and squeeze until no breath was left in her medically enhanced body.

Luckily, Vet happened to be in my office when the paperwork arrived from my attorney's courier. After hitting me with some self-talk crap from his college psychology days, I calmed considerably.

Convincing him I wasn't going to call or see Elizabeth against my attorney's wishes, Vet headed back to Beacon whistling about the ass kicking he'd be delivering during our Thursday night workout. He cryptically alluded to a possible surprise for me when I got there. *Interesting.*

With my duffel bag in one hand, I palm my phone in the other, checking messages as I walk into Beacon. I'm stoked to burn through some laps against Vet tonight. I welcome my best friend's competitive nature, a byproduct of years of grueling training that earned him two gold medals and the nickname "Corvette" for his speed off the block in Sydney.

Seeing no urgent messages, I mute my phone and take a deep, cleansing breath. I love this place. I have never once regretted investing in Vet's vision.

It is nearing eight p.m. on a Thursday night, which signifies closing time is drawing near. I give a quick wave to Tracy, who works at the center and locks up on Tuesdays and Thursdays.

"How is that new baby of yours?"

"Ooooh, he's getting so big. His little legs look like the Michelin man."

"I miss those days."

"Come now, Shaw. Surely, you've still got time to have a couple more."

I shake my head and look down, not willing to let her see the disappointment in my eyes. "Not impossible, but not likely, Tracy."

Slowing my steps, I walk toward the locker room. It's been a long while since I thought about having more kids. By the time I felt ready, Elizabeth was riding the Crazy Town Express. I had always hoped to have more children, but as each year passed, my hope had been reduced to a fleeting whim.

After changing into my suit and athletic shorts, I prowl the building in search of V. As I walk to his office, I glance out the front door to see him waving goodbye to a woman as she leaves the parking lot in a sweet Land Rover. *Hmmm. Does Vet have a new lady friend?*

I catch a ghost of a smile on Vet's lips as he walks back to the building.

I let out a low whistle as he walks through the door. "So...that was a nice Rover."

"Yeah, pretty sweet." V gives nothing away as he walks to his office.

"Not as sweet as the dark-haired beauty I glimpsed behind the wheel."

He shakes his head, a rusty sounding chuckle parting his lips. "You should see her head-on. She'll take your breath away, man."

I stare at V, assessing his thoughts. "Are you slipping or just turning over a new leaf? You actually told one of your women where you work?"

"She's not one of my women." The vehemence in his voice surprises me.

"Yeah, why not?"

"Because *she's* our new volunteer as of last month, *and* she's your daughter's new boss."

"Damn, that was *the* Ms. Waters? The way Sarah talks about her, you'd think she's a female Steven King."

We turned the corner and walked into V's office. "Yep. That was *Kate*. Sarah's new hero, and your worst nightmare."

"I don't follow."

"She's got a sharp tongue, quick wit, and is as guarded as they come. Sarah will castrate you if you scare her off. Tread lightly with this one, dude. She's special, but your baggage looks like a damn carry-on compared to what I've seen of hers."

"She's important to Sarah, so she's already on my nice list. Looks like I won't be meeting her tonight. Probably best, considering the day I had." I clap V on the back. "I need to drown today's frustrations. Get changed and meet me at the pool. But be warned. It's a 'take no prisoners' night."

V shoots me a self-assured grin. "Wouldn't have it any other way, man."

10

EVIL ONE

PAST...

I study her. She's laughing and smiling as her baby babbles in the car seat resting on the chair beside her. I'm annoyed and losing patience. Stilted best describes our conversation. The infant monopolizes her focus. It's a baby, not the president.

Truthfully, I don't want to be here. My time is a valuable commodity. But...the access this woman affords me is priceless. The temptation is too great to ignore.

No one deserves all that she has.

Her usefulness lies in her connections and what they can give me...perfection and money.

I continually remind myself to be patient.

Patience is key to having it all.

11

KATE

THE ROUGH DRAFT FOR A PIVOTAL SCENE FOR MY UPCOMING book is done. Sarah has been amazing, her innocence providing refreshing insights. She is truly a gifted writer.

Over the past two weeks, I finished outlining my next project and wrote about a quarter of the scenes. Sarah's help has been priceless.

She and I have bonded, growing closer during the extra hours we spent together. While I am still hesitant to share information about myself, Sarah has used me as a sounding board as she shared pieces of her family situation.

Her parents divorced about two years ago, with full custody being awarded to her dad. From what I gather, the two of them are very close. When she speaks of him, her eyes reflect the same admiration as her words. He is a successful businessman who works long hours but still tries to spend quality time with his daughter. Reduced quality time now because Sarah is working with me each week. Sarah said her dad was supportive of her job but cited some disagreements of late.

Sarah's relationship with her mom is totally different than the one she shares with her dad. It appears tenuous and stilted.

From the information I've pieced together, her mom isn't employed but keeps herself busy socially. According to Sarah, Elizabeth organizes fundraising for a local private school and spends quite a few hours at the spa. While I haven't met her, I am fairly certain she and I would not mesh well.

Looking outside, I see the sun is minutes from falling behind the skyline. Time has flown while Sarah and I were writing. Darkness will soon descend, and Sarah needs to be on her way before it gets too late.

I back up the computer, shut it down, and stand up, stretching my back. "Great session. Let's pack it in for the day."

Sarah, who has been staring at her phone screen for the past five minutes, gives me a limp nod. She's worked well today and hasn't seemed preoccupied until now.

"Everything OK?"

"Yeah. My dad is stuck in traffic."

"Not a problem. I'll stay until he gets here. Or I can take you home to save him a trip."

"You don't have to stay. Jon's here. I'll hang with him."

"I don't mind." I gather my note cards, sliding a rubber band around the stack before depositing them in my purse. I catch Sarah's stare from my periphery. As I wait, her inquisitive nature wins, and she turns, completely facing me.

"Kate, how can you tell if someone is happy?"

Not knowing where her line of questioning is going, I pause to ponder my answer. "Have you ever heard the saying, 'Beauty is in the eye of the beholder'?"

Sarah nods, and I continue. "Happiness is kind of the same idea. Happiness is dependent on the person. Is there a reason why you're asking?"

Sarah stares at her fingers, twisting them together. "It's my dad. Besides spending time with me, I don't know what makes him happy. He rarely does anything besides work, sleep, and hang with me. I worry. What's going to happen to him when I leave for college?"

My heart melts for her. Sarah is an old soul, pondering life and examining how each person is a cog in its wheel. Always a problem solver, she is already worried about what will happen to her dad when she goes to college.

"I don't have experience with this, but maybe you could talk to him? Maybe he feels his time with you would be compromised if he branched out on his own."

"I guess I could talk to him. I just want him to be happy. Sometimes, I think my mom sucked every bit of happiness right out of him."

At that moment, I hoped I never had the *pleasure* of meeting Sarah's mom knowing I'd be hard pressed to keep my opinions to myself.

Sarah's phone chimes with an incoming text, her face lighting up with surprise as she reads it. "My dad's here. He's waiting out front." She slings her backpack over her shoulder as she stands up. "I guess we're going to dinner. Do you need any help out to your car?"

"I'm good. Have fun, and think about talking to your dad."

Sarah gives me a wave and disappears out the door.

Not five minutes later, Sarah meets me as I exit the building.

"Dad thinks you should come to dinner with us. He says it's time to meet you and your awesomeness. His words, not mine." Sarcasm drips from her tone.

Could I go? Yes.

Should I go? Probably.

Did I want to go? Maybe.

I had been in Chicago for nearly three months. Besides volunteering at Beacon, I'd done very little outside my own house. My only friends were Amy, Jon, and Sarah. A strong, but small, circle.

I should do this.

"Why don't you give me the name of the restaurant, and I'll meet you guys there in a few minutes?"

"Woohoo. Deal. Lino's Pizzeria, just around the corner on Ohio. I hope you like pizza. Theirs is to die for." Sarah throws her hand in the air and gives a little whistle.

I watch as she skips out the front door, jumping into the back of a black town car as I walk to my SUV, wondering if I can handle what I just agreed to.

12

KATE

The restaurant is not what I expected given my view from the street. The dining room is double the width of the storefront and accented by small booths running down the outer walls. Resembling small cottages in an Italian village, each booth has windows with working shutters that can be closed by patrons who desire privacy from other diners.

Delicious aromas of garlic bread and mozzarella cheese waft through the room. Families and couples engage in loud conversations while enjoying their meals. The lighting is low, highlighting the twinkling ceiling lights meant to mirror stars in a clear night sky. This place is sure to become one of my new favorite restaurants, and I haven't taken a single bite of food.

Following the hostess, who had obviously been instructed to look for me, I admire the emerald green of her shirt, as she winds through the dining room toward a secluded booth in the back corner. This booth is larger than most. A curtain falls across the entrance, and the shutters are pulled closed. Sarah and her dad obviously enjoy the privacy Lino's affords its patrons.

Flutters of anxiousness and excitement dance in my

stomach as I approach the table. The internal pep talk during the drive over had done an adequate job in calming most of my nerves.

I am ready to reach out. Expand my experiences.

At the same time the hostess pulls back the booth's curtain, a tall, dark-haired man backs out, a phone attached to his ear. He gives the hostess a quick nod and walks toward a back hallway just beyond the booth.

My breathing quickens.

My skin buzzes.

My stomach somersaults and churns over a man my eyes barely glimpsed. Sexual attraction floods my limbs, a feeling I rarely experience. Taking a steadying breath and forcing a smile, I slip into the seat next to Sarah.

She rolls her eyes, annoyance evident in her manner. "My dad. Couldn't even make it through dinner without having to take a call. Story of my life."

Trying to be understanding while validating her frustrations, I shrug. "Sometimes work seeps into personal time. It happens to me." I lean over, nudging her shoulder. "Gives us a few minutes of girl talk. You said you're going out of town soon. Anywhere exciting?"

I listen to Sarah as I peruse the menu. Asking questions here and there, I learn she and her dad plan to boat across Lake Michigan. I do poorly at hiding my surprise at her disclosure.

"You mean, just the two of you? By yourselves? Across Lake Michigan? Isn't that a tad dangerous?"

"Dad was born and raised to love water. It's in his blood. He can handle himself."

"So, your dad, what does he do?"

"He designs boats, among other things too boring to mention."

My stomach crawls up my throat.

Tall.

Dark hair.

Designs boats.

Raised to love water.

Memories ghost into place.

Fate surely isn't this cruel.

A riot of conflicting emotions screams through my body. Outwardly, I'm granite. Smooth, cool, strong. Needing to hear what my heart already knows, I continue.

"I don't think you've ever told me your dad's name."

At the same moment, a large hand enters my periphery, held out in introduction. He's standing, waiting for my acknowledgment before taking his seat. His voice is smooth. The no-nonsense cadence forever etched on my heart. "Shaw Graham."

Two words.

The man who fractured my heart so many years ago.

My past has collided with my present.

Jagged pieces melt together.

Turning my head, I see my heart standing before me.

"Shaw?"

13

SHAW

"KATE? WHAT ARE YOU DOING HERE?"

In business, showing surprise is a form of weakness. Drawing upon years of training, I struggle to find my voice while dropping a mask of indifference over my face.

Where has she been? Why is she here?

Confusion floats across Sarah's face. Sensing the underlying tension, she jumps in with an unnecessary introduction. "Uhh, Kate Waters, this is my dad. Dad, this is my friend and, technically, my boss, Kate."

I stare at Kate.

What the hell is going on?

The din of the restaurant disappears, my full attention directed toward the beauty sitting in front of me.

Her features are a sixteen-year tattoo on my memory. Ocean blue eyes, fringed with thick lashes. Chestnut hair, disappearing down her back. Her full lips part, small wisps of air fluttering between them as I continue to drink her in.

My memory has served me well. She is a refined, exquisite version of young Kate. Years of maturity make her even more beautiful than her teenage self.

"Um, Dad? You're staring. Like full-on creeper staring." Sarah's voice pulls me from my reverie. Being called out by my daughter reminds me of where I am.

Pent-up anger, hidden for years, rises within me. I'm stretched like a rubber band before snapping back to reality. Sharp, biting words build within me, waiting, poised for release.

Kate continues to meet my gaze. Challenging me. The fear I saw during our introduction has been replaced by an uncontrolled inferno. Her eyes blaze blue, daring me to speak, knowing doing so will open the door to the past. A past she and I have not shared for over sixteen years.

Like a veil shielding a bride on her wedding day, Kate's emotions drop from her face. Smooth confidence, laced with indifference, takes anger's place.

This Kate is a worthy adversary. One I have not met. Strategy, sharp and keen, seeps from her pores like a general preparing for war.

Unsure of her tactics, I ready myself for a fight. Her skills for trickery were legendary back in the day, and my guard is up.

Game on.

I sit down across from the woman who has owned my dreams for over a decade. Subtly shaking my head, I pierce Kate with a smile. "I'm sorry. Thrown for a minute. You look like a girl I once knew."

"Oh?"

"Really liked her. *Loved* her, in fact. Apparently, not enough. She left me with a kiss and was gone the next day. Ghosted me, with no way to contact her."

"Surely she left you something? A phone number? A note, perhaps?"

"Nope."

Layered below her anger, I see surprise register in her eyes before it disappears seconds later.

Kate raises an eyebrow in challenge. "If you loved her, why didn't you look for her?"

Nope.

I. Wasn't. Doing. This.

I refuse to satisfy her morbid curiosity through a pretend third-party story. I'll be damned if I am going to roll over and make this easy for her. She has obviously forgotten who she's dealing with.

Her questioning eyes betray her, revealing the importance of the answer she seeks.

Ignoring her question, I take control by asking one of my own. Mentally pulling on my sparring gloves, I step into the ring.

"You're the *Kate* Sarah can't stop talking about?" Purposely devouring her with my eyes, I linger on her chest until she visibly squirms. "Frankly, I expected you to be older."

Kate bristles from my insult. She's a master at disguising her emotions, but I'm better at exposing them. She opens her mouth with what is sure to be a venomous reply, but it's cut short by the arrival of the waiter.

"Your pizza has gone in the oven, sir. Is there anything else I can get you in the meantime?"

Challenging Kate to speak up, I raise my eyebrow and stare at her while taking a swig of my house draft. "Anything you need? Dagger? Undetectable poison, perhaps?"

A full-watt, one hundred percent fake smile spreads across Kate's lips. "A 1990 Latour, please?"

A thousand-dollar bottle of wine?

Had I not been prepared, her face would have been the recipient of the beer trying to escape my lips. I swallow, a smirk slowly spreading. *She thinks an expensive bottle of wine will be a hardship on my wallet?* Her naïveté both excites and disappoints me.

Excitement for her boldness in trying to anger me, disappointment in her lack of knowledge of my success.

Had she never tried to find me? While I didn't flaunt my riches or success, my ex-wife did a good job of keeping us in the public eye over the years.

The waiter looks to me for confirmation of the order. I give an affirmative nod, which sends him scurrying away from the table. He's probably running to the kitchen to boast about scoring the big-ticket table of the night.

Returning my attention to Kate, I realize I'm smiling. While her presence threw me, I'm actually enjoying sitting across from her and reliving the memories swirling between us.

Sarah, who I belatedly remember is present, eyes us with the weariness of a homeless dog eating dinner for the first time in weeks. I can see her mind working all the angles. By now, she has to realize Kate and I know each other. Beyond that, I'm not sure what she has deduced.

Feeling guilty, but not enough to deter my next actions, I engage Kate in questions about Sarah's job.

"So, Sarah tells me you're a volunteer at Beacon? How did you find the center?"

Kate takes a sip of her water, seemingly gathering her words. Plotting and preparing to release only those that will paint her as a dedicated, loving volunteer, not the deceitful liar she has obviously become. "I recently moved to Chicago, and I'd been looking for a place where I could volunteer my time. A little online research led me to Beacon."

"New to the area? Where did you live before?"

"Out of state." Her reply is fast and blunt.

"Your work schedule must be very forgiving to afford you so much time to volunteer."

Kate stares at me, hands crossed and resting in front of her on the table. *Questions, Shaw. You need to ask questions for her to answer.* This conversation is infuriating, yet exhilarating, all at once.

Trying to ignore me or feign indifference, Kate's eyes bounce around the booth like a pinball. She is unsettled and uncomfortable. Call me a jerk, but any emotion I can elicit is a win in my book.

Kate had been such a passionate person. I have no doubt that passion still resides within her, and I accept the personal challenge of releasing just a bit of it tonight.

"What is it you do to earn a paycheck?" *Blunt, right back at you, babe.*

"I write."

"For? A magazine, a newspaper, a blog? A marketing company? Corporate PR? Children's books, best sellers, cookbooks?"

"Yes."

Kate smiles and takes another sip of water. Her one-word answers remind me of talking to a stubborn toddler.

"Sarah, since your boss is having some problems speaking tonight, maybe you can fill me in on what she does?"

Sarah stares at me with shock and contempt. I can already feel the sting of the tongue-lashing I'll be getting on the way home. Her eyes dart to Kate, trying to gauge how she should answer without offending her mentor. Kate gives a nearly imperceptible nod, indicating it's OK for her to respond.

"She volunteers, and she writes. She hired me to help with research for her next project. I've researched small, coastal resorts, as well as lakeside resorts in the Midwest."

Interesting.

"What places have you found?"

As the last word leaves my mouth, the waiter returns with two wine glasses, a bucket of ice, and the overpriced bottle of wine. Nodding to me, he tilts the bottle in front of him like one would display fine art, making a production of the uncorking and the tasting pour. I wave my hand, indicating a tasting is unnecessary. The bottle is already open. He can't pour it back in if I'm unsatisfied with its taste. He fills both glasses and places the bottle in the ice bucket.

"Your pizza will be out in just a few minutes. Anything I can get for you in the meantime?"

Again, I wave him off, anxious to return to my interrogation.

Kate takes a tentative sip of her wine. Had I not been watching carefully, I would have missed her slight wince, presumably from the tart taste, before swallowing. Let her suck on the sour taste of her trickery. Her glass will remain full throughout the meal. I'll make sure of it.

"What are your favorite places so far?"

Sarah pauses and looks up at the ceiling. I can practically see her research notes flying through her memory as she searches for her favorite. I lean back, taking the last drink of beer as I wait.

"Well, I found one place that sounded like fun." Sarah smiles nervously as she glances at Kate. "Kate vetoed the place quite quickly. She didn't feel it fit the vision for her project."

Curiosity keeps me on this path of questioning. I'm interested to see if I can piece together random clues that will offer me a glimpse into the woman Kate has become. "What was it called? What state was it in?"

"It was just a little, resort in Wisconsin. It was called White Bird? White Seagull? Something like that. I thought it looked pretty cool. Thought it might be a place to check out and visit one day."

My eyes cut to Kate, the force of Sarah's words reverberating through the look we both share. Barbs of guilt and disappointment prick my eyes, sliding painfully down to my heart where they land and dig in. Loving images of our summer, our adventures, our promises, assault me before being replaced by pain. Memories burn hot and bright before turning to ash—gray, suffocating and dead.

I take a moment, doing my best to bury my feelings before I do or say something I can't take back. "Was the resort called White Eagle Inn, perhaps?"

Sarah's eyes light up. "Yes! That's the place. Maybe we could go there. Check it out sometime?"

"Yeah, maybe." The words quietly slip from my lips on a cough, as I attempt to hide the pain crawling up my throat.

My pocket vibrates, and I cannot remember a time I've been more thankful for a business interruption. Standing and looking at my phone while it rings, I prepare to use this call like the lifeline it is. Sarah's anger will be legendary, but I will deal with her later. "I'm sorry. I'm going to need to head back to the office to return this call. Sarah, Michael will drive you home."

Sarah's jaw nearly hits the floor. Steam is practically pouring from her ears. I am in for a fight of epic proportions the next time I'm alone with her.

I thought I could handle seeing Kate again, talking to her, sitting with her, but I grossly underestimated the feelings coursing through me.

Seeing her is like being hit by lightning—unexpected, sudden, and painful. I need to retreat and regroup before our next meeting. Fate has thrown us back together. Kate wants to flee, I can see it in her eyes, but I'll be damned if I let history repeat itself.

14

KATE

Shaw sits in front of me. Handsome and magnificently built. His blue eyes shoot straight through my heart. I have lied to my heart, convinced I never wanted to see him after receiving the devastating letter years ago.

You left me without a word.

I stare at him, trying to find a glimmer of the young man I once knew. The years have given him a maturity he wears exceedingly well.

Physically, he is breathtaking, in both looks and stature. He bears an authoritative air accentuated by the tailored Armani suit, starched Oxford shirt, and impeccably straight red tie.

My lips part, my brain gasping for the oxygen stolen from my lungs when I see his face. I barely register Sarah's words as she chastises her dad after our introduction.

I struggle to maintain a calm outward composure. Inside, I'm the antithesis of calm. Confusion, resentment, and anger begin to bubble within my veins.

Shaw had turned his back on me. *He* closed the door. The fault lies at *his* feet. Why is anger emanating from *him*?

Confidence begins to flow through me. I can do this.

Emotions buried, composure relaxed, I stare at him, giving nothing away. Once a participant in my happiness, he no longer qualifies to be anything more than a silent spectator.

Shaw has braced for battle, his professional arrogance in place and ready.

He's pretending I'm not the woman he knew years ago. That *I* left *him* without a word or explanation.

He's sorely mistaken. I left him a note. Taped it to his door myself.

That note was me. My heart bleeding, seeping onto the paper and mixing with my tears of devastation and anguish. I told him I'd return. I gave him no indication my feelings were anything but true.

He had every opportunity to contact me. He had a phone number and an address. He chose to ignore my words, my promises, my heart.

Lost in the past and looking for an escape from this encounter, I'm disoriented when Shaw abruptly transitions the conversation.

Laced with verbal jabs disguised in innocuous comments, Shaw questions my writing abilities while blatantly staring at my chest. It appears Shaw has cornered the market on Grade A asshole distinction. He's baiting me, in hopes I'll lash out, into revealing personal information he wants to know but doesn't have the balls to ask.

Barely able to contain my reactions to his rudeness, I open my mouth to give him a piece of my mind at the same time the waiter appears, requesting my drink order. As the waiter fawns over Shaw, I bite my tongue, biding my time.

This man is an enigma to me. *What is he thinking?* Is this encounter shredding him the way it is me? Questions about the past swirl through both of our eyes.

I have a life. I'm content. That's all he has a right to know.

Shaw has no claim on me, my time, my words, or my life. His expectations are laughable, considering he's dealing with me, Kennedy Willow. Time has created a facade and strengthened my resolve. He has no idea the persona he's so ruthlessly attacking was ironically created to deal with scars left by him.

When the waiter returns and pours the ridiculously overpriced bottle of wine, asked for solely out of spite, my eyes dart around the table, stopping to focus on my full glass.

I take a sip of the tart liquid, trying to mask my distaste, as I silently pray Shaw is reaching the end of his obtrusive questions. *Note to self: Stick with the tastier, ten-dollar bottles of wine.*

Unsatisfied with the answers he receives from me, he tries to pry them from Sarah. The most damage Sarah relays is her research involving jobs and coastal towns near water.

Shaw shows immediate interest in the information.

Does he remember the time we spent in our lakeside town?

When Sarah brings up the White Eagle Inn, I nearly break, and I can see it clearly affects Shaw as well. Sarah found the place that connects us.

A phone call interrupts us, and Shaw uses it as his excuse to abandon this conversation, issuing Sarah a hurried, half-assed apology before he leaves the table.

Sarah's outrage shows on her red face. She repeatedly apologizes, both angry and embarrassed for her dad's behavior. She suggests finishing dinner, and I reluctantly agree.

What happened tonight?

Silently taking inventory, I feel pieces of my heart have already started to loosen. The glue I've spent years applying becomes brittle, threatening to splinter and break.

Destruction is coming. I don't know when, but it's coming, and there's nothing I can do to stop it.

15

SHAW

ANGER AND CONFUSION GRIP ME AS I HEAD HOME. *WHERE HAS she been? Why was she so angry?*

She was the one that left me.

What did she mean, she left a note? There was no note. There was nothing.

My mind is like a pinball, bouncing between questions and memories. My nightmare weeks ago had not done her justice. Fragmented memories pieced together by my subconscious had created a poor substitute for the woman she had become.

Kate is refined in a way that is foreign to me. She has nervous energy hidden behind an air of professionalism.

New Kate's beauty is wrapped within a mysterious edge. An edge I have never seen. An edge that turns me on, physically and mentally.

She is a puzzle, secretly holding the pieces I so desperately sought.

Plan.

It's what I do best. I need to create a plan before I see her again. I have questions. She has answers. Answers she *will* be giving me, whether she wants to or not.

It's been sixteen years. Seeing her melted those years, decimating them like fast-flowing lava.

I'm hot.

For answers.

For explanations.

For her.

My body knows what my brain refuses to acknowledge. She had been my *one*. The *one* I'd wanted and the *one* for whom I still yearn.

Her appearance is unexpected and may prove problematic, given my current custody situation. Yet, I can't deny her presence feels right.

I need to convince her.

Get my answers.

Work through forgiveness, then erase our years apart.

Today is the day I reunited with my heart. It is bruised and broken, yet beats a strong, steady rhythm. Tomorrow is a new day, and I will be ready.

16

KATE

BRIGHT RAYS WARM MY FOOT AS IT POKES OUT FROM THE END of my sheets. I have never been able to sleep unless one foot is exposed to the crisp air. It's a personal quirk I embrace.

As I stare at my ceiling, I sift through last night's dinner, trying to decipher information: relevant versus irrelevant, factual versus false.

Questions, ones that shouldn't matter, plague my mind. *Why was he so angry? How did he have a child? When was she born? Why did he ignore that note I left him?*

...My mom had an emergency. I have to leave. My number and address are listed. Please call me as soon as you can. I can't do this without you. You are my promise, my heart. I love you...

Leaving him had been necessary, but losing him had been agony. Revisiting my questions had the potential to rip open the loose stitching of my resolve. I had tied off and tucked away my memories like an heirloom quilt. They were never forgotten, but too fragile to use or display in the open.

He has a child. My math couldn't be far off. Sarah had to

have been conceived not long after Shaw and I were together. *How long did he wait? Did he try to find me? Did he make the same promises to Sarah's mother as he did to me?*

It took years to realize our relationship had been a fantasy. A mirage misread by the innocence and naïveté of my youth. His "I love you" more like "I love you when I'm horny in Wisconsin" endearments.

While my mind was happy with its assumptions, I couldn't convince my heart it had been wrong. It clung to the hope he loved me just as much as I had loved him. He had been my *one*. My heart committed to forever the minute he spoke the words and handed me his heart in return.

I want to embrace the hope of my youth. Yet, letting go will close the door on all that passed between us, and some things are too precious to let go.

I stretch and check my phone. I'm dreading facing Sarah and her plethora of questions. She is bright and intuitive, two traits that guarantee awkward working conditions the next time we're together. Luckily, today isn't my day of reckoning. My only obligation is teaching a one-hour "How to fill out a college application" class for eight Beacon "regulars" this afternoon.

I ease out of bed, stopping at my closet to grab clothes before heading to the bathroom to turn on the shower. When I moved in, I needed just one shower before I learned. Run the water first, or enter at your own risk. I loved this house, but the plumbing was old with a capital "O." Jumping in without letting the water warm up was like dousing yourself with a bucket of ice.

As I pull my clothes from my body, I scrutinize the woman in the mirror before me. If I squint, I can see remnants of the scared girl I once was. No matter what I had done to bury her, she would always remain as a reminder of the successful work I had done to move past her. Always silently judging me for the decisions I made.

Giving myself a mental shake, I roll my shoulders and step into the shower.

A scared girl may live within me, but she wears the armor of a warrior. And I am ready for the war I sense is coming.

17

KATE

COULD THIS DAY GET ANY WORSE?

My favorite coffee shop somehow ran out of my favorite breakfast blend. Thinking I wouldn't notice, they switched it out with some caramel hazelnut crap. I sat down, took one drink, and almost made it to the trash to spit it out.

Almost.

As I pushed away from the table, my throat developed a tickle. You know the one. The kind of tickle that usually rears its ugly head during a church prayer or the four-hour SAT. You try to hold it in, but it just doesn't let up.

Yeah.

I made a valiant effort, but couldn't hold it in. In the middle of pushing to my feet, a cough erupted, causing me to spew coffee down the front of my shirt, with the brunt of the eruption landing in the middle of my lap.

Warm, pungent coffee immediately seeped through my linen shorts, soaking my panties. After spending ten minutes in the bathroom, trying to salvage my drenched underwear, I opted for going commando. I stripped out of the panties, dabbed them with a paper towel, and slid them in my pocket.

I know I should have just thrown them away, but I'm frugal. I may be a well-paid author, but I'm not wasteful. They were still perfectly serviceable. Nothing a good soak and wash wouldn't fix.

Now, I'm fighting what feels like my entire closet hanging from my arms and wrapping around my body like a boa constrictor as I make my way to my car. *Seriously, when had I dropped my entire closet off at the dry cleaners?* My bicep muscles are screaming, and I know I'm in danger of them snapping within the next fifteen steps. *Is snapping a bicep a thing?* If it isn't, I will be the first casualty. Twelve articles of clothing, plus bags and hangers, are freakishly heavy. Not to mention, the threat of "suffocation by plastic bag" is a high possibility, as the plastic dances and blows in the wind.

What I wouldn't give for a personal, non-writing assistant right this minute. My mental note to find one two months ago is getting an instant pass to the top of my to-do list. Why and how I've made it this long without one is beyond my comprehension.

OK. I'll be honest. I don't know the "how," but I do know the "why." Letting someone in my mental headspace and my personal physical space is nearly impossible for me. Four people in the history of my life had made it there. My parents, who were dead, Amy, and *him.*

Arriving at my SUV, I pull a circus act, shifting all of the hangers to one hand so I can open the door with my other. Praising myself for having a vehicle with keyless entry, I hold the door handle, watching for the "wink, wink" of the lights, letting me know my SUV has unlocked. No flashing lights. *Hmm, maybe I missed the "wink, wink" because I'm hyper-focused on my screaming biceps?*

I try again, pulling the door handle a little more forcefully, only to have it spring back into place, nearly ripping off three fingernails in the process.

What the hell?

Trying to figure out what is going on, I shift the clothes, managing to drop one of the hangers on the ground. I'm totally thankful now for those plastic bags of mass suffocation that managed to keep my silk shirt from getting dirty.

At this point, the street can keep the annoying, albeit clean, piece of fabric. I would leave it right here on the street, if it didn't happen to be my favorite Michael Kors silk blouse.

As I bend to retrieve my errant garment from the ground, shiny Oxford shoes saunter into my periphery.

"Kate?"

Deep, smooth, intoxicating voice. Shit.

No number of years will ever erase his voice, nor the reaction my body has to it.

I slowly stand up, holding the offending blouse while holding the other eleven in my other hand. *Damn you, Michael Kors and your fashion wizardry.* I should have left the shirt in the gutter where it fell.

"Shaw."

Surprise and, dare I say, a bit of satisfaction, graces his face. "This is a pleasant surprise. What are you doing here?"

What does it look like I'm doing? Handing out clothes to the homeless? At this point, I should just ditch the whole lot and run.

Looking anywhere but his face, I quickly remember my locked car. I need an exit strategy before my biceps truly snap. "Picking up some dry cleaning. Now, if you'll excuse me."

"Of course, let me help you with your door." Assuming I already unlocked my vehicle, Shaw reaches around me, giving the door handle a little tug. "If you can just unlock the door, I'll open it for you."

Frustration for the situation burns within me. Taking a deep breath, Shaw's smell assaults my nose. Clean, fresh laundry and citrus soap.

Just like my ears, my nose remembers him. A memory of us

in the shower flashes through my mind, and I'm frozen in the past before being dragged back to the present.

"The door, Kate. Unlock it." Impatience seeps into his tone.

I beg your pardon? I raise an eyebrow and scowl. He thinks I'm doing this on purpose? Like I'm being difficult and trying to toy with him. Like his nearness, his voice, his smell, hasn't sent me spiraling back to the past.

I stare straight into his mesmerizing eyes and lean toward him like I'm about to share a closely-guarded secret. He leans in expecting a soft whisper.

"*I can't* open the door! It's not *working!*"

He whips away from me and winces, probably from his burning eardrums. He holds out his hand and snaps his fingers. "Here, just give me your keys."

Loathing my life and looking to make the fastest getaway possible, I angle my hip toward him. "They're in my pocket."

Like lightning, he plunges his hand inside my pocket. It's right at that moment I remember the events of my utterly craptastic day. "No!"

Confusion is written across Shaw's forehead as he withdraws his hand like my shorts are on fire. His fisted hand extends between us, and both of us stare at the delicate lace peeking between his fingers.

Kill me now.

Uncurling each finger like he's doing a countdown, Shaw looks between me and his hand which is now fully open. A smirk stretches across his face.

Sitting in the center of his palm is my soaked key fob, tangled in my pink, lace thong.

18

SHAW

Pink tinges Kate's cheeks as she stares at what I'm holding. It had taken me a second to figure out why my clenched hand was wet. To be honest, a scrap of pink lace never hit my radar for what would be sitting in Kate's pocket.

It was like sticking your hand in one of those boxes in grade school and trying to tell your brain what you were feeling.

It had been a long while since I held a pair of her panties. To be honest, I don't think I ever truly held them. More like skimmed them down her body to reveal the treasures beneath.

The swimming debacle returns to me in a rush. Kate daring me to swim out to Birch Island in the freezing waters of Lake Michigan, only to have her hightail it back to my cottage with every stitch of my clothing in her hot little hands.

I'll admit, the walk back to the cottage was a bit freaky, not knowing if I would encounter a bear or the local sheriff out for his nightly rounds.

I had stomped back, angry and surly, only to find Kate waiting for me on the deck in nothing but a pair of lace panties. Lace panties very much like the ones I had pulled from her pocket.

My dick stirs as I stroll down memory lane. I need to lock him down before I embarrass myself in the middle of the sidewalk.

Clearing my throat, I look at Kate. She is doing her best to avoid eye contact while simultaneously attempting to hoist her obnoxious load of dry cleaning to her shoulder.

I click her key fob a couple of times, but it fails to unlock her door. I suspect the wetness of her underwear has something to do with its malfunction.

"Seems like your key isn't working."

"You sure? Maybe you just don't know how to click it." Sarcasm as thick as molasses drips from Kate's lips.

I meet the challenge and innuendo in Kate's eyes. Looks like *Feisty Kate* has come out to play. "Yeah. Knowing how to click it has never been a problem for me. What about you? Ever have problems clicking it when you're alone?"

"Nope. Every time I click it, it just opens right up. Even though a double click is sometimes needed when it's been sitting for a while."

I swallow, my brain having no problem imagining Kate. Reclined on her bed, eyes closed. Her small hand creeping across her stomach, angling further down... Shit. *Down boy. Baseball statistics, stock prices, mind-eating zombies.*

I glance at Kate, her lips barely containing a smirk. She knows the spiral my mind has taken, her words sent me from zero to horny in three short sentences.

My mind had forgotten how she could turn me on with mere words. Unfortunately, my dick has the memory of a starving elephant. His short-term experiences may be lacking, but his memory is long and vivid.

I squeeze my hand, balling her panties within my fist.

"I'm keeping these, by the way. I had intended to grab a

coffee just up the street. Ward off that afternoon energy slump. It seems you killed two birds with one stone."

"What do you mean?"

I pull her panties to my face and inhale. Closing my eyes, I slowly exhale before sliding them into the inner pocket of my suit coat. "Apparently, I was craving the sweet, tangy *aroma* of...*coffee*. You know the kind? Strong, sweet, just a touch of spice? Best coffee fix I've had in months. Energy restored."

Kate's face is a blank mask. Locked down tight. But the Kate I knew wouldn't stay quiet for long. She's thinking, plotting, planning. Time for me to exit.

Slipping her key fob back in her pocket, I turn and start walking toward my office leaving her to solve the vehicle issue on her own.

Shaw—one, Kate—zero.

My ears are just sensitive enough to hear a muttered "Asshole" as I step off the curb.

After finishing my email to the yacht company in Wisconsin, I pull my phone from my pocket. It's well after seven p.m., but I don't want to head home yet.

My impromptu meeting with Kate has excited and riled me up. I reach my fingers into my coat pocket, fingering the delicate lace that had been nuzzled up to Kate's body at some point today.

I had taken a walk earlier under the guise of going for a coffee. My frustration had been an unwelcome distraction since our dinner a few days ago. The questions swimming around in my head were getting louder.

As I approached and saw her struggling on the sidewalk, my adult maturity flew out the window. I wanted to taunt her and tease her, hoping she would react and the unreserved, unfiltered Kate would respond.

She had always been shy, but now she's aloof. Haughty. Guarded. I don't like it. She isn't the Kate I had known, and I have an almost obsessive need to know why.

Why does she hide behind a mask? What has she been doing since we ended?

We never truly broke up. The words were never spoken, and my heart never felt the clean break of closure. Seeing her had unearthed a desire for answers.

When she left, my sadness and desperation tricked me into thinking I didn't need or want her. After seeing her now, I know my mind has played an elaborate shell game, transferring and compartmentalizing my feelings until I couldn't remember their weight or significance.

I stand from my desk, crossing my massive office to the closet where I keep a bag of workout clothes and swim gear. A long grueling swim has always done wonders for clearing my mind. Whether it comes from exhaustion or clarity, I intend to catch some sleep tonight.

I walk into the bathroom attached to my office, stripping down and pulling on a pair of athletic pants over a Speedo. My eyes drift across my reflection, landing on the tattoo on my left pec. Small and faded, it's a daily reminder of the woman whose panties are currently stuffed in my suit pocket.

I had gotten the tattoo the day Kate left. At the time, I planned to surprise her with it. More than once, we agreed to each carry a piece of the other's heart.

Looking at it, I feel the past rush back, filling me with the unwavering confidence I had in her. In myself. She was my heart.

As the days following her disappearance bled together, hope replaced confidence.

Uncertainty replaced hope.

Despair replaced uncertainty.

The tattoo, a small letter K shaped like a jigsaw piece, rested right above my heart. Kate had been the person I had deemed worthy of sharing my heart. She had held it and promised she would keep it safe. I had mistakenly thought I held hers. When she left, a piece of me went with her, my tattoo a daily, unwanted reminder of what she took when she left.

I had been searching for Kate for sixteen years, never once stopping, though my reasons for finding her had changed over the years. Even when Elizabeth and I were married, I had someone looking for her.

Call me what you will. Lowlife. Bastard. Cheater. In the beginning, I thought finding her would erase her reasons for leaving. She would see me. Remember me. Love me.

Over the years, I grudgingly accepted she'd left. For whatever reason, she had abandoned what could have been for a reality in which I didn't exist. My feelings for her devolved into bitterness and blurred my memories.

Wanting to rid myself of the poison her memory had become, I continued to look for her, desperately yearning for closure. I wanted an ending and the ability to cut the jagged piece of her memory from my heart for good.

Seeing her showed me how much of a liar I had become. I still want her. I yearn for her smiles. Her caring words. Her acceptance. Her love. My heart denies my mind its revenge, protecting her memory and refusing to taint or mar what it holds dear.

Seeing her brings a clearer perspective. Unknowingly, my time with her had shaped me as a person. My professional drive. My unconditional love for Sarah. My efforts to be a good husband.

Years of decisions had been unconsciously shaped by her. I bought a boat slip in Milwaukee because she had grown up there. I spent more time with Sarah because it had been Kate's wish to have spent more time with her own dad. In retrospect, I had probably chosen Elizabeth because she was the complete opposite of Kate.

I thought I had been successful in smothering my memories of Kate. In actuality, she lived within some of my most important actions and decisions.

My thoughts are a chaotic mess. I need to man up. Live for what I want.

My heart is screaming. It wants her. *I* want her. Our years of silence are over. Fate has brought us back together. Her reasons for leaving all those years ago no longer matter. Sure, we need to talk about it, but I know now I want to move forward.

She may struggle, object, and refuse, but I am never letting her leave me again.

19

SHAW

I STROLL INTO V'S OFFICE, NO LONGER ABLE TO AVOID MY obsessive need to gather information about Kate.

Always an early riser, V is already sitting behind his desk, engrossed in emails, his damp hair indicating his morning swim has come and gone.

Sensing my presence, his gaze lifts from his computer screen. It isn't one of surprise, he's just assessing why I'm at his office early on a Friday morning.

His interest is piqued.

"Tell me everything you know about Kate Waters." I get straight to the point, not one to mince words. Especially about this woman. V knew about my past. He knew I had found "the one," and it ended horribly. He didn't know the whole story, no one truly did. But he knew I never cared for Elizabeth in the same way.

V leans back, folding his arms across his chest as he smiles from his seated position. "She's a volunteer and a damn good one at that."

"Why didn't you tell me about her when she started volunteering?"

"Why would I? She's a volunteer. Her background check didn't raise any red flags. She's always on time and damn good with the kids. They like and respect her, which, as you know, is a huge victory."

V turns around and grabs a file from the cabinet directly behind him. I stare as he places the file on his desk, flipping it open to her one-page application.

"Her off-the-charts hotness level is an added bonus for my eyes on the days she's here."

Heat rises through my body. V purposely didn't tell me about her. "You didn't tell me because you're interested in her for yourself, aren't you?"

V's smirk confirms my suspicions before the words leave his mouth. "She *could* be a woman of interest to me if that's what you're asking."

"She works here. She's off-limits." I smile at my quick thinking. No way in hell is he going to worm his way into Kate's life. There's only room for one guy, and that guy isn't V.

The smirk slowly fades as V's eyes lock with mine. "Why are you asking about Kate? And why the possessive caveman shit? Have you even met her?"

"I met her last week. Sarah and I invited her to dinner. I thought it was harmless. The way Sarah has been talking about her, I thought she was an old English teacher type."

V takes a sip of his coffee, trying to hide his smile. "Blew that impression out of the water, did she?"

Taking a seat in front of his desk, I rest my elbows on my knees. "Yeah."

"She gets your blood racing? Thinking of her under you instead of across from you, yeah?"

I look directly at him before delivering the blow. "She has already been under me."

Confusion and annoyance cross V's face. He thinks Kate and I have hooked up since last week.

"Please tell me you and she didn't bump uglies after your dinner?"

"We didn't 'bump uglies' last week, as you so crudely put it. It's been a while."

"Shit. I thought you never stepped out on Elizabeth."

"I didn't, you ass. Kate came before Elizabeth."

I watch as V's eyes narrow before going wide. His brain slowly connects the dots from what he knows of my past.

"Kate. Your new volunteer. Sarah's boss. She's the one fate stole away."

20

SHAW

I STARE OUT THE WINDOW AS MY DRIVER INCHES THROUGH RUSH hour traffic. I'm distracted and restless, wishing I would have driven today.

Rush hour. More like rush *hours*.

I don't recall a time when traffic hasn't been an issue in Chicago. It could be five a.m. and people would still rush wherever it was they needed to go.

At one time, I liked the hustle. The adrenaline rush of being on the go. Fact is, the adrenaline wears off. It gets old. Boring. Exhausting.

Maybe *I'm* just getting old. After the past couple of days, I feel like an old man.

Since seeing Kate on the street, my brain has been on overload. The lock on my memories has sprung, pushing out every thought, memory, and feeling ghosting through my brain.

A summer of memories materializes, unbidden. Memories, vivid and real, vanish as quickly as they appear. *Maybe it's my brain's way of testing my sanity. Or maybe it's fate's way of giving me the middle finger. The jury is still out on that one.*

The year after Kate left was hell. She loved me, and I was

positive she was coming back. She was the thread in the fabric of my future. Two sewn together as one until she cut the thread and took off, leaving me with a mess of frayed edges, broken and limp.

It took every minute of that year to realize she wasn't coming back. I was lost. Still would be, if I hadn't had Sarah.

Sarah became my reason. My hope. My life. She came into my life when I needed to focus. To move on. To let go. I didn't feel it at the time, as nervous and scared as I was, doing what I could to provide for this helpless little human.

Sarah was, and still is, my saving grace.

After Kate left, I didn't know if my heart would ever heal enough to love another. Having Sarah proves I have the capacity to love.

My love for my daughter is woven with titanium threads. Unbreakable.

With Kate, I loved. With Sarah, I lived.

As my car pulls up in front of my building, I realize Sarah is going to bombard me with questions. I'm ashamed to admit I've been avoiding her since our dinner. Avoiding questions I have no desire to answer, but knowing I will when she asks.

Sarah is an intelligent, sharp girl. No doubt she felt the blanket of tension at dinner. Her anger regarding my departure was evident in the string of scathing texts I received over the past few days.

I've never been one to shy away from confrontation unless it involves my daughter. She is a formidable opponent, one I've had no energy to face. Call me a coward, but I know how I've raised my daughter, and I've had no desire to face her wrath in my current mental state.

I flash my driver, Michael, a tired nod and exit the car. Jonathan, the doorman, opens the door as I approach.

"Good evening, Mr. Graham."

I keep my head down as I skirt around Jonathan's body,

giving him a muttered reply before walking to the elevator. Answering to Sarah after how horribly I treated her has me feeling like I'm on my way to the principal's office.

I wave my access key across the panel and the elevator doors close. My breath quickens as I realize what I've done. In my distraction, I stepped into the elevator instead of taking the stairs. My hands start to shake and sweat beads across my forehead.

My breathing becomes more labored with each floor. Shit. I can't breathe. I need air. Seconds before I push the emergency call button, the doors open on my floor. I stand immobile, trying to calm my nerves enough to move my feet. Minutes pass before I'm composed enough to step off the elevator.

I'm greeted by darkness as I step through the door of my condo. I toss my keys and briefcase on the entry table, then peel off my suit coat and throw it on the back of a nearby chair. Making my way down the hall, I stop at Sarah's closed door and hear the steady hum of her shower. It seems my execution has been stayed for the moment.

I continue to the master bedroom at the far end of the hall. Opening the door, I see the orange and pink hues of the setting sun. The floor-to-ceiling windows opposite the bedroom door are the main reason I bought this place. *Lord knows it wasn't for the elevator ride.* I'm awed by the sight of the sky reflected in Lake Michigan.

The water infuses me with a feeling of tranquility. This room is my shelter from life's chaos.

After shedding the rest of my suit, I grab a pair of well-worn jeans and a Northwestern T-shirt. Dragging my feet down the hallway in search of Sarah, I no longer hear the shower, and her door is open.

Slamming cabinets alert me to her whereabouts. Turning the corner into the kitchen, I am struck with a sensation of déjà vu. Her thick, caramel hair is thrown on top of her head in a messy, wet bun. Her beauty and mannerisms hit me with a familiarity that is misplaced and confusing.

Is peanut butter and jelly OK? Answer wisely because it's my favorite.

Sarah looks up, surprise in her gaze. "Did your rude pill wear off?"

I see frustration in her eyes. She wants to pick a fight, but she also wants answers. Her mind is pulling her in two directions. Anger would be instantly gratifying, but answers would be more satisfying.

She slams her peanut butter and jelly sandwich down on a plate, stalking to a bar stool and slouching down on it. She takes a bite of her sandwich, giving me laser eyes as she chews and swallows.

I can see her anger ebbing, her curiosity winning. I busy myself making a sandwich while I wait for her questions.

"Why did you leave?"

"I had a call. Strell and Johnson wanted to cut a deal."

"She was a guest. One you treated like gum stuck to the bottom of your shoe. What's your deal? You would have taken my phone for a month if I did that."

"I'm also your father. I make the money and pay the bills. I have to work."

Narrowed eyes bore into mine. "Doesn't mean you have to be a jerk."

"Noted."

"How do you know Kate?"

The question gives me pause. I knew it was coming. Sarah's sharp and direct as a missile. "I met her a long time ago. We parted ways. I haven't seen her since."

Silence coats the kitchen before a sly smile appears on Sarah's face. "You dated her, didn't you?"

I wipe my mouth with a napkin. "Briefly, yes."

"Who broke it off?"

Could I say she broke up with me? More like, vanished into thin air. "No one, really. She just left one day."

"Did you love her? Why didn't you try to find her?" My daughter, the romantic.

"Yes, and I did."

"And...what happened when you found her?"

"I bought her a thousand-dollar bottle of wine."

21

EVIL ONE

Present...

I lean back against the headrest, staring at the city lights as they pass my window.

Irate doesn't cover my present mood.

My meticulous plan went to shit tonight.

The fault lay at the feet of one of Chicago's finest. Officer Johnson had been the perfect ally until she got greedy and wanted more than I was willing to give. I shut her down before she knew what hit her.

She is dead to me. And so are years of patience and planning.

Feeling the stare of the driver, I look in the mirror attached to the windshield. Fucking service couldn't even send my usual driver.

Our eyes lock, and I feel my blood surge. I sense a darkness hidden within the green orbs. An evilness I can mold and exploit.

"See something you like?" My voice is husky as it drifts to the front seat.

A wide smile fills the mirror. "Do you?"

Undoubtedly.

Just like that, my mood lifts, replaced by excited desire. My smile returns as my plan falls back into place.

22

KATE

FINISHING MY FIRST ROUND OF EDITS, I STAND AND STRETCH, happy with the progress of my current project. It has been a long day.

Who was I kidding? It's been a long couple of months. My predictable, orderly, albeit dull, life has taken a turn on a tilt-a-whirl, and I am still struggling to get my bearings.

I'm amazed I've completed my edits considering the turmoil of my thoughts. Shaw's abrupt, unexpected entrance back into my life has been wreaking havoc on my mental state. Over the past weeks, sleep has been a commodity I haven't been able to afford. My body is physically exhausted, but my mind is wired. It's like my brain is speeding down the Auto-bahn on a never-ending tank of fuel.

I am confused, frustrated, angry, and hurt. But I'm also energized and excited.

I convinced myself years ago that I hated his actions. His unspoken words. His ability to make me fall in love with him. The coldness of his abandonment. All this left me no choice but to bury what we had and move on.

For sixteen years, I've been denied the luxury of questioning his motives and receiving closure. I willed myself to accept my own version of closure. In doing so, Shaw gradually disappeared from my everyday life. Like faded, old photos, I kept him tucked away in a box within my heart, able to retrieve memories when I wanted, but never trusting myself to have them displayed in the open where I would dwell upon the images.

Amy has been the model best friend, loving me like the sister I never had. She is my rock, holding me up when my body doesn't have the energy to move. My debt to her is larger than I'll ever be able to repay. She spent hours rubbing my back, listening while I cried myself to sleep the night of "the dinner." I barely made it back to the house before I collapsed from shock. She'd embraced me as I fell apart and stuttered through the explanation for my meltdown.

She is the only person who knows Shaw's significance to my past. She knows of our relationship and how it ended.

There's one detail I have never shared. Not with Amy, not with anyone. I still have difficulty accepting the decisions I felt forced to make from my limited set of choices.

Amy has been an angel, but she is also a working woman who can't afford to babysit her mentally distraught friend. She'd been needed at a client meeting in Los Angeles, and while she swore she could send her office manager, Eric, I insisted she go. Her company is her livelihood, and I'd never forgive myself if she lost money or clients because of my breakdown.

She made me promise to call, no matter the time, and she would fly home if I needed her.

Deciding I wouldn't sit alone at home wallowing, I'd thrown my notes and laptop in my purse and headed to Beacon.

Beacon is my safe place. Its calming atmosphere envelopes me like a warm hug. I had been fortunate to find this place. I love its vibe. I can write and shut off the world, which is what I had needed today.

No past. No memories. No Shaw. I did what I had to do. I became Kennedy Willow, the strong, independent woman. The woman in control of her choices, her life, her future.

I roll my shoulders and stare at the wall. I am strong. I am prepared. Shaw is a hiccup in my life's path.

He's a storm on the horizon, building strength, and placing me in the path of swirling chaos. I need to harness an inner strength, holding myself together until the storm of Shaw moves through. I just hope it doesn't destroy me before it clears.

23

KATE

A WEEK HAS PASSED SINCE "THE PANTY EXCHANGE" AND MY nerves, while still on edge, have calmed. Shaw has made no effort to contact me, and for that, I feel relieved.

Sarah and I have been working through scenes quickly. We are like partners in a well-choreographed dance. In charge of research, she develops general ideas for scenes, and I expand them into full-blown scenes.

As the scenes start to form a more cohesive story, I can see Sarah piecing together the direction of my manuscript. So far, she has held her tongue, but I can see her brain working through ideas and questions as we work.

I have become comfortable with her, often forgetting she is just fifteen years old. She is such an intuitive young woman, I find myself wanting to open up to her.

I am beginning to trust her. With those feelings, I know I need to share my hidden truth.

I have to trust she will not share the information with anyone. Telling her could put my carefully constructed facade at risk. While I have volunteered with many teens, I never quite know what they are thinking. Telling Sarah could end poorly, but I hate deceiving her almost as much as I hate giving up the information.

I've decided to tell her I am Kennedy Willow, but I'd yet to find a perfect time, until today.

It's my day of reckoning as I prepare to work with her. She doesn't have school, her dad is out of town, and she's looking to avoid her mom's house.

My eyes roam her form. Her head bent. Earbuds in. She's alternating between writing notes and staring into space, and note cards of varying colors are fanned out before her. Some are organized in lines, while others are in a haphazard array, waiting for inclusion in a scene.

So much of Shaw is woven within her. Every time I work with her, I recognize a little more of him. She has the Graham confidence. Like a magnet, people are drawn to that confidence, as it exudes an underlying feeling of trust.

She has a keen intelligence that looks at the world from all angles. She will never allow herself to fall prey to a life of heartbreak and forced choice. It is something I envy with the same conviction as my thankfulness for the bond we have formed.

Needing to calm my nerves, I take a sip of my lukewarm soda, nearly choking as it burns my throat. I return my cup to the table and clear my throat, hoping to garner Sarah's attention.

She is in the zone. No amount of subtlety will divert her attention. I take a deep breath, releasing it before tapping her on the shoulder.

True to the reaction of a person immersed within her own mind, Sarah's body jerks. Embarrassed by her action, she gives a small smile while pulling out her earbuds.

"Sorry. I guess I was more focused than I thought. Do you need something?"

"Yeah. There's something we need to talk about."

Her eyes grow big, reflecting nervousness as she sits straighter in her chair.

"Nothing's wrong," I rush to reassure her.

I take one last breath, knowing the next thirty minutes will determine my future with Sarah. An eerie feeling crawls down my neck, and I spin around, hoping to catch a glimpse of what had spooked me. Nothing moves and nothing seems out of place from my vantage point at the computer.

Will she be angry? Surprised? Hurt?

"There's something I haven't told you." Sarah looks at me, wide-eyed and waiting. "I'm not quite the person you think I am."

Sarah pulls her bottom lip into her mouth, nibbling while she stares at me. "I don't understand."

I stand, running my hands through my hair and tugging the roots. *How can I write best sellers, but I'm having difficulty explaining myself to a fifteen-year-old girl?*

"I'm screwing this up." I pace while trying to gather words into a coherent string. "You know the project we've been working on? Do you have an idea what it is?"

Sarah pauses, her eyes scanning left and right, like a person trying to retrieve information stored in the far recesses of her brain. "A book? A novel of some kind?"

I give her an affirmative nod and smile, encouraging her to continue. I hope she uses every ounce of her intelligence to piece together what I'm trying to say. It may be a cowardly way, but I cannot come up with an easier solution. I'm hoping she'll be more receptive to my information if she puts it together on her own.

"Some kind of psychological thriller, right?"

Again, I give her an affirmative nod. If she's the fan she claims, my next piece of information will get to her to the finish line. "The main character is a forensic anthropologist named Emma Jansen."

Sarah sits for a moment. I see the minute she figures out what I'm too much of a coward to say. Her eyes grow large as a wide smile stretches across her face. "Holy crap! *You're* Kennedy Willow?" Her voice hitches at the end like she's asking a question, even though she already knows the answer.

I raise my eyebrows and lift my shoulders in a shrug. She obviously wasn't lying about being one of my fans.

Sarah jumps from her chair and paces the room like a caged animal. I let her, knowing she's processing my information and looking for clues she may have missed.

Her excitement and nervous energy are contagious. I rise to my feet from my propped position against one of the computer tables.

"I can't believe I didn't figure this out. She...I mean...you are, like, my *favorite* author! You've sold millions of books. You've been published in something like fifty countries. Why didn't I see it?"

As sudden as her outburst hit, she stops and looks at me. "Wait a minute. I've seen pictures of Kennedy Willow. Her picture is on the back of all of her books. That isn't you."

Her mind works so fast, but at least we're already through the most difficult part of my confession. "True. Those pictures aren't me."

Sarah's eyebrows lower and her nose scrunches. "Are you Kennedy Willow or not?"

"I'm Kennedy Willow, but the woman whose picture appears on my books is the public's image for Kennedy Willow."

"Why? If I was the awesome writer you are, I'd have my picture plastered all over my books. You're famous!" She speaks with the certainty and conviction of a fifteen-year-old product of the social media age. For all of her introspection and intelligence, her answer is true teenage girl.

"It's not something I can explain right now, but let's be

content to say I like my privacy. Fame is not something I'm focused on."

Sarah seems mollified, yet a little disappointed, with my answer.

"It's very important to me that no one knows Kennedy Willow is actually Kate Waters. I've spent a very long time separating my personal life from my author life. It was necessary for me at a difficult time in my past."

Sarah listens, the shock of our conversation setting in and stealing questions I'm sure will come.

"Will you be able to help me keep my secret? It maintains my anonymity and lets me be Kate Waters, not Kennedy Willow." I bite my nail, a nervous habit that rears its ugly head when I'm highly stressed.

Sarah stares into my waiting eyes. "I will guard it with my life. I won't tell a soul."

The butterflies in my stomach immediately dissolve. I love this girl. I didn't fully realize until now how strongly we'd bonded. If I would have lost her over this, it would have been like losing a loved one.

Sarah stares at the ground, and an energy surrounds her as the first questions bubble to the surface. I owe her this. She has given me her trust, and I must do the same. "You have a question for me, don't you?"

Sarah keeps her head tilted down, raising just her eyes in my direction. "Why did my dad say your name was Kate Bradley?"

The storm I could feel brewing puts me on edge. My life is predictable, orderly, and safe. I'm currently walking a line of uncertainty, a line that is slowly, inexplicably, pulling me closer. Like the ripple from a skipped stone thrown across the water, it is moving and changing.

I study Sarah, trying to determine how much to reveal, and how fast. I've already shared so much. While I trust her curiosity is strictly for her own information, I'm weary, standing at the end of a dock, staring into the dull water. It's eerily calm, yet dark enough to hide the uncertainty that is the bottom.

Once I jump, there's no turning back. I'll be drenched in memories, filled with both happiness and pain. My muscles twitch, urging me forward toward the water.

I am strong.

I am ready.

"That was once my name."

"Why did you change it?" A voice devoid of accusation and filled with curiosity passes across Sarah's lips.

Painful memories of that time bubble through my consciousness. "A situation beyond my control was pulling me under. I was drowning in memories. A very good friend urged me to focus on a new path, choosing something I loved to pull me out of my depression. A new focus. My love of writing became my salvation." My lips turn a half-smile. "To truly move forward, I had to shed the aspects of my life that were weighing me down. A new focus. A new name. A new me."

Sarah sits, silently processing. As I watch her, I see Shaw. His focus. His quiet contemplation. The very best pieces of him are reflected in her.

I am sadly thankful. Sad our future died, yet thankful his dream of being a father didn't.

A small voice breaks me from my reverie. "You didn't totally let go."

Lines of confusion crease my forehead. "What do you mean?"

"Your new name, Kate Waters. Dad's job. His love of sailing. He loves the water, always has. You chose a name that meant something to him."

A flutter runs through my stomach. Waters. I remember, it just came to me at the time. Waters just seemed to fit. It had felt calm and soothing to me. *Had I unknowingly chosen the name because it reminded me of Shaw? In trying to forget him, had I subconsciously linked myself to him?*

Sarah assumes my silence confirms her theory. "He loves the water. He told me about a place he used to stay as a kid. Right on the water. Said some of his best memories were created there."

My heart stutters like someone just jumped out and yelled "boo." *Had he told her about Door County?* "What's the place's name? Has he taken you there?"

Focused on any scrap of information about Shaw, I wait impatiently. For all the energy I spent thinking I hated him, I realize I was wrong. My hate is love, disguised by the thorns of betrayal, hurt, and abandonment.

"Don't know the name. We've never been there. He said it lost its pull after he started working for Pierce Industries. Mom suggested going a couple of times when I was younger, but I remember him saying something about wanting to preserve his memories of the place. No big deal. If it was anything less than a five-star resort, Mom wouldn't have been happy anyway. It was probably why he made the excuse."

Preserve his memories? Did he want to remember? He was the one that slammed the door on me.

"Hmm. You're probably right." I'm suddenly tired, our conversation emotionally draining me. Sarah now has private information very few people know, and I have to trust she'll respect my wishes and honor my anonymity. It's a gamble on my part, but I feel calming relief about my decision.

Did Shaw's ability to calm me extend through his daughter too?

Sarah seems accepting of my revelations. Like her dad, she will probably reflect on the conversation and hit me with a bevy of questions the next time.

She has won me over. She's the daughter I would have chosen if I ever had the chance.

24

KATE

"Did you love my dad?"

It's been a week since I told Sarah I am Kennedy Willow. A week of silence obliterated by five words.

I sit, stunned. Of all the questions Sarah could have asked, I didn't think she would start there.

How much did she know of our old summer relationship?

"Ahh, that's a bucketful of questions all rolled up into one." Looking to distract her and deflect the question, I study her note cards, moving some from one line to another in her organized rows. "I like what you've found here. The readers need breadcrumbs leading them where I want them to go. You're quite a talented writer."

Her curiosity isn't swayed. "So, did you?"

A fine sheen of sweat starts to coat my body. My chest grows damp, my shirt clinging to me like a baby monkey clings to its mother. I owe her the truth or at least a semblance of truth. *How much of my old life am I willing to peel back and expose?* I shy away from the total truth, settling for an easier version. "At one time, yes."

Spying my soda can, I walk across the room and swipe it

off the computer table. Clinging to the momentary distraction, I tip the can and allow the sugary liquid to dribble down my throat. Reveling in the burn, I tap the can on the table, wondering if I appeased her curiosity enough to change topics.

Silence fills the room as my heart beats uncomfortably. My previous life had somehow slithered into my present one, this discussion a culmination of fears festering for over a decade.

"What changed?" Her voice is a small, unsure whisper, like that of a child asking a parent for forbidden information.

Could I do this? Could I open up and let the memories bleed from the darkened corners of my mind?

My thoughts are a chaotic mess of feelings attached to words vying for a turn to burst from my mouth. I'd spent years folding, intertwining, and packing away my feelings. A single question has become the broken thread, unraveling my years of pain, hurt, and denial.

"I met your dad when I was twenty. It was the beginning of summer. He had just graduated from Northwestern and was staying at your family's cabin. I was working in the dining room of a small inn." My memories evoke a smile as I remember the first time I met Shaw. His boyish charm, yet confident nature, drew me like a honeybee to nectar. He had been the epitome of perfect, or at least my vision of perfect.

"He was persistent, patient, and very determined. He wore me down, and I finally agreed to go on one date with him."

Sarah grins and nods her understanding. "My dad is a firm believer in the long game. Every time I've gotten in trouble, it has been by my own confession. He is a silent extractor of truth. It's creepy sometimes."

Sarah's statement is valid. Shaw is the ultimate master of the long game. My heart had been the loser in the game we played. I had been naïve, grasping for companionship and acceptance when I met him. I played the game, risking my heart for the ultimate prize, only to lose much more than that.

"We spent every free moment together that summer. We had fun. We were carefree. I hold some great memories of that time."

Sarah's brows lower as she looks at me with confusion. "I don't understand. If you had fun together, what happened?"

Our bubble burst. My heart died. I lost myself.

"I had an emergency and had to leave. By the time I was able to make it back, your dad was gone, and the cottage was closed up."

"Wait, *what*? He left? He didn't try to contact you?" Sarah stands and begins to pace. Her agitation is evident in her posture and gait. "Didn't he leave a phone number?"

Stifling a sad chuckle, I gently remind her of life before social media and prevalent cell phones. "The only phone was the one at the cottage. I found the number in the phone book, but every time I called, the line just rang. I never received a response to the few letters I sent to the registered address."

That wasn't entirely true. I did get the letter. The one that broke my heart while giving me the answers I so desperately wanted.

Sarah stops pacing, silently mulling over my words, looking for holes and inconsistencies. "That doesn't sound like my dad. For all his harsh edges, he still looks for the best in people. He looks for the morsels that give people their personality and individuality. He told me that's how he reminds himself that perfection is not reality."

Sarah's words are a salve to my tattered thoughts. The man she describes sounds so much like twenty-two-year-old Shaw, looking for the good in everyone. That's one of his traits I had most admired.

Like the rays of the full, warm sun, Sarah's face suddenly lights. "Maybe he *tried* to find you. Did you leave him a way to contact you?"

"I did leave him a short note." My mind rewinds to my shaking hands as I taped my note to the wooden front door of the cottage. Shaw had been gone, most likely taking advantage of the cloudless day with his small sailboat. "He wasn't home, the door locked. I just attached it to his door."

The spinning of Sarah's mind is nearly loud enough for me to hear. "You don't know if he ever got your note?" Her stare pins me with a force so strong I can't look away.

Sheltering the shred of hope my heart had harbored for sixteen years, I nearly spit my answer at her. "Of course, he got my note. He just chose to ignore it. He was the only person at the cottage, it was taped to the door. I have no reason to doubt he saw it." *He had chosen to ignore me.*

"There's an easy way to find out. I'll just ask him. Problem solved."

No. The problem wouldn't be solved. It could only cause more hurt. If he hadn't seen my note, then our separation would be just as much my fault as it was his. The stones of hate and distrust on which I'd rebuilt my life would crumble, crashing to the ground in a pile of rubble.

25

SHAW

THE CREAK OF MY CHAIR DISTURBS THE QUIET OF MY OFFICE. Today had been a day of small victories. Following a long-awaited ruling, Elizabeth had been eradicated from nearly every aspect of my life. I suspect the judge's private interview with Sarah had been the deciding factor.

Elizabeth had clung to her petition for shared custody of Sarah, a pawn in her quest for more money to fill her pool of greed. Elizabeth had attempted to discredit and abuse my social standing, citing petty arguments that were as false as a prostitute's moans of pleasure.

Her hope in winning child support until Sarah turned eighteen had been crushed, and Elizabeth's ugliness had oozed out of her perfectly manicured and coiffed self. I was relieved the judge saw her complaints for the lies they were—greed.

I had immediately contacted Sarah to give her the news. Given Sarah's current age, the judge had also ruled Sarah, and only Sarah, would determine the time, duration, and frequency of visits with her mother.

The ruling is a double-edged sword. Sarah will be in charge

of her relationship with Elizabeth. She will have the freedom to make decisions previously out of her control, and she will no longer be a victim to the whims of her greedy mother. However, with the ruling comes the real possibility Elizabeth's interest in a mother-daughter relationship will wither and die in the absence of child support.

My hope for Sarah is she will someday have a mother-daughter relationship filled with love and respect, regardless of money or social standing. If not with her mother, then with her own daughter. Scars of indifference fade but never disappear. My own relationship with my mother is the perfect example.

As I look out my window and across the city, I imagine a life according to my original plan. A life where a ruling like today's wouldn't be celebrated nor would have happened in the first place. What would my life look like? Would I leave for work, excited to return each night to the mutual love and respect of my wife? Would I have more than one child? Would my wife have embraced pregnancy as she carried our child?

I want nothing more than to answer those questions. I know the woman I want, and I don't want to let another day pass without her.

It may have taken me nearly sixteen years, but my life's plan is still valid. Kate is *my one*. She had been the girl my twenty-two-year-old self had fallen for. My first love. At the time, the center of my plan. A plan made in the innocence of a perfect summer.

At thirty-six, Kate is still the woman for whom my heart longs. I am captivated by her inner strength. She has transformed from a shy, innocent, young girl to a refined, confident woman.

It is going to require fierce determination to convince her my plan for us has not changed. Luckily, I have never met a challenge too great. Winning her trust and love is a challenge I gladly accept, no matter how long it takes to reach the finish line.

I want Kate by my side as my partner, lover, and wife, and I won't give up until she walks beside me.

Inky black darkness permeates Chicago. Cocooned within my hired vehicle, I watch the city skyline flash across the window matching the speed of my thoughts.

Where is Kate? Is she safe? Do thoughts of us plague her mind?

The faster the car drives, the more restless I become. Giving myself no time to reflect, I instruct my driver to drop me at Beacon. Its calming effect subconsciously calls to me, a whisper silencing my thoughts.

Ten minutes later, we pull up to the familiar building. A swim would quiet my fears and swallow my secrets as it so often did.

Michael pulls up to the front door. His expectant eyes meet mine in the mirror, silently gauging how many hours separate him from seeing his wife.

"Tonight's swim promises to be long. Go home to your wife. I'll find my own way home."

"It's no trouble, Mr. Graham. I can stay."

"Go home. Give my apologies to Beth for keeping you as late as I already have."

Michael grins, no doubt imagining the ways he'll pass the time with his new bride.

I open the door and step out, tapping the roof of the car to signal Michael's departure. As I walk up to the entrance, I realize my gym gear is back at the office, an oversight that could prove most embarrassing if Beacon wasn't as dark as

Soldier Field two hours after a loss. I have no problem with improvising.

I unlock the door to Beacon with my key, making sure to flip the lock, lest any kids decide to wander in after hours and get an eyeful. Knowing the building layout like I do, I opt to keep the lights off and use the red glow of the exit signs as my guide.

I pass by the technology lab Sarah loves, and open the door to the locker room. My stealth mode ends as the automatic lights spark to life. Somewhat disoriented and nearly blinded by the bright light, I move to my private locker.

I noiselessly slip out of my suit coat, hanging it up before loosening my tie and unbuttoning my Oxford shirt. As I do, my thoughts return to Kate.

I feared our years of silence had tricked me into placing her on a pedestal, embellishing her looks, her voice, her personality. Rather, my mind had subdued her beauty and dimmed my memory of her. She is more. More than I remember. From what I have seen and heard, she is exquisite.

She's also angry and hurt. I gathered that much from our interactions during dinner that first night. While I'm unsure why she would be so upset, considering it was her who left, I'm fairly certain there are lingering emotions from how we ended —or failed to end—our relationship.

How will I polish her tarnished memories of me?

I finish undressing and my mind reels. My rote muscle memory aids me when my mind remains focused elsewhere. Naked as the day I was born, I shut my locker and walk slowly through the door leading to the pool.

Underwater lights, installed at the insistence of Vet during construction, throw a blue cast throughout the room. The *click* of the closing locker room door pierces the silence with a stark echo.

Four steps to the pool, then I'm diving in. Warm water

welcomes me, enveloping me in heat like a well-loved blanket in the dead of night. I surface and move into the front crawl as I make my way down the lane. The water washes away my chaotic thoughts and fills me with a sense of calm as I fall into a steady rhythm.

26

KATE

I SAT DOWN IN THE TECHNOLOGY LAB WITH THE INTENTION OF writing for a few minutes after helping Jenny and Damon, two of my favorite teens who frequent Beacon, finish an English Literature project. A quick check tells me a few minutes morphed into four hours.

An eerie feeling crawls down my neck. I spin around, hoping to catch a glimpse of what spooked me. Nothing moves or seems out of place from my vantage point at the computer.

It is well past eleven p.m., and a good time to call it quits before my active imagination realizes sitting in the dark in a deserted building is the perfect time to freak out.

After saving my work, I gather my notes and throw them in my purse while the computer shuts down. I stretch one last time, then step out of the lab and turn down the hall toward the back door.

Earlier, Jon had told me I could stay late as long as I set the alarm and left through the back door, which locks automatically. Jon said he would "lock" me in before he left. Having no reason to believe Jon forgot, I felt safe enough to lose myself in my writing.

As I approach the back of the building, I see a light from under the locker room door in my peripheral vision. *Strange the lights would be on in the locker room when the rest of Beacon is dark.*

Intending to shut off the lights, I swing the door open in time to hear a distinctive *click* on the opposite side of the locker room. *Are my ears playing tricks on me or is someone else in the building?*

I reach into my purse, pulling out my phone and readying it to dial 9-1-1. My finger hovers over the button as I inch toward the door on the other side of the room. To my knowledge, the door leads to the pool. I have never used it, but I remember the building layout from Jon's guided tour.

I set my purse down, my heart racing, and ease the door open as quietly as possible while gripping my phone tightly in my other hand. The room is not fully lit, only bathed in a blue glow.

Ripples radiate across the pool, and I freeze. Someone is in here. My eyes zero in on the intruder.

From the muscles rippling across a naked back, I can see it's a man. One who swims with strength and purpose.

The fear I felt seconds before falls away, morphing into a morbid fascination. His body cleaves the water with ease. My will to move disappears as I stand, mesmerized by his sleek movements. His muscles are steel molded by a singular focus. He is beautiful. And he has no idea I'm staring at him like a crazy stalker.

Regaining my equilibrium, I inch toward the pool intending to get the intruder's attention. He is on the opposite end now, making the turn that will put him at my end within a minute.

As he swims closer, I continue to watch him.

Anticipation buzzes through me.

Then shock courses through my body.

His stroke, his position, his focus.

I *know* this man.

He captivates my vision as my mind tries frantically to reconcile who I'm seeing. I am a moth, and he is my flame. Like a drowning woman nearing the safety of shore, I am drawn to him. He is a beacon.

As my mind trips over the events of the last few minutes, he draws nearer, focused and unaware of the stalker watching him.

Forgetting my cell phone sits poised in alert mode, I shut it off. The sound, normally disregarded and unheard, is like a cannon within the quiet of the cavernous room as he reaches my end of the pool.

He immediately snaps his head in the direction of the sound.

Somewhat startled, Shaw holds the side of the pool. His blue eyes scream a dozen questions while his lips remain silent. Anger quickly shrouds his surprise.

"Kate? What the hell are you doing here?"

Anger creeps into my lungs, fueling the harsh words poised on my tongue. "I was working. This place was closed and locked. How the hell did you get in here? I should call the police."

A slow smile grows across his full lips. "If you must, go ahead."

I know that calculated look. His response was too quick. *What am I missing?* Still holding my phone, I raise it and turn it on. Explaining his presence to the cops will wipe the smirk from his face.

"Are you absolutely sure you want to call the cops? They'll have to come, take your statement. You may even be asked to go to the police station. They'll have to call the owner and bother him in the middle of the night." *A mind reader now, are we?*

Shaw is baiting me. Yet, I am not sure if it is to make a fool of me or to avoid making a fool of himself.

"Give me one valid reason why I shouldn't call the cops."

He stares at me, raising an eyebrow as if to say, "I'll give you a reason, all right." Even though my heart is beating faster than a hummingbird's, I refuse to be intimidated. I stare him down while I hold my ground. As much as I want to remain angry, excitement and physical desire have taken its place.

Without warning, Shaw places his hands on the pool deck and pushes. His biceps are large and tight as they hold his body for a split second before he climbs out of the water.

I struggle to maintain eye contact, refusing to give him the satisfaction of a visual perusal of his naked torso. He stands in front of me, arms at his side. Rivulets of water drip from his hair, cutting a path down his toned chest.

He closes the distance between us and shakes his head. I jump back, failing to avoid the water leaving his body and hitting me in the eye. I growl—yes, *growl*—at him as I lift my hands to wipe the water from my face.

He throws his head back and laughs. A deep laugh. One that wraps around me like a fur throw on a winter night. It is familiar, yet foreign, and it's disarming. For a few seconds, I forget how much of an ass he is.

Stripped of my earlier resolve, I look at him. Not just his eyes, but his face, his chest. I look at his entire body. His one hundred percent "naked as the day he was born" body.

A gasp flies from my mouth, saliva sneaking down my throat, causing a spontaneous choking fit. As I repeatedly cough, my eyes watering and face turning red, Shaw watches me with calculating eyes.

"This is just speculation, but I think I just gave you a reason not to call the cops." Self-assured cockiness drips from him like the water running in lazy paths down the hard planes of his face. "Calling the cops would require the gift of speech." He leans toward me, voice low like I am his confidant and we're exchanging forbidden secrets. "Correct me if I'm wrong, but you appear a little speechless at the moment."

His sarcasm is mocking, as I struggle to take a full breath. If I could conjure some of the spit currently choking me, I would nail him dead center in his smug face.

Determined to rip him from his cocoon of arrogance, I will myself to calm down. "Kindly shed your coat of flattery, Mr. Graham. My choking was problematic because you made me wet, not because you're naked."

Shit. That sounds bad.

I back away, looking for an escape. Shaw steps forward, pursuing me in all his glorious nakedness, as my back hits the locker room door. I feel behind me for the door handle as Shaw crowds me. Bracing his forearms against the wall on either side of my head, his eyes are lasers, racing to read my thoughts before I lock them down.

He tilts his head and leans down, just inches from my ear. Turned on, but refusing to give him any indication, I snap my eyes toward the floor. His proximity steals my escape plan, making his torso my unintended visual target.

I stare at his naked chest. My traitorous tongue begs me to open my lips and collect a sample for comparison—the man in front of me versus my lover of the past.

His breath softly caresses my skin, tickling the sensitive area just below my ear. My heart beats furiously, as his pulses strong enough I can see the fluttering movement just below his skin.

"I remember every single time I have been naked before you." His words are a reverent whisper like he fears someone will steal them before he gives them voice. "Every single time you looked at my body, touched my body. Every single time I made you wet for me. Every. Single. Time. That is a problem that has ghosted me for sixteen years."

He leans back, my eyes immediately straying to his. For just a moment, I lower my walls and let him see what our past has done. My fear, my hurt, my loss of hope all stemmed from his unfulfilled promises. I'm fully clothed, yet I feel naked in front of him.

He sees it. We both feel it. A crack appears in his spirit. His confidence has teased him into thinking we can return to who we were and what we had.

I look back to his chest, no longer willing to share my vulnerability. My mind tells me I've moved on while my heart urges me to reconsider.

Close again, our hearts are calling to each other, trying to establish the synchronous rhythm of the past. A past Shaw left and the one I've so desperately tried to forget.

Finding the door handle, I push backward, releasing the lock and creating my escape. Not expecting the sudden movement, Shaw reaches out, bracing his hands on the doorframe and narrowly saving himself from a face plant.

Unconcerned for Shaw's physical well-being, I turn and flee on rapid feet. I'm thankful my brain can function on autopilot, allowing me to navigate through Beacon in the dark. I continue toward the safety of my car, which sits outside the back door in the lot behind the building.

Our conversation has caused a burn I can feel radiating through my veins. I look down, noticing for the first time, I'm still clasping my cell phone in my hand. I completely forgot about my phone and the reasons why I'm holding it. I slip it in my back pocket and immediately pull my keys from my front pocket.

I open the building's door just enough to squeeze through the opening, in pursuit of the safety of my SUV. Chastising myself for my erratic behavior, I unlock my door and slide into the driver's seat.

I take deep breaths, slowly releasing each one, in an attempt to calm my racing heart. My mind lingers on our conversation.

The longer I stood before him, the more I saw *my* Shaw. The boyish smirk. The way he listens with his eyes, consuming pools of rapt compassion and unwavering attention. The way he wears his arrogance wrapped within a tinge of shyness.

Forgiveness hovers in my periphery. I feel myself wavering as the drive to ask him my unanswered questions becomes almost overwhelming.

After a few minutes, I've calmed myself enough to drive home. As I start my car and pull out of the parking lot, I desperately recall my internal chant.

Shaw is the enemy. He lied. He left. He loved...without me.

My mind knows all of this, but my heart begs me to see it his way. After all, I also left. I changed. I lived...without him.

I want to hide from my shortcomings. Blame Shaw for our mistakes and my pain. My pain has bound me to him for so many years, and I have no idea how to release myself from the bindings.

I pull into my driveway, realizing I have no idea how I made it home. I barely remember pulling out of Beacon, yet somehow, here I am.

Finally free of his questioning gaze, my mind has circled back to contemplation of forgiveness and what that would look like for me? For Shaw?

Truth: We each made decisions that changed our futures. If I can accept our choices, can I free myself from years of pain?

Will freeing myself cut the bindings that secure me so intimately to Shaw? Am I willing to live without him and his memory?

27

EVIL ONE

PRESENT...

My eyes survey the SUV, parked in front of me, from the privacy of my black BMW rental. Luxurious, yet a dime a dozen in this city. Perfectly nondescript and indistinguishable to the downcast eyes of the homeless trash who roam the nearby streets like cockroaches.

Shaw's been inside for half an hour, and I'm already bored. My phone does little to keep me occupied as I wait for his departure. His jaunts to Beacon are a thorn in my side. A large amount of effort yielding little reward, and a waste of my precious time.

As I debate the merits of leaving, the back door flies open, releasing a wild-eyed Kate.

Interesting.

It seems my reward may exceed my effort after all.

Shaw and Kate. A two-for-one deal.

Kate runs to her car, her attention far away from my assessing eyes. The lights of her SUV blink as she approaches. She jerks the door open and slides in. Her vehicle idles for a few minutes before she pulls away.

I hate that she's here.
And for that, she'll have to pay.

28

KATE

I barely close my eyes and the light from my window jars me awake. After a restless night cursing my bedsheets, my pillow, and every other offensive object in my room, I think I finally drifted off around five a.m.

I glance at my phone—seven a.m. *Great. This day is going to be fabulous.* Being a person who cannot ever fall back asleep, I growl in protest and get out of bed. Hoping a shower does wonders for my groggy mental state, I step under a spray of warm water.

Reveling in the warmth as it spreads across my skin, my mind drifts to Shaw's body. How the water droplets descended down his neck, making their way across his chest and below. His body was perfection. Remnants of the body I had known so intimately had been visible, yet defined and perfected over the years.

Years had been more than kind to him. My own body's reaction had pebbled my nipples, heating my skin. I'd attempted to disguise my physical reaction with harsh words and fake bravado, but something tells me I may not have been as successful as I hoped.

Thoughts of Shaw pelt my mind as the water and soap from my shower softly mesmerize my skin.

I remember every single time I have been naked before you.

Trails of heated sensation run across my breasts, making them heavy as they beg for attention. My hands slowly drift upward. My fingertips dance across my rib cage, barely touching the sensitive skin just below my firm breasts. My breath stutters, becoming faster, shallower.

My hands continue to my nipples, erect and hard. I feel strong hands, firm and unforgiving, as they knead my breasts, grasping each nipple as they pull outward.

Heat travels directly to my core as wetness pools between my legs. One hand continues to knead and pull as the other seeks the wetness between my legs. One finger slides effortlessly between my folds, eager for its target. Silky warmth coats the finger as I move, pushing in and slowly pulling out, building a rhythm.

Every single time I made you wet for me.

The whisper of his velvet voice acts like gasoline to my already heated body. I pinch my nipples and add another finger to my swollen, dripping core. My head falls back as a thumb grazes my clit.

A third finger pushes in, spreading me with a slight burn as I stretch to accommodate the girth. Large, firm fingers reward me with burning pleasure. My body is on fire.

His head dips, and I grab his hair anchoring him to me as his tongue teases my nipple. White hot pleasure shoots to my core as his teeth bite my sensitive flesh. My orgasm builds as pleasure consumes me. Lips graze my ear. *You hold my heart. I love you.*

The words hit me, and I explode. Pleasure washes through my body. Overwhelming sensations pulse through me, robbing my limbs and ripping my footing out from under me. I sink to the shower floor as the aftershocks of my release continue to pulse through me.

The spray tattoos my body. The water, like fine needles, assaults my oversensitive skin. I'm dazed, yet alert.

Never has an orgasm of that magnitude come from my own hand. Only one person has ever owned a response that powerful.

As I reach up and turn off the shower, I hear his faint whisper.

Every. Single. Time.

I feel a buzz and look at my watch. I have thirty minutes to get to a meeting with my editor, and I cannot find my purse. My designer bag houses my computer, my notes, my life, and a large assortment of sugarless gum. If needed, I could fit a Labrador puppy in it. It is, by no means, small and unnoticeable.

Where is it?

My mind runs through yesterday and all the places I can recall having it with me. Minutes later, I remember.

Beacon. Late night. Strange noise. Naked Shaw.

Shit.

I set it down in the locker room while I investigated the pool.

I look at my watch again. There's no way I can make it to Beacon and still be on time to my meeting. I pick up my cell phone, pulling up my contact number for Jon.

His smooth pre-recorded voice hits my ear after the fourth ring, and I end my call without leaving a message.

Shaw. He would have surely seen my purse when he went back into the locker room. Would he have picked it up? Left it there? Known whose purse it was?

You left it in the men's locker room. Do you know any guy who carries a Hermes purse? Get real, my sarcastic inner child rolls her eyes and snarks at me.

I'll have to call him.

I allow myself a few minutes to pace and think of other options—*there are none.*

I pick up my phone and realize I don't know how to contact him. The only detail I know is he's CEO of Pierce Industries, but his contact information isn't going to be just a Google search away.

Wait, I have Sarah's number. I'll just shoot her a text and ask for it.

Kate: Could you give me your dad's phone number?

I glance at my watch again as I pace and wait for a response. Five minutes slip by, and my panic begins to rise.

Teenagers have their phones on them at all times, right?

Sarah: Um, sure? 555-6920. Did I do something wrong?

Kate: Absolutely not. You're fine. I think he may have something of mine. Thanks.

Sarah: OK

I mouth a silent "thank you" that Sarah gave me the number and accepted my reasoning without question.

I call my editor and reschedule for next week. She asks if everything is OK which I fake a half-hearted, "Fine," before ending the call.

I punch in *his* number and hear the first ring before realizing I didn't plan what to say.

I frantically run through the conversation, barely getting through a practiced "Hello," when I hear his caramel-coated, yet annoyed, voice.

"Hello."

"Uh. Hello?"

I hear the initial annoyance in his voice rise. "Who is this? I think you have the wrong number."

Silence. Pulling my phone away from my ear, I see the call has ended.

He hung up on me. What the hell?

My cheeks heat as my anger starts to build. I redial his number and wait. My anger mounts as the phone rings for the third time.

His hardened and perturbed "Hello" barely clears my ears before I unleash my frustration directly at my intended target.

"Do *not* hang up on me! You arrogant ass!"

His strong breath caresses my ear ahead of his words. "You have a nanosecond to tell me who this is. No one has this number."

"I can see why, if you hang up every time someone calls you."

Silence fills the air before I hear a more subdued, "Kate?"

"Yes."

I hear the creak of a spring. *A chair or a door, maybe? Did I catch him at work?*

"What can I do for you?" His calm voice, void of his initial annoyance, is a soothing balm to my anger and frayed patience.

"I think you may have something of mine."

"Oh, yeah? What do you think I have?"

I can hear his smile as he starts to flirt. That voice. I

instantly flash back to this morning's shower. His voice is intoxicating. And so *not* the reason for my call.

Pull it together, girl.

"I left my purse in the locker room last night. Did you see it or pick it up, by chance?"

"No. No purse. But...I did find a ten-pound leather suitcase. Looked expensive. Heavy as hell."

"That's my purse, you ass!"

"Wow, a purse, huh? Could have fooled me."

My exasperation is high and my patience thin. "You have it then?"

"Yeah. I've got it."

"Great! I take back my comment about you being an ass. Give me your address, I'll stop by and pick it up." I hustle around my place to find paper and a pen as I await his directions.

"No can do, Kate."

Wait, what?

"I have your purse, it's safe. But I don't have it with me today."

A frustrated groan escapes as I hit my forehead with my free hand. "Where is it? When can I get it?"

"I'm a businessman, Kate. How about a trade?"

My mind races, trying to pinpoint his angle. *Trade? What does he want that I have?* Suddenly, I narrow my eyes. *If I still know Shaw, he knew I would call, and he already had a plan for when I did.*

"How about your purse for a date?"

Silence. That's all I can offer. If I agree, I'll have to spend time with him. If I don't, I can kiss my computer and all it holds goodbye. I'm the mouse caught in the lion's trap, and Shaw knows it.

I release a breath resigned to Shaw's manipulation. "Fine. When and where?"

"Saturday. Email my secretary your address. I'll pick you

up at eight in the morning. Wear comfortable layers and athletic shoes."

He rattles off his secretary's information, then ends the call. As I stare at my phone, I'm left to wonder if I could really do without my purse and its belongings. Looks like I have three days to figure that out.

29

SHAW

A SATISFIED SMILE SLIDES ACROSS MY FACE, AS I END THE CALL. I knew she'd find a way to get my number and contact me. Her purse—I swear it's larger and heavier than my athletic bag—sits on the backseat of my car forty floors below me.

After she left Beacon like the devil was in pursuit, I had walked into the locker room to find her purse on the floor. Uncertain whether her fear or her forgetfulness had caused her to leave it, its discovery had been the key I needed to get my foot in the door. Her loss had been my gain, one I was fully willing to exploit to get what I wanted.

Satisfaction fills me as I replay our exchange. I adjust my pants, hiding the evidence of my reaction to her call. Angry Kate was a turn on, even when I couldn't *see* her anger. Her tongue delivered barbs that got under my skin, but not in the way she hoped.

She'd resisted my deal, not wanting to trade her time for the return of her purse, but I held my ground until she finally agreed, like I knew she would.

Her words ignited a slumbering hunger. A hunger I keep masked in the stark light of day. The Kate I knew had been a master of words. Creating feelings of warmth and passion, hunger and desire, simply by opening her mouth.

I cannot fathom the fact she has always been within my reach. Had I known where to look, I would have gone to her.

I intend to rectify sixteen years of failure. I have finally found her, and have no plans of letting go.

The "trade" is my ticket to talk to her. We'll be alone, and she'll be a captive audience while I work through all the questions floating between us.

Saturday morning can't come fast enough. It's going to be me, Kate, and the open water.

Saturday morning, I arrive at the address she emailed my personal secretary. I'm briefly confused before I become wise to her plan. Sitting outside Sunnyside Bakery, I catch a glimpse of Kate in a line ten people deep.

The little vixen is smart, yet I won't be deterred. I am positive she gave the address of the bakery for three reasons: One, so I wouldn't have a clue where she lived; two, the popularity of the bakery could make us late for whatever I had planned; and three, having her vehicle would allow her a variety of transportation excuses.

She had honed her skills of subterfuge in the years since I'd known her. I have to admit, I'm both excited and eager to see whatever she plans to do. She has forgotten one can never bullshit a master card player, and I am currently holding four aces. I intend to remind her of that fact, but not before having a little fun at her expense.

Someone happened to back out of a parking spot right next to her Land Rover, so I do some quick maneuvering and back in tight to her driver door. I step out of my vehicle, lock it, and walk to a vantage point allowing me to keep an eye on both Kate and her SUV.

I continue to watch her as she looks around the bakery, peeking out the front window every now and then. Looking for me, no doubt.

Twenty minutes later, she steps up and speaks to the woman behind the counter. One Styrofoam cup and white paper bag later, Kate emerges with a small smile on her lips. She pulls her phone from her coat pocket and looks down, her lips parting in a full smile at the message I'd just sent.

Shaw: Sorry, I'll be there in ten minutes.

Her fingers tap across her phone, her smile growing more pronounced.

Kate: No problem. Take all the time you need.

I watch as she drops her phone back into her pocket and practically skips toward her car.

I stare at her retreating back as realization hits me. She's planning to stand me up.

Kate's not a liar. She will claim she showed, would even show a receipt if questioned. My text gives her the perfect "out" to leave before I arrive. No doubt she thinks I'll second-guess the address and drive away.

As she gets to her car, she notices what I've done. I watch as her face drops, realizing there's absolutely no way she can squeeze in through her driver door.

I recognize her panic as it starts to set in. Her ten-minute escape window is dwindling. She turns, scanning the parking lot for the driver. Her eyes dance right across my body, wrapped in my coat and ball cap, without recognition. Anxiety has blinded her. She walks around to the passenger door, and I hear a scream of frustration. Both passenger doors are blocked by the cement posts holding the enormous bakery sign.

She's trapped, and I can't help but watch in entertained fascination. She paces in front of her car, continuing to scan the parking lot. After a few minutes, her anxiety must fuel her appetite because she sets her coffee on the hood of her Land Rover and rips into the white bag like its presence has offended her.

She reaches in, withdraws a frosted long john, and takes a vicious bite. Custard filling spurts from the end, hitting her chin and igniting a chain of sailor-worthy cuss words.

No doubt her suitcase of a purse, tucked safely in my car, would have a napkin or...twenty.

Like she's reading my mind, I watch her reach to her side, flailing her hand like she's feeling within an invisible purse. Another exasperated scream hits my ears as she tries to clean her chin by alternately wiping and sucking her fingers.

My eyes are glued to her fingers. Saliva pools in my mouth as my brain starts down a dirty road.

She leans toward my Jeep, peering into the darkened windows. I sense her anger has hit a crescendo, and my Jeep may be her next target. As I start my walk across the parking lot, I see her tip her cup dangerously close to my passenger window.

Too nervous to see the lengths she will go to appease her anger, I pull my keys from my pocket and hit the "panic" button. The Jeep goes crazy, horn blaring and lights flashing.

Kate startles and screams, her arms flailing to her side. I can't contain the laugh that flies from my mouth. Had I been recording this, I could have made bank on the video I'm sure would have gone viral. I cancel the alarm on my Jeep and approach her.

Stopping in front of her, I see coffee covers her face and is creating a maze of wet brown streaks down the front of her shirt.

I stifle a laugh under a strangled cough as Kate attempts to maim me with her laser stare. "Hi, Kate, sorry I'm late. Looks like you're wet...again."

30

KATE

Anger and frustration pour out of me as my latte literally drips down my face. I can't catch a break when it comes to embarrassing myself in front of Shaw. It figures he would get here when I'm dripping wet and battling tears.

His comment is successful in making me momentarily forget my intention to leave him high and dry. "Listen! Some jackass just gave me a heart attack, which made me spill my drink. And he hasn't even shown his cowardly face yet. He probably ran back into the bakery before I could identify him."

Shaw reaches into his pocket and produces a wadded up napkin and hands it to me. *One* napkin. That's like giving me an ounce of milk after accidentally eating a ghost pepper.

As I stand before Shaw, wet and uncomfortable, I remember our "trade." I thought I had a foolproof plan for ditching him today, but it seems I'm the fool because I didn't foresee bringing a forklift to move cars belonging to drivers who can't park.

"So, probably not ready to go, huh? Might want to change, first?"

"You think?" My sarcasm knows no bounds. Looks like I'll

need to change and, somehow, I don't think I'm going to be able to lose Shaw on my way home. I'm livid. Not only will I have to go through with his stupid "trade," but he'll also know where I live. Two things I didn't plan on when I woke up this morning.

Shaw opens his mouth, then closes it, deciding against the words he planned to say. "I'll follow you. We can leave your vehicle at your house, and I'll drive from there. No sense taking two cars. Plus, where we're going, there won't be parking for yours."

"And that would be where?"

He gives me his All-American grin. "Wouldn't you like to know."

I reach into my pocket and click my keys to unlock my car. Nothing. I pull my keys out and look down to see wetness seeping from my key fob. *Perfect. Could my life be any worse right now?*

Shaw's eyes sparkle beneath his ball cap as he licks his lips. "Seems like your keys had a run-in with coffee again."

"It would seem so." Bitter sarcasm laces my voice as I picture the last time this happened.

"Forget it for now. I'll take you to your house to change. We'll go on our date, then I'll bring you back here tonight. We'll figure your car out then."

As much as I want to argue or complain, I just want this day to be done. "Fine, let's go."

He walks around to the driver's side of the Jeep. The obnoxious car I've been standing next to this whole time, flashes its lights, indicating it's been unlocked. "I'll just pull forward so you can get in."

Son of a bitch. The Jeep is his.

An hour later, I sit in the passenger's seat of Shaw's Jeep, contemplating the gift of his demise. He had returned my purse when we got to my house. A quick scan indicated everything still remained inside. Pity. It appears I cannot add "thief" to my running list of the "violations" I'm keeping in my head. Nudist. Skinny Dipper. Cocky CEO. Captain. But not a thief.

I haven't said more than ten words to him since the bakery. His attempts at conversation have failed, so we ride in tense silence while listening to Imagine Dragons. His choice, not mine.

As we inch through Saturday morning traffic, I wonder what he has planned and how I'm going to avoid talking to him for the better part of the experience. My anger from earlier has morphed into indifference for this sham of a date.

Turning right into a marina just north of the city, I survey all the boats. It is a travesty calling them boats when most are the size of small houses. I spy several people milling around. Some are washing their yachts, while a few fish from the dock. Others are having coffee as they lounge on comfortable chairs on their boat decks.

I can understand their fascination with being around water. It has always had a mesmerizing, relaxing effect on me. Surprising, considering all of the memories I share with Shaw. I hear my name and realize Shaw has parked the car and is trying to get my attention to step out.

I raise my eyes and find him studying me.

"I haven't been on a boat since I was twenty." My voice sounds small and unsure. The heat in Shaw's stare tells me he is picturing the time he and I spent together on his parents' boat.

"You'll find it's much like riding a bike. Once a seaman, always a seaman."

I reach toward him, pulling back at the last second, afraid

to feel the warmth if his skin touches mine. "I'm not sure if I can do this."

He leans into me, invading my space. "You can do this. I dare you."

His words extinguish my anxiety. Neither one of us can refuse a dare, and he knows it. I look at him and make a decision.

Today is for me. I am not weak. I am strong. I am exhilarated. I will do this.

With firm words and strengthened resolve, I turn to him. "Lead the way, Captain."

I recline on the deck as Shaw steers effortlessly around the final buoy before hitting the throttle and pushing us into the vast waters of Lake Michigan.

As he stands, feet braced apart, scanning for debris and potential threats in the water, I am transfixed by his profile. As we motored through the marina, he turned the bill on his Cubs cap backward, allowing small wayward curls to escape around his face. Those curls are now being caressed by the wind. It is an enticing glimpse of a younger, freer man who looks identical to the only Shaw I have known.

His eyes have shifted to deep, sparkling blue, reminding me of a geode I once saw during a presentation in my college geology class. His well-worn T-shirt and faded, relaxed jeans make him nearly irresistible. The wind has done me a service by tightly molding his shirt to his well-defined chest. He is truly a handsome man.

I quickly push away the regrets I feel creeping into my thoughts. So much has happened in the years since we were together. Absolute and irreversible things put more distance between us than lost years.

Shaw turns, catching my blatant perusal of his body. His smile, soft and genuine, shows fully on his lips and in the sparkle in his eyes. "You're so lost in thought, I'm going to need GPS to bring you back to this date."

A chuckle slips through my lips, covering my embarrassment of being caught a captive to my thoughts. "First, this is *not* a date. Second, no GPS necessary. Just doing a little thinking. The water relaxes me. Where are we headed today?"

"I thought we'd cruise for a while. Maybe stop for a late lunch before heading back." He looks at me with sudden concern. "Sorry, I should have asked if your entire day was free." He busies himself, adjusting dials on the massive dashboard near the wheel. "Chalk it up to my excitement of having you...on my boat."

Is it just me? Did he intend the innuendo or is my brain headed to more nefarious territory than his? He's a curveball to the small amount of romance "game" I have.

"As much as I loathe to admit, I didn't have any plans today outside of a random errand or two. That said, I may be without shirts next week since my Saturday allotted laundry time will be severely depleted."

Shaw leans toward me like he intends to share a shameful secret. "The only thing I heard was 'without shirts.' Can't say I'd be sorry to see that happen."

Placing my hand on my chest and widening my eyes, I purr my mock outrage in my best Southern drawl. "Mr. Graham, you are an incorrigible rogue."

"I would tattoo that title on my chest as long as it involved you, your best assets, and no shirts."

"Watch what you wish for, I may just hold you to that bargain someday."

After our banter, I lean back, face to the sky. The sun feels heavenly. I fail to convince myself that the warmth spreading throughout my body has nothing to do with the rogue standing across from me.

As we continue at a steady clip, Shaw checks some gauges and makes some adjustments before securing the wheel and taking his seat in his captain's chair. He's situated his seat so he can scan the water, and face me a bit more.

We sit in comfortable silence, content to be on the water, listening to the waves as they rock the boat. I can admit this part of the day is turning out to be close to perfect, even if I had tried in vain to ditch Shaw earlier. I find I'm more thankful for his persistence than I would ever willingly admit to him.

Conversation starts, but it's a bit stilted and slow. We've exhausted the weather, favorite TV shows, and what we love about Chicago. Slowly, we work into a rhythm that seems to take off once we start talking about Sarah.

Shaw's love for Sarah is evident in his words, his expressions, and his body language as he tells animated stories of her schooling, friends, and his recent experiences with boys. I openly laugh as he admits to purposely trying to intimidate some of her boy "friends" on more than one occasion. He seems both embarrassed and proud of the lengths he is willing to go to protect his daughter.

As I listen to his stories, I become overwhelmed by the feelings swirling within me. He spoke of his nervousness and his fears of inadequacy when Sarah was a small toddler. He is such an involved and compassionate father.

He is a father and, for a period of time, he had been a husband, belonging to someone else. They had shared family experiences I only dreamed of having when I was younger. Shaw experienced everything we had desired, but he had done it without me. I feel cheated. He had lived what we had dreamed.

I'd wanted so badly to have a family of my own. I wanted

my children to feel the same love I felt initially, growing up in my small family.

It had been the three of us, and we had been happy. Until it had fallen apart in high school, with the physical death of my dad and the emotional death of my mom. It only took a single day for my family to disintegrate.

Shaw's sudden silence snags my attention. He's caught me stuck within my own thoughts for the second time today. I try, without success, to keep my tears at bay. I tip my head toward the sky, making a production of running my hands across my face, trying to erase any evidence of the melancholy I feel.

His eyes search mine, looking for an explanation for the sudden shift in mood. He isn't stupid. He knows I'm upset, no doubt scanning through our conversation to find the words which caused my reaction.

Knowing I can't distract him from the questions swimming in his eyes, I offer a bit of truth wrapped in sarcasm. "Kids. It seems they drastically change your life."

He swallows as he continues to look at me. "Absolutely. She was the best change I could have asked for."

His response causes another batch of tears to well up, begging for escape. I fight to keep them from falling, knowing I can't hide my pain with Shaw just an arm's length away.

He had known my dreams and desires. We talked about them for hours. The dock at his cottage was our favorite place to talk, to dream, to plan.

Footsteps on the deck grow softer, only to return minutes later. A water bottle enters my periphery as Shaw extends his arm. I see it for what it is, a peace offering. I turn my face toward him, reaching for the water bottle at the same time he gives me a sad smile.

He read my pain through my silence and chose to back off.

Can he read my mind? He may suspect, but he can never truly guess the source and depth of my hurt.

31

SHAW

I'm an idiot. Why didn't I think about what I was saying? I silently berate myself as I sneak glances at Kate. Our conversation had started flowing, both of us laughing, settling into a comfort level I haven't felt with a woman in forever. She peppered me with questions, and I had charged ahead without a care or concern for how she would interpret my answers.

I can tell she truly enjoys working with Sarah. She said as much during our conversation. She thinks Sarah is intelligent, insightful, and compassionate.

Kate's departure from the conversation was instant like I had walked into a room and shut off a light. Her eyes dimmed, and her mind pulled her inside, slamming the door in my face.

Now, her mind hides behind that door as she stares at the water. I continue to curse myself, as well as the four-hour trip we have ahead of us. I comb through each story I shared, but I'm lost. *What pulled her away so quickly?*

As we talked, I shared little stories of Sarah as a toddler, a young girl, and a teenager. Stories of sleepovers, first days of school, and even a hair-raising trip to the emergency room for stitches.

I'd even shared the somewhat comical day Sarah learned to ride a bike, explaining Sarah had been determined to learn before her friend, Josh. We visited a store and bought a bike and helmet before heading to a path near our house.

I had recounted Sarah's fear of falling and my own assurances I wouldn't let her fall. By the time we left the bike path that day, Sarah was riding confidently on her own. I told her it had been one of my proudest moments as a dad. To see your child conquer a fear, with your help, is both humbling and exhilarating.

As my mind sifts through our conversations, I happen upon a memory. Flickering to life, like a naked bulb in an old limestone cellar, the realization hits me. The day I taught Kate how to ride a bike.

Too scared to learn as a child, I had coaxed her to give it a try. I admit it may have been the motivation of a naked sleepover that tipped her over the edge in her decision to try.

I'd located an old bike at the cottage, yet it was still sturdy and serviceable. Kate's fear had been palpable. I simply held her and encouraged her, determined to help her succeed and not let her fall.

Kate sat astride the bike, both feet on the pedals, hands firmly gripping the handlebars.

"I don't know if I can do this. You won't let me fall, right?" Her eyes were like saucers as her teeth assaulted her lower lip. My dick stirred to life as she continued to look at me, so innocent and trusting.

"I will never let you fall. You can do this."

She inhaled and exhaled, schooling her features into a look of determination. "OK. I'm ready."

I held the bike, slowly pushing it as she pedaled. Loosening my hold, I continued to give her words of encouragement. Her face was a picture of pure concentration. She hadn't let fear rule her. She may have agreed to humor me, but she was doing this for herself.

I let go as she continued to pedal, not even realizing I was no longer supporting her. She continued pedaling, stopping when she reached the end of the long driveway. She turned to me, her smile the biggest I had ever seen. She jumped off the bike, letting it fall while she ran to me. At the last second, she jumped, wrapping her arms around my neck and her legs around my waist. Her momentum took us to the ground amid laughter.

"I did it! You're the best teacher ever."

I squeezed her in a tight hug. "Think of the story you can tell our future children."

She instantly got quiet, her body stilling under me. My words had stunned her into silence. Glancing up through her lashes at me, she whispered, "We'll tell them together. I'll promise to be their cheerleader."

I swallowed, thinking of the dreams we had, the plans I was already making. "And I'll promise to be their teacher."

"I'll tell them their teacher is the best in the world."

Pulling her closer, my forehead meets hers. "The best in the world, huh?"

Her innocent eyes held uncompromised trust as they gazed into mine. "Because, just like with me, you'll never let them fall."

"That I can promise you."

As I held Kate that day, I realized she was the only woman for me. Over the course of just a few weeks, I had fallen in love with her.

I hadn't told her my plans, but I had requested assignments within my family's company. Assignments allowing me to fast track my plans to take care of her. The biggest obstacle, at the time, would have been convincing her to marry me before she finished school.

Her determination to be self-sufficient was one of the traits that had initially drawn me to her. Even though I supported her drive, it scared the crap out of me. I had been scared she would wake up one day and decide she didn't need me.

Little did I know, one month later, that day would come. The day she disappeared, leaving me with unfulfilled plans and a decimated heart.

Our promise to teach, encourage, and protect our children was one of the many fractured promises floating under the bridge of our past.

Once again, I want to know. Why did she disappear? My inner self is screaming today is the day to demand answers. Push her to extremes, hoping the answers I crave will spill from her in anger. My mind wants to question her if only to rip her answers to shreds. But my heart wants to hold her, protect her, and never let her fall again.

After three hours of tension-filled silence, I motor into my slip in Milwaukee's harbor. A few gray clouds have moved in to mar the perfection of the blue sky. It's like the clouds are a direct reflection of my mood.

I jump from the boat as the dockmaster secures and ties her off. I turn to collect Kate, only to find she's already hopping onto the dock.

I slowly tilt my head. "Still independent, I see." My response is tinged with disappointment in the stolen opportunity to touch her.

"In all things." Her statement is punctuated with a smile I could easily mistake for genuine if I didn't notice the firm set of her jaw.

She is upset, giving me little hope of returning to the camaraderie we shared as we left Chicago.

"There's a deli just across the street. I thought we could pick up lunch and bring it back to the boat while we relax for a bit."

"I guess I could eat."

I thank the dockmaster, who I notice is making appreciative side glances of Kate. I narrow my eyes, giving him the unspoken message to stay the hell away. He seems to understand and turns on his heel, heading back to his post.

I turn, gesturing for Kate to proceed in front of me. As she passes, I place a possessive hand to the small of her back, giving all men a subtle cue she's mine. Warmth and awareness jolt through my arm as I feel Kate stiffen.

Touching her is like flipping a switch on an old movie reel.

Her hair fanned around her head as she rests on my pillow. Kate tackling me to the ground, my face covered in kisses. Her blue eyes, wet with unshed tears, as I push into her for the first time.

My body responds instantly, my dick jumping to half-mast before her forward movement causes my hand to fall away.

My reaction to her is like a wave. It knocks the wind from me, only to pull my feet out from under me as it retreats. She holds power over me that compares to no other.

As we walk toward the deli, I attempt to steer us back to a level of comfortable conversation.

"Sarah said you haven't lived in Chicago long. Where did you live before?"

Her raised eyebrows tell me she thinks, for some reason, I already know the answer to the question. "Milwaukee, actually."

"No shit. How long did you live there?"

She side-eyes me as teeth capture her bottom lip, pulling it into her mouth. "A little over fifteen years."

Her answer hits me like a brick to the chest. There's no way she lived in Milwaukee this whole time. If she did, my investigators would have found her. *If they would have known her new name.* When I first hired them, I gave them explicit instructions to start in Milwaukee, knowing it was where she had gone to school. I'm shocked, recovery coming slowly as I try to piece together my next question. "Composed" Shaw has left the building. "Soooo...after us, you came back here?"

"Yep." Her voice pops the P like Sarah does when she's

annoyed and doesn't want to talk to me. "Where have *you* lived?"

"Well, let's see. China, the Netherlands, Italy, Chicago, and Milwaukee." My eyes roam her face, hoping to gauge her reaction to our living in the same city at the same time.

Her jaw tenses as she slowly swallows. "I know." Her response is so quiet, I find my ears straining to catch her words.

What? How did she know about me when I didn't know about her? I'm unsure how to process the information from our short conversation. Luckily, we've reached the deli.

I hold the door for her, all the while hoping she doesn't glimpse the turmoil racing through my mind.

32

KATE

Back at the boat, Shaw remains quiet as we dine on lunch from the deli. Crab cakes for me, a pastrami on rye for him.

His silence allows me to contemplate our trip. *Am I happy I was tricked into coming? No. Am I glad I was forced to come? In a way, yes.* Our conversations have given me a glimpse of the man who has been shaped by the boy I once knew.

Shaw is an excellent father. My opinions formed in the months I have been working with Sarah are solidified following today's conversations. He has done his best, even with his busy work schedule, to make time for Sarah, taking her on excursions and giving her experiences to remember for a lifetime.

I'd known he would be an excellent father. Shaw had been determined to break the mold of "hands-off" parenting he claimed was so popular in the social circle in which he was raised. He seems to have done what he set out to do, not that I'm surprised. He's accomplished so many of the goals he set for himself.

Our conversation on the way to the deli had confused me. He knew I returned to Milwaukee. At the very least, he had known that's where I went when I left.

Then there was the letter that arrived a couple years after our separation. The one he'd instructed a lawyer to send. The one that sent me into a darkness from which I almost didn't return. He knew. He had always known. Yet...if I read him correctly, his words and his body language represented confusion and surprise. He seemed hurt and possibly a little angry. It didn't make sense. I am obviously missing something.

I continue to obsess as we eat, stealing glances at him as he looks at the water. Half of his lunch sits, untouched, on his plate. *Where do we go from here?*

Shaw is interested, at least, in the physical sense. Our bodies respond to each other like time has stood still. His body calls to mine like a beacon in rough waters. I may not see his intentions, but I move toward him just the same.

Maybe a quick roll in the hay would cure our physical desires and quench the burn.

I finish my crab cakes, tidying my area and throwing away my garbage. I look across the harbor and see more dark clouds. They look darker, more sinister. Appropriate.

"We should probably get moving. Looks like we could be in for a rough trip home if those storm clouds are any indication." His teasing voice from earlier has disappeared and been replaced with one of resignation.

I give a smile and jaunty salute, hoping to lighten the mood ahead of our four-hour return trip to Chicago. "Ready when you are, Captain."

He responds with a quick shake of his head as he prepares the boat for poor weather should we get caught on the way home.

Ten minutes later, we leave the marina. Both of us are quiet except for the racing thoughts burning through our heads.

I move closer to Shaw, at his insistence, putting me next to him on the double captain's seat. He voiced concerns for me hitting the floor, ass first, should we encounter large waves. Happy he harbors concern for my ass, I get comfortable in the seat beside him. The tension brought by the weather outweighs any emotional strain between us.

Shaw was correct in his weather prediction. Thirty minutes in, a storm has whipped up a fine display of power. The wind makes the lake an angry host, banking the waves and tossing the boat, much like a ball in a tennis match.

Shaw's eyes are vigilant, yet his body language reflects none of the worry or stress within my own. In fact, I'm starting to feel hot and clammy. My head seems fine, but cramps are starting to twist my stomach, and I feel the onset of queasiness.

Nerves explode within me. I'm going to be sick, I just know it. I start reasoning with my stomach, hoping the promise of a new Hermes purse gives my brain the incentive it needs to bring my stomach under control. My stomach gives my brain the finger and kicks into gear, twisting with such force I nearly fall out of my seat.

I look to Shaw, whose eyes are pointed straight ahead. Sensing my anxiousness and pain, Shaw glances over at me, his eyes widening as he sees my face.

"Oh, shit. Kate, are you OK?"

I shake my head, afraid opening my mouth will bathe him in the contents of my stomach. He hits a gauge in front of him and stands, scooping me up—one arm under my knees and one under my arms—in the process. Cradled against his chest, I close my eyes, only to open them seconds later when my nausea gets worse.

Shaw holds me carefully as he stumbles through the cabin while trying to brace himself against the rocking of the boat. His steps are efficient as he carries me to the small bathroom on the other side of the galley. Using his shoulder, he wedges us through the door.

His careful maneuvering is precious seconds too late as my stomach misunderstands my small hiccup as permission to empty its contents. Without consideration for myself or those around me, my stomach continues its revolt. My body feels like a used, inside-out T-shirt.

When I stop heaving, I feel strong hands bracing my arms from behind while holding me upright. Two seconds later, I smell the vile evidence of my nausea. My body revolts again, sparing my mouth of acid, but twisting my stomach as I dry heave.

"Do you think you can stand on your own?" Shaw's concern is twisted around each word.

I nod and feel him release his hold, listing me toward the wall to support my weight should I need the extra help.

As I became cognizant of my surroundings, I hear a deep rumble from Shaw's chest. "I haven't been thrown up on since Sarah was five. She got sick at the fair, and I tried to catch her vomit in my hand. I thought nothing could ever be nastier...until today. Always full of surprises, Kate."

Embarrassed doesn't even scratch the surface. Mortified, with a heaping side of humiliation, is more like it.

I open my eyes and look at the devastation. Shaw stands sideways in the tight hallway. His shirt is plastered to his body by a mucous glue dotted with red, pink, and white chunks. The stench is unbearable and nearly brings another bout of retching.

The bathroom has fared no better, the floor a mess of putrid smelling goo.

I lean against the wall, feeling a bit dizzy, as darkness rims my visual field. Struggling to speak, I lift my eyes to his face. "I'm so sorry. And utterly embarrassed."

Shaw shrugs, turns, and makes his way back to the kitchen. "I'll help you clea—"

Then my world cuts to black.

33

SHAW

SHUTTING THE NOW CLEAN BATHROOM DOOR, I WALK TO THE kitchen, returning the bucket to the sink and throwing my gloves and sponges in the garbage. Cleaning the evidence of Kate's sickness nearly turned my stomach inside out more than once. I think the host of *Dirty Jobs* would have taken one look and said, "No." And I had once seen the guy wade through waist-high shit.

I amble back to the bedroom, my footing surer since the majority of the storm has passed. Kate is tucked on her right side, eyes closed, facing me.

She scared the hell out of me when she fainted. In a flash, she had crashed to the floor, nearly taking her eye out on the door handle as she fell. Two steps had returned me to her side, unable to rouse her from her stupor as I checked for injuries.

I carried her to the other bathroom and stripped her of her clothes. No easy task, considering they stuck to her like a second skin. Luckily, she remained unconscious, unable to protest as my hands removed her undergarments from her toned body.

Since she was unable to stand on her own, I had stepped

into the shower, working quickly and efficiently to wash her hair and body. It was a struggle to detach my body's desires from the task of bathing her. She was sick, and I had no right to even think sexy thoughts while she was in her weakened state.

My willpower waned as my eyes fought my resistance, traitors as they were. My gaze drifted across her delicate collarbone, taking a detour for a quick, salacious glance at her puckered nipples.

The sight had burned through my retinas straight to my long-term memory.

After checking on Kate and grabbing some clothes from the supply I keep on the boat, I return to the bathroom to take a quick shower. The fully-clothed rinse I'd taken with Kate hadn't been successful in washing away the stench that clung to my body.

I allow the water to run, giving way to today's stress as it circles the drain. Knowing my depleted fresh water is in danger of hitting empty, I grab the bar of soap, giving extra swipes to my chest, which had been Kate's unintended target.

My mind wanders to her small, yet toned body, as my hand runs over my semi-hard cock. As thoughts of her invade, my cock hardens, begging me for attention. Her body is so small compared to mine. Strong, yet fragile.

Guilty as I may feel, the draw is too close, too real, too much temptation.

Fisting the base of my now fully-erect cock, I give it a firm squeeze. Twisting my fist, I slowly pull upward. I open my hand when it reaches the tip, watching my palm rub over my slit, and groan as the roughness of my skin opens the slit, releasing a slight burn. I repeat the process. Fist, squeeze, twist, rub.

My fist becomes Kate's mouth, squeezing and twisting as her hair sifts through my hands. My palm, her tongue, as she uses the tip to open my slit, drawing my saltiness into her mouth. She was born to control my cock, picking up speed without my instruction.

The push and pull of her mouth promise the release I crave. My balls draw up. The hum from Kate's throat is a whisper to my ears, but a canon to my cock. I come on a yell that echoes through the bathroom.

As I watch the last drops of my release fall through the drain, guilt sets in. I used Kate. She's just given me the most explosive orgasm I've had in years, and she isn't even aware it happened.

I'm going to hell.

Tortured moans pull me from my guilt. I quickly finish my shower, sparing thirty seconds to dry my body before throwing on a pair of sweatpants and a T-shirt.

My ears catch stronger moans as I approach the bedroom. I enter, noticing Kate is still asleep, but restless. She has kicked the majority of her covers to the end of the bed, leaving her body completely naked from the tip of her head to the bend of her knee. The sight of her knocks the breath from my lungs. I struggle to contain my reaction, which is magnified by the orgasm I experienced, just minutes ago, at her expense. She is sick and disorientated, and I am a grown man. I can remain indifferent to the swell of my own body while I focus on caring for her.

I force my brain to understand she is off-limits, both physically and mentally, for the foreseeable future.

I cross the cabin and pull the covers over her and up to her chin. The small bucket I left lies empty on the bed next to her. My hand moves to her forehead, brushing her hair from her face. She feels hot and feverish, and I see shivers dancing across her features as she whips her arms from under the covers, exposing her naked chest.

I walk to the bathroom, pull a washcloth from the small cabinet, and soak it with tepid water. I return to the bed, placing the cooler cloth on Kate's forehead in a feeble attempt to make her more comfortable. While she tolerates the cloth, its presence stirs agitation as she sleeps.

I sit on the side of the bed and listen as she starts to mumble. Jumbled words, interspersed with clearly coherent ones. She continues, and I am a voyeur in her one-sided conversation.

Her voice sounds labored and raw like she ate sandpaper before speaking.

"Sorry…tried…you…"

I'm confused, continuing to listen as shivers wrack her body.

"Beautiful…miss this…ours…miss this…"

Her voice fades to indistinguishable whispers. I am drawn to her. Past memories and current desires are braided into a single rope as it pulls me closer.

I love her. It's been angry and peaceful. Ugly and beautiful. Broken and perfect. But always love.

34

KATE

A SHARP KNOCK ON MY FRONT DOOR ROUSES ME. FRAGMENTS shoot through my brain. Date. Boat. Sick. Home. Tired and achy, I roll over and stumble to the foyer.

My hair sticks to my face as I try to push it behind my shoulder. I look down, checking to see if I'm decent before opening the door. Hot mess is the perfect definition of my appearance. Lacking the energy to care, I open the door to an older man with a long, white beard and curly white hair.

Think Santa Claus in coveralls. A perfect nickname, considering the covered basket, thermos, car keys, and envelope he hands me before turning and walking back to his truck.

I hang the basket from my arm as I finger the envelope. It's white, stationary type. Expensive. Elegant. I open the flap, pulling out a matching piece of card stock with a typed message.

Kate,
Never a dull moment with you.
Rest & renew your strength.
Not sure what you'll be able to keep

down, so I sent a little of everything.
Looking forward to you feeling better. - S.

I'm willing to dwell upon Shaw's note until my nose picks up the scent of buttery goodness wafting from Santa's delivery basket.

I open the cover, my hungry eyes dancing at their fortune. Nestled within are warm croissants, a container of chicken noodle soup, a thermos, a box of crackers, and a plethora of other goodies. My nose tells me the thermos is filled with herbal tea. As I eye the food, my stomach whines. It begs me for sustenance while offering apologies for yesterday's embarrassing behavior.

I lift a croissant and nibble the corner while I ponder Shaw's motives. I'm lost, not sure what to make of his intentions. I reread his note.

Looking forward to you feeling better.

Amy startles me from my contemplations as she ambles over and practically sits on top of me. Always a smartass, she smirks as I huff and move over. She eyes me over her coffee cup before her gaze settles on the basket covering the majority of our small coffee table.

"If those are Shieldman's croissants and you didn't save me one, I may have to kill you." No one gets between Amy and her insatiable desire for baked goods.

"First, I didn't know you had returned from your trip. Second, I can't assure you they came from Shieldman's, but I did save you one or two."

She leans over, her eyes growing wide, as she peers into the basket of yummy food. "Shit, I think the whole front case of Shieldman's in sitting in here. Croissants, eclairs, cake donuts, turnovers. Who have you done and when did you do it?" Her crass humor puts a smirk on my lips.

Her eyes practically roll back as she bites into a cherry

turnover, smearing red gooeyness across her lip. Small flakes fall from her mouth and hit my arm.

"Have some dignity, girl. It's called manners."

She carefully hits me with a pillow, making sure her coffee doesn't spill on her beloved Pottery Barn couch. Her attachment to this couch is over the top. No lie, she would cut someone if they did anything to it.

"Seriously, where did you get all of this? And while we're revealing all of our secrets, why don't you tell me what the hell you're wearing?"

I wipe my mouth and look around the living room, studiously avoiding her penetrating glare, knowing my answer could possibly release the hurricane known as Amy's protective nature.

"Shaw sent them, and I'm wearing his shirt."

I feel her surprise as her eyes stare at me. I look over at her, her angry glare pelting me with words her mouth does not say. I fidget, her silence making me nervous.

"I'm giving you two minutes to get your story straight and start spilling your guts. But first, go change that shirt. I can't talk to you while that picture stares at me."

Knowing Amy won't let me off the hook, I roll off the couch. *What's the big deal about this shirt?*

I look down to see a cartoon picture of a man in a rowboat sitting in a school of fish. Only those aren't fish. They look like a bunch of little tadpoles. I scan the words.

Row, row, row your boat
gently down the stream.
Merrily, merrily, merrily, merrily
life is in the cream.
No, he did not.

He put this damn shirt on me when I was barely coherent. I vaguely remember grunting, followed by a string of muttered curses before my body was wrapped in warm, cozy softness.

In toddler fashion, I stomp toward my room, debating how best to respond to his clothing atrocity.

Five minutes later, I sit back, angled into the corner of the couch and wrapped in my fluffy bathrobe. A mug of tea, compliments of Shaw and poured by Amy, sits on the coffee table. Amy faces me, licking sugar from her fingers.

"Seriously, you are still eating from the obnoxious basket?"

Amy scrunches her face like she's confused why I asked such a question. "Treats from Shieldman's Bakery are like Charlie's Chocolate Factory golden tickets. Rare, sought-after morsels of gold. Even if Shaw was the vilest person on the planet, there's no way in hell I'm depriving my taste buds of this golden ticket experience. I'm your best friend, but I'm not crazy." She pulls her legs under her and faces me. "Now, I believe you owe me a story."

I send off a quick prayer of thanks as I stare at Amy. She is my very best friend. There isn't anyone on the planet I trust more. She has seen me at my worst, and she still stands by me.

Amy had been gone for the better part of two weeks, and I had no idea how much I missed her until this very moment. She'd been stuck in Miami, dealing with the mess created when an entitled teenage gymnast, who didn't have a driver's license, decided to take her coach's Tesla for a spin. *News flash: gymster needs to make better choices in the future.*

I often question how Amy deals with the shenanigans of her clients while maintaining her sanity. She always laughs and tells me it's easier to feel better about yourself when you are surrounded by the stupidity of others. I guess she has a point.

While she was gone, we shared upbeat texts. We kept in touch by sending pictures of food, funny people we saw at the gym, and the occasional strange-looking Uber driver.

I had not shared my random experiences with Shaw. She knew of our initial meeting and "panty gate," but she didn't know about naked Shaw or the boat ride from hell.

I feel like I'm tiptoeing through a minefield since Shaw returned to my life. I'm also nervous to see Amy's reaction to our continued interactions. Shaw is a strong factor in my past, and I'm afraid of discoloring Amy's view of me.

The unforgiving truth is I never totally let go of my feelings for Shaw. I grew as a person and moved forward in my life, but my love for him never died.

Time, the ultimate healer, has turned that love into puckered jagged scars. Unsightly on the surface, but the same passionate, consuming, love underneath.

I'm not sure how to explain my complicated feelings to Amy, considering I don't fully understand them myself, but I can't hold out any longer. My moment of truth with my friend has arrived.

I need to share my feelings, broken as they may be, with her. Deep down, I know she'll never leave. There's nothing I can tell her that will drive her away. Yet, I still fear the stark reality of exposure.

It's time to rain my shitstorm of a story upon Amy's head, and I pray she doesn't think less of me. I begin by recounting the Naked Shaw Story, describing how I had forgotten my purse, which then turned into the shared phone call, which ended in a date. I tell her about the bakery, his trickery, and the coffee spill. I finish with a detailed version of the worst bout of sea sickness-slash-food poisoning I have ever experienced in my life. Amy listens, mouth dropping and eyes bulging at all the appropriate times until I've finished.

I watch as Amy's thoughts play across her face. She opens her mouth to speak only to close it without saying anything. Finally, she looks at me as a grin stretches across her face. "You give new meaning to 'Go big or go home.'"

"Shut it," flies from my mouth at the same time the pillow I tossed hits her smirking mouth.

She tenses, a seriousness dropping over her face. "Respect the couch at all times."

I roll my eyes and wait for her further assessment of my muddled story.

Amy reaches for my hand, giving it a squeeze before speaking. "You know how much I love you, right?"

I nod and stare at her, wetness making her eyes sparkle as I wait for her to continue.

"All these years, and you still love him." The awe, laced with disbelief, squeezes my heart. Her assessment is a statement of fact, not the angry judgment I feared. "All these years, you struggled to move on while protecting him within your heart."

Tears leak from my eyes as I listen.

"You are either the strongest or the most stupid woman I know. Hiding your real feelings. Why?"

Her question is one of curiosity, not scrutiny. Words fail me as I attempt to speak.

"Shaw hurt me. I loved him, and he threw us away. Yet, I can't reconcile the Shaw I knew treating me the way he did. He gave me all of himself, just as I did with him. No one is that good of an actor." She nods in understanding, encouraging me to continue. "I was hell-bent on creating a new persona, one that allowed me to leave my broken pieces in the past. Even though I questioned why we ended, I couldn't eradicate him from my heart. As the years passed, I gave up searching for answers and tried to live my life. Interesting fact—you can't fully live life with half a heart."

Amy gives my hand another squeeze and pulls me to her, wrapping me in a tight hug. Words aren't needed, her hug says it all. She is, and always will be, my person.

She sits back and tilts her head toward my own. "I only have two questions. First, does he still make your heart flutter and get your blood pumping?" *More than ever.* I nod, and she gives me a smirk. "Second, do you need my help with a plan to win him back?"

Amy is the real deal. She is blunt and direct, but she is also caring, understanding, and always has my back. With Amy in my corner, I have the strength to move mountains, win marathons, and conquer Shaw's heart. For a second time.

35

KATE

It's been two weeks since my conversation with Amy and twenty-four hours since I've heard from Shaw. He's texted me daily, checking to make sure I've recovered. He's even called twice when I didn't respond to a couple of his texts.

Every time I end one of his calls, I'm amazed how long we talk. Our conversations are easy, whether the topic is about the weather, my current writing project, Sarah's love for being my assistant, his current work projects, or his continued love for boating and being outdoors.

Hearing his voice is like wrapping myself in my grand-mother's quilt. Happy, comfortable, and content. Granted, our conversations have only skimmed the surface, neither of us willing to rock the boat by digging deeper.

Every time Shaw and I speak, he hints for another date or "do-over" as he jokingly refers to it. Every time he hints, he throws it out more as a suggestion than an actual request. *Feeling the waters, maybe?*

Waiting for a more formal request, I skirt his suggestions, change the subject, or just plain ignore his hints. I have apologized profusely for the rudeness of my stomach and the horrific mess I made on his boat. While he assures me he holds no grudge, he doesn't miss an opportunity to tease me about it. He treats the whole experience as water under the bridge, and I've finally started to feel comfortable enough to throw out a few of my own jokes.

As I pick up my phone for the third time in the past hour, I realize I've started looking forward to his daily communications. They are fun, playful, and easy.

I can feel it. He has surreptitiously slid his way under my skin. He's been stealthy, careful, and quiet. I had been oblivious, and over the past few weeks, I let him in without realizing his intent.

After analyzing the past two weeks, I conclude Shaw's game is the same as when we met. Hand-feeding me snippets of himself through small conversations and stolen moments while he works his magic. Over time, I became unsatisfied and wanted more than bits and pieces of him. Just like then, he is slowly wearing me down. Now I'll wait for the right moment, and when he asks again, I'll agree to go out with him.

His tactics make me wonder if he's still the Shaw I once knew, or if this is an elaborate charade designed to destroy what is left of my heart?

Doubt holds my hand, pulling me toward her friends— Uncertainty, Mistrust, and Fear. They are doing their best to make me their blood sister. I am resisting, but I occasionally catch myself listening to their whispered warnings.

I promise myself I'm going to talk with Shaw. Hopefully, I'll get some long-awaited answers. I still have strong feelings for him, but the answers I seek have the potential to bring us back together or destroy any possible future between us.

My phone chimes and I pick it up faster than a Southern mama's backhand in church. I can feel the buzz as he crawls deeper under my skin.

Shaw: Dinner, tonight?

Me: I've been working all day. Casual attire, OK?

Shaw: If by casual, you mean a tank top and tight sleep shorts like a Victoria Secret model wears? Yesssss.

Me: Nope, my modeling days are over. I meant yoga pants and a T-shirt.

Shaw: Mmmm. Yes, that works, too. I'll pick you up at 5:00.

Me: I'll be ready.

A pleased smile paints my lips. We've cleared the first hurdle. He has officially asked me out. Tonight could be the last straw or the cherry on top. Only time will tell.

Amy knocks on my bedroom door just before five to find me standing in a lacy, black bra and yoga pants, as I'm frantically trying to decide between an old, comfy Marquette T-shirt or a new, off-the-shoulder sweatshirt. It's comfortable, but it also screams sex more than the old T-shirt.

"I'd ask what has your panties in a twist, but you have on your booty-hugging yoga pants. No way they can twist when your pants are strangling your ass."

My laser stare does little to deflate her humor as she laughs and falls on my bed.

"Seriously, what's the deal? I haven't seen you this stressed since Target quit stocking Gentle Glide tampons and you had to switch brands."

I set my jaw, my words fighting to make it through my clenched teeth. "Like I've told you before, you can't just *switch brands*. The potential for humiliating consequences is huge. If the fit, the absorbency, or the contour doesn't mesh with your body, you're just asking to ruin your favorite underwear. How many times do I have to tell you this?"

"And...there you have it, folks. I'm the master. Mention the tampon switching debacle, and it distracts her every time."

"You're such a smartass."

"I know. Quit stalling, what gives?"

I pick up the sweatshirt and slip it over my head, then turn to the mirror to survey my look. It says casual, but down for a little action if needed. Perfect. I remember my mom joking, "It's always better to look marvelous than to feel marvelous." I may be stressed and terrified out of my own damn mind, but I'll look sexy.

"Shaw is picking me up in a few minutes. He asked me to dinner. Casual dress."

"Oh, I see how you're looking to play. Show a bit of bra strap. Let him get a little peeky peek, so he knows you've still got the goods."

I'm shaking my head before she finishes.

"Don't shake your head 'no' at me. You forget, I taught you nearly every one of my tricks. Progress, my little grasshopper."

The bell rings, and I whip my head in the direction of the door. Indecision wars within me. I need to brush my teeth, but I'm nervous about leaving Shaw and Amy alone in the same room. I know Amy's interrogation techniques she covertly disguises as friendly conversation. If I allow her to entertain him, I fear I may find Shaw on the floor in the fetal position, incoherently chanting his own name, by the time I enter the room.

As I'm debating whether to skip brushing my teeth and head out to answer the door, Amy winks and jumps off my bed. "Don't worry, take your time. He's in good hands."

"Yeah, that's what scares me." I turn and hurry into my bathroom to finish getting ready.

As I enter the living room, my ears ring with both female and male laughter. Amy and Shaw are sitting on the couch, like two peas in a pod, and I'm instantly suspicious. Amy doesn't like any guy on first sight. Her nickname in college was "Ice Queen," and she took her role very seriously.

Shaw is smooth, but not smooth enough to win Amy's favor so quickly. I look at Amy, and I spot it. A bag from Shieldman's Bakery is cradled within her arms like a newborn baby. At one point during a conversation, I jokingly mentioned needing to share my previous bakery basket with Amy to quell my fear of waking up with only one eyebrow.

It seems his listening skills are on point. He must have filed the trinket of information away for the day, like today, when they would meet, and he'd need to win her favor. I'm surprised he remembered something so innocuous and impressed he listened so intently during our recent conversations.

Turning my eyes to the man in question, I nearly swallow my tongue. He is delicious perfection. As my gaze rolls over him from my position behind the couch, I see dark jeans and a blue shirt collar peeking out from under a black leather jacket. His thick, dark hair is wind mussed like he's driven with his window down. My fingers itch to run through the silky strands. Without seeing his eyes, I know they shine like Caribbean waters, clear aqua blue.

My secret perusal does nothing to tamp down my growing interest and everything to ramp up my nervous excitement. I've made up my mind to ask my questions and hear him out, the anticipation bringing a delicious awareness to my physical senses.

"Am I interrupting comedy hour?" I tease, as I walk around the couch. Both cast sidelong glances at each other while trying to keep straight faces, and my skin prickles like it does when I enter a room and everyone stops talking.

Amy smiles at me, not bothered in the least by the death stare I give her. "Yep. Your stomach and its reflexive actions have given me material for the next year. No lie, I couldn't come up with a more hilarious story if I tried."

Shaw stands, his look pensive and a little nervous. "We were just sharing some of our embarrassing moments. It happens to everyone."

Amy's eyes bounce between us. An uncomfortable silence blankets the room, and I suddenly feel compelled to race out the door. I force a smile. "Ready to go?"

Shaw reaches down and picks up a second bag. "I had a feeling I'd need two of these. Something told me one bag wouldn't cut it if I arrived and both of you were home."

The sweet smell of cinnamon and sugar hits my nose, making my mouth water. I glance at Amy, who protectively cradles her bag like a mother grizzly bear protecting her cub.

"This smells heavenly. Do you mind if I bring it with me? It ensures I'll be able to eat full donuts and not just lick crumbs from the bag, which could totally happen if I leave it here with Amy."

"One time. *One* time, five years ago, I ate your dessert. Get over it!" Amy smiles, affection softening the strength of her tirade as I hand her my bag.

I walk to the foyer and grab my coat from the peg by the door. Shaw comes up behind me, opening the door with one hand while placing his other on my lower back, steering me outside.

Amy's raised voice filters toward us. "Shaw, remember what I said. I'm damn good at my job. I can decimate a reputation with a few pictures and keystrokes. I will stop at nothing to protect my girl, no matter who your friends are."

Shaw gives her a quick head nod. "Heard and noted."

36

KATE

I slip my house keys into the pocket of my coat and set off down the sidewalk, making sure to step over the raised crack that seems to trip me at least once a week. I throw a quick word of warning over my shoulder, but as I look forward, I stop dead. Apparently, my notice wasn't quick enough. Shaw falls victim to said crack, which puts him flush against my back, his hands holding my arms for support.

His front, hard and warm, is plastered against my back. His hands, strong and unyielding, send electric currents down my arms. My body immediately feels buzzed and floaty. He leans in, and the smell of sandalwood and mint drift around me. His nearness banks the smoldering embers he ignites with his presence. One touch has me fantasizing.

"What's wrong?" He leans in closer, and his breath tickles my neck in a warm caress, stealing my ability to respond.

"Are we walking, or is your Jeep wearing an invisibility cloak at the moment?"

His amusement rings through his answer. "No walking. No Jeep. We're going old school tonight."

"What does that mean?" My voice rises slightly as I scan

the driveway for his definition of "old school." I don't like surprises, and my inability to find a vehicle, coupled with Shaw's nearness, is making my heart race.

His hands rise from my biceps and settle on either side of my head. His fingers delve into my hair and turn my head slowly toward the curb, where a sleek, black motorcycle sits on its kickstand.

I whip around to face him, effectively extricating myself from his firm grip. "Oh, hell no! If you think I'm getting on that death trap, you are sorely mistaken. Old school? More like death school, Mr. Graham."

Shaw takes my hands in his, bending down to catch my eyes still trained on the motorcycle. "You'll be perfectly safe with me. You can do this. I'd never let us fall."

I'll never let you fall.

My mind is transported, back to Shaw teaching me to ride a bicycle. He was trying so hard to convince me as I stood in front of him, terrified and nervous, yet willing to trust him. *I'll never let you fall.* His words had rung true that day.

Tonight is important. It has the potential to change my life. Just as I rode the bike years ago, I would ride this motorcycle tonight. I don't have to drive it. I just have to trust Shaw to keep me safe. Somehow, trusting him is even more terrifying than getting on the back of his motorcycle.

I look to Shaw, who has walked to the sleek bike and started putting on his helmet. He's either sure I'm going agree to ride this death trap, or he's planning to leave if I don't. Knowing I won't sleep if I allow fear to ruin my chance at answers, I look to him. "OK, I'll do it. But I have a few conditions."

"I would be disappointed if you didn't."

"No trying to scare me. No riding after dark. No funny business."

"Gotcha. No scaring, no darkness, no fun. I promise." His

mouth tips in a smirk as he places a helmet on my head and straps it under my chin.

Shaw moves to the side of the motorcycle, taking hold of a handlebar as he effortlessly swings his leg over the massive piece of machinery. He makes some adjustments to mirrors, turns the key, and kicks the motorcycle to life. The black combat boots, I missed when I'd shamelessly checked him out earlier, are a sexy addition to his bad boy look. A visual responsible for the wetness currently making my panties a bit uncomfortable.

"Step up and swing your leg over the back seat." He points to silver rods sticking out behind his calf. "Once you're on, rest your feet on these pegs." His voice is a strangled yell over the roar of the motorcycle's engine.

I follow his directions, swinging my leg over and settling on the seat, which is surprisingly soft and comfortable. Good thing I wore pants with stretch or mounting this thing would have been more than awkward.

"All set?"

I jump, surprised to hear Shaw's voice as it comes through the helmet.

"I think so."

He reaches back and grabs both of my hands, bringing them around his waist. "Easier to hold on. Also, easier to catch you if you start to fall off."

I note the delicious hardness of his abs where my hands rest around his waist, but then his words register. "What?!"

His chuckle tells me he's trying to rattle my already frayed nerves. As he turns the throttle and takes off, my scream nearly drowns out his, "Hold on, beautiful."

What am I thinking? We're both going to die.

37

SHAW

I watch Kate as she fights an inner war. I know she'll agree to get on, it's just a matter of how long it will take before she psyches herself up for the experience. Just like when I taught her to ride a bike and sail, she has to overcome her fear on her own before she can embrace the freedom of a new experience.

I know she'll love the speed, the exhilaration, and the freedom of flying down a road with the wind as your guide. The vibration of the motor a constant reminder of the power harnessed between her legs.

Riding is a release for me. I love the freedom I feel, and the clearness of my mind, after a long ride.

Kate's eyes are a window into her soul, which harbors a sea of doubt and pain. The night at Beacon, as I stood before her naked, she lifted the shutters, allowing me to glimpse the scars she held within before slamming them closed once again.

I goad her, knowing my teasing will likely have a favorable effect on her decision. She agrees to go, given a few conditions. Conditions to which I agree in exchange for having her arms wrapped around my waist and her chest pushed firmly against my back as we cruise along Route 20.

I'm doing a fine job priming my fantasies. My cock twitches, attempting to jump in front of my good intentions. I make quick work of mounting my bike, adjusting my swollen dick, along with my jeans, under the guise of getting ready to ride.

I give Kate instructions to get on the bike, making sure she knows where to put her feet. She swings a leg over and shifts around, her legs rubbing my outer thighs. Her crotch is pushed tight against my ass, and her chest is pressed firmly against my back. Suddenly, I'm starting to second-guess my decision to take the bike tonight. I tease Kate about holding on before I release the clutch and pull away from the curb feeling like tonight could be the first night of our second chance.

My body betrays its age as it continues to twitch like a virgin choir boy at a Pussy Cat Dolls performance. I will my body to relax, lest I gun the throttle and terrify Kate into making me turn the bike around and take her home.

It's the end of May. The nights still cling to a coolness that becomes more pronounced as we travel along Route 20. As we pass through small towns sandwiched between cornfields and rolling meadows, I'm entertained by Kate's surprised delight.

Her initial fears have been replaced by wonderment at the vastness of the open fields. It's hard to believe we are so close to the hustle and rush of Chicago.

Kate's fascination with farm animals is damn cute. My ears are ringing from her squeal of excitement upon seeing two bison meandering through a farm field. I have to admit, I was awed. They are such interesting creatures. Big, burly, and completely oblivious to the two people gawking at them as we passed.

I pull into Joe's Place, a casual restaurant known for mouth-watering ribs. My mouth starts to salivate, either from the scent of food or watching Kate as she scrambles off the back of my bike before I hit the kickstand and slowly dismount. It's been a while since I enjoyed such a long ride, and my aging body makes sure to remind me I'm not the twenty-two-year-old I once was.

Kate pulls off her helmet, giving her head a quick shake to release her hair from its confines. I'm struck dumb as I watch her. She is gorgeous. Long brown hair, blue eyes, and full pink lips, made for sensual kisses and soft caresses.

I remove my own helmet and hold out my hand. "I thought we could eat here, then we'll head back before it gets too dark." She hesitates for a few moments before placing her hand in mine.

Having her body pressed against me for the past hour has been tortuously sensual, and my need to continue touching her is fierce. I want to hold her, touch her, climb under her skin, and set her body on fire the way she has done to me.

My heart stutters as she takes my hand. My blood sizzles below the surface as warmth travels up my arm. Her small gesture is a victory in my body's desire to pull her close.

Mistrust is the armor separating us from the happiness we once shared. Time has healed, but it has also molded us, changed us, and made us strangers.

I refuse to be a stranger, relegated to reminiscing about past events and lost love. I intend to find out exactly what happened between us so it can be fixed, overcome, and forgotten.

Failure is not a choice, nor an option. She belongs with me, next to me, loved by me. I will settle for nothing less.

Kate's eyes search my face. For what, I don't know, but damn, if it doesn't make me a little nervous. She was always quiet and tended to get lost in her thoughts, and I used to kiss her to pull her from them. That strategy may not be regarded as helpful at this point. Don't get me wrong, while every nerve south of my waist is completely on board with the idea, my brain squashes all thoughts of kissing. *Best not to have two failed dates with this woman.*

I look around, finding about half of the tables occupied. A two top in the back corner catches my eye. It's a quiet corner, with no one else using tables on either side. It's as intimate as we can get at a family restaurant, and my feet take off, on a mission.

A server arrives and takes our order. Broasted chicken for Kate, and a full rack of ribs for me. We agree to share an order of hand-cut fries, which the teenage girl assures us are well worth the extra calories.

As Kate and I wait for our food, the conversation is non-existent. Neither of us knows how to approach the conversation without blurting our demands. I have to admit, sitting at a table across from Kate, sixteen years after she walked away, is unsettling. The hurt I've nursed is muted by the stark clarity of the feelings I have for the woman who sits in front of me.

"Kate, I have to ask. Why did you leave?"

Her discomfort is a living, breathing entity pulsing between us. She shifts her body, withdrawing as far as she can without leaving her chair. Her eyes bounce around the restaurant, like a housefly searching for a way to escape to the outdoors.

I wait as she remains silent, wondering why it's so difficult for her to reply. If the reason for our separation is my fault, as she so adamantly believes, her reasoning should be simple.

After being denied an explanation, years have brought me to this moment. I've imagined and planned it. I'm determined to receive an answer, and I refuse to let Kate retreat without breathing the words for which I've waited.

She is at my mercy. At a place she's never been, in a town with a name she's never heard, without a car to secure her getaway.

Her eyes finally fall to mine, the pain of a thousand regrets threatening to pour from her damp eyes. "Why did *you*?" Her voice a thread of sound nearly obliterated by the noise of the restaurant.

What the—? Why did I leave?

"What are you talking about? I never left. That was all you, Kate." My voice rises to be heard over the boom of my heart. "You went to work, I went sailing. When I came back, you were gone. In what universe does that equate to *me* leaving *you*?"

Tears escape, and she frantically tries to dry them with a paper napkin. "We shared our dreams. We made plans. You held my heart. You held so many parts of me. You left, and I barely had enough pieces left to breathe. I *never* left you." The venom pouring from Kate gives her voice a firm edge. Patrons turn to glance at us, questions of curiosity reflected from their eyes.

I look to them, trying to convey my apologies while my head is bombarded by Kate's accusations. *What is she talking about? I never left her. I loved her.*

I reach across the table, but Kate pulls her hands to her lap. Her rejection stings as I try to make sense of the last five minutes. The answer I sought is not one I expected, nor one I even understand.

"Maybe we should go outside, away from prying eyes, yeah?"

She wipes more tears, rivulets of pain and lost dreams, broken plans, and misunderstandings. Each tear kills me. Her pain is so great, her tears cannot be contained, overflowing from the dam she keeps within herself.

She nods her agreement, then slowly stands, making her way to the door. I signal the server as she approaches our table with our food. "Just leave our food on the table. We may or may not be back for it. Thanks."

I pull a one hundred-dollar bill from my wallet and hand it to her as she stares, wide-eyed, at me in confusion. I don't have time, nor do I care to explain, as Kate is falling apart near the front door. I reach her quickly, placing my hand at her back as I push the door open and guide her into the crisp evening air. Unsure if my hand will ever be allowed to touch her again.

38

SHAW

KATE SITS ON THE GRASS IN FRONT OF THE MOTORCYCLE. I pace, trying to reconcile what I've heard with the day I remember. That day is vivid, from the number of times I have replayed it within my mind.

Soft fingertips trace up and down my neck. I open my eyes and come face-to-face with crystal blue diamonds shining from Kate's smiling face.

The sun has already risen and the heat of the day promises to be stifling. The open window in my bedroom brings a breeze cooled by the refreshing temperature of Lake Michigan. The rhythm of the waves is a calming song to welcome the new day.

Kate's smile warms my vision as she moves her hand to my hair, fingering the strands as she likes to do. She lays her head on my naked chest as her fingertips skate over my sensitive skin.

I love this girl. She understands me, my goals, my motivations, and praises me for my ambitions. To find someone like her is a gift. Sacred. Priceless.

Mine.

My desire to protect her is strong. While it doesn't matter to me, I know she would have a difficult time assimilating into the social circles my life requires. Because of this, I've made my plans. I'd disappear from this life and its expectations, right now, if it meant having Kate in my life and being able to provide for her and our future children.

I pray the next two years will be fast and kind. I hope she can hold on to her innocent nature and won't be torn apart by the sharks that masquerade as innocuous debutantes. Heaven knows my mom, the largest great white, won't be supportive. My plan just needs to stay its course. If it does, Kate and I won't have to worry about conforming to the rigors of high society. Together, we'll be untouchable.

I run my fingers down her cheek. Stopping at her chin, I tilt her head toward me. I lean down and brush my lips across hers. The tip of my tongue wets her lower lip before delving into the warmth of her mouth. Our tongues duel, advancing and retreating in a synchronous pattern. I tug her shoulders, and she rolls on top of me, understanding my unspoken cue. Her long hair falls like a curtain, hiding us from life's expectations.

My hands cup her head. "When I was a teenager, I always hoped I would have children. I could imagine them, but I could never imagine what my wife would look like." Kate silently begs me to continue, knowing I rarely talk about my childhood or lack of one. "I think I know why. My mind couldn't have created a woman as perfect as you. You are the other half of my heart. I love you."

A lone tear slips from Kate's eye, and she's silent as she looks at me. A blinding smile lights her face. "I love you. I've loved you since the day you taught me to ride a bike. You are my forever love."

She leans up, placing a kiss over my heart, which nearly bursts from my chest. Her words feed my arousal, and my cock grows impatient between us. She laughs and rolls off me. "Tame that beast, Mr. Graham. I have to work a double shift in twenty minutes. No time for play."

I slide my arm under Kate's back and roll on top of her, careful not to crush her. "He and I will concede to your schedule, maybe kill the day sailing, as long as you pencil us in for tonight."

Her teeth graze my lips. "I will do no such thing."

I pull back and look at her, confusion and surprise on my face. "What?"

"No pencil for you. After this morning, you've definitely graduated to permanent marker in my schedule."

"Funny lady, you are."

"Absolutely. I'll see you back here at eight."

I focus on Kate, knowing the next few minutes could determine how we spend the rest of our lives. Lowering my voice in an effort to soothe, I start arranging my words with the care of a man walking through a minefield.

"I woke up. You were watching me, playing with my face, my lips, my hair. It felt incredible. I loved waking up that way." I smile, hoping my words can penetrate the debilitating poison that has festered for so many years. "We talked. I told you I loved you."

The memory nearly chokes me with the pain of its release. I glance at her, attempting to gauge her reactions, her thoughts, her memories of that day. Tears flow freely down her cheeks.

I want to wrap my arms around her and absorb her hurt and pain. Yet, I know she'll have no use for my touch as she processes my words. "You said you had to work two shifts."

She nods, head tilted toward the ground, like the weight of the memories are too heavy to raise her head.

"I was going to go sailing, and we'd meet back at my house that night by eight. I was waiting, but you never showed."

She starts to shake her head, unwilling to believe my last comment. "I left that day, yes. But I didn't leave *you*. I came back. I told you I'd be back. You *knew* I was coming back."

Anger tints her voice, giving it a strength I don't expect. Her eyes plead with me, as her words pierce my skin like a thousand bullets.

What the hell is she talking about? She left. No word. No explanation. "I had no idea you were coming back. I. Knew. *Nothing.*"

Kate's head whips up, her stare pinning me in place. She

slowly stands, and her eyes never leave mine as she stalks toward me. She stops close enough for me to feel her breath as it leaves her lips in stuttered steps. Anger pushes the words from her mouth, each one a brick hitting my chest. "The note. I. Left. You. A. Note."

My world implodes. We have been apart for sixteen years. I refuse to acknowledge what this could mean. We nursed hate and anger for over a decade.

She didn't leave me.

I didn't leave her.

Pain, the fabricated purpose of our separation, was for nothing.

My voice gentles, devoid of anger and filled with defeated sadness. I knew my next words were going to hurt her just as hers had decimated me. "Kate, I never saw a note."

"No." The whispered anguish held within that one word could wound a thousand warriors. Her legs buckle as she stumbles to her knees, her hands reaching out to catch her fall as her body convulses.

Needing to touch her, I drop to sit beside her, reaching around and twisting her body to fit against mine. Her back to my front. My head rests on her shoulder as I hold her tight and rock her. Tears stream down Kate's face, and her body shudders as years of pain soak the fabric of her shirt.

The tension in her body ebbs as the initial shock dissipates. Aftershocks ripple through her, and she turns her face into my neck, craving my silent support.

My mind races. Possibilities swirl through my consciousness, like tornadoes ripping through memories, erasing the years of lies created to foster the hurt of abandonment.

So many times, I've looked for her, hoping I could find her and close the door on unanswered questions. I had been positive the truth would cure my curiosity, figuring nothing she could say would ever fully purge my anger toward her.

Years had not prepared me for her words. Like shards of glass, sharp and jagged, they pierced me, lodging themselves in the rough exterior of resolve.

As she quiets, I begin to run my fingers through her hair. I remember my sister doing the same to me when I was upset as a child, the action calming in its silent simplicity.

When she finally speaks, her words are quiet, yet strong and purposeful. "That day was the worst day of my life."

My hand momentarily stills as my mind transports me. In many ways, I share her sentiment. There has only been one other day that competes for the worst of my life.

I will my fingers to continue their movement, hoping my presence and gentle touch will encourage her to continue.

My pulse starts to climb. Its fast rhythm—a soundtrack for words that have the ability to slay me—leaves me barely breathing and almost wishing fate never allowed our paths to cross again.

As much as I crave the truth hidden behind her lips, I suddenly long for the anonymity of my story. The one that convinced me to move on. I wrote a story to fit my life. Painting me as the injured party, it had no surprises. I created *my* truth.

Kate was going to share *hers*. *Mine* and *hers* would be gone. *Our* one truth would be the only survivor. I honestly didn't know if I could handle what that meant for us.

Conflict rises within me. My compulsion to kill her words, before they fall from her mouth, grows with each shared breath.

Today will change me.

Change her.

Change us.

39

SHAW

"My mom...she broke. A neighbor found her. Called the ambulance. Got her to the hospital."

Kate sits in front of me as she speaks, each word a nail painfully piercing my flesh for what she went through. Her voice is monotone. Absolute. Her eyes are vacant, staring straight ahead as she continues.

"It took the hospital nearly twelve hours to find me. A social worker ended up calling her boss. As fate would have it, he vaguely remembered her telling him I worked in a restaurant somewhere in Door County. Knew it had a bird in the name."

My fingers stop at her shoulder, giving her a squeeze to let her know I'm here. Listening. Sharing her heartache.

"The social worker finally got me on the phone at the fifth restaurant she called. It was the middle of the breakfast rush. My brain was running a mile a minute. I didn't know what to do. So, I left. Went straight to your cottage, hoping I could catch you." Kate turns to me, an anemic smile on her lips, her eyes red, but present, like she has returned to the conversation to include me.

"I was too late. You weren't there. I had no way to reach you. My mom was lying in a coma over two hours away, a vent the only thing keeping her alive, while I tried to figure out what to do."

My mind spins back to my memory of the day. I hadn't left until near lunchtime, a problem with the rudder stalling my trip. If she got a call during the breakfast rush, I would have missed her by mere minutes. Seconds of time had created a chasm of years.

"The only solution was to write you a note and tape it to the door. I was sure you would find it. Know what happened. Come to me. Or... at the very least...wait for me to return." Her voice fades to a whisper as she releases a strangled breath.

My fingers move to run the length of her jaw, splaying wide as they skim her ear before cupping the base of her skull. I tilt her head toward mine as I lean in.

"Look at me." My voice is gentle but firm, and she reluctantly lifts her eyes. "I. Didn't. Know. I never would have left you to deal with your mom on your own."

Glassiness returns to her eyes as we sit, each silently watching the other.

I recognize the look as I stare at her. Under the anger, the resentment, and the hostility, her heart is still tied to mine. No matter how thin the string that binds us together, our hearts harbor our love and recognize it in each other.

"My mom. She...died before I made it to the hospital. Her heart broke. Cardiac arrest, they said. They were wrong. Her heart had broken when my dad died. Without her heart, it was her sanity that broke. It slipped through her fingers, just like each pill she swallowed slipped down her throat."

As she relives the day, the story of her mom and not making it to the hospital before she passed, causes my own eyes to blur from unshed tears.

"What was left of my family disappeared that day. I was a

mess. The life I'd known was gone. It was a lot to process. I had to plan a funeral, organize bills, make plans for the house, my mom's car, her belongings. I honestly don't remember a lot from those weeks."

I lean forward and brush my lips across her cheek. "I'm so sorry."

"When I wasn't mourning my parents, I was questioning why you didn't show up or call. I didn't understand, but I didn't know how to contact you."

I sit, frozen in my memories, as a lone tear slides down Kate's face.

"We didn't have cell phones. The only thing keeping me sane was knowing I could find you waiting at the cottage when I came back. As confused as I was, you were my light, shining on my path back to you."

I rail against myself. *Why didn't I know? What happened to the note?* Then, I register what she just said.

The confusion clouding my mind paints an unintended harshness to my tone. "You said you came back? When?"

Kate pushes herself to her feet, fleeing from my embrace like a spooked kitten. She quickly walks toward the end of the parking lot before spinning to face me. "I did. August fifteenth. Fourteen days after I left, I came back." Her voice is emphatic, pleading with me to understand her, believe her, trust her.

I jump to my feet as well, my body needing to move as my mind works over Kate's words. I run my hands through my hair, pulling hard in an effort to focus. "August fifteenth? Fate isn't that cruel."

She stops, her body rigid. "Wh-What do you mean?"

I take a breath and let it out, unsuccessfully releasing the tension gripping my body like a vice. "When you left, I was confused, worried, hurt. I searched for you. Your boss was the only person who knew anything. He told me you left quickly and wasn't sure when, or if, you'd be back."

I glance at Kate. She is stock-still, and tears run down her cheeks as she listens to the pain of my own memories.

"I stayed at the cottage for two weeks straight, convinced if I left for any reason, you would return and I would miss you. I ignored calls from my family. My sister freaked and showed up, scared out of her mind when she couldn't get me on the phone." I pause as my sister's face flashes in my mind. She was frantic the day she showed up. Her hair was messy, her face completely missing all traces of makeup. I don't ever remember her yelling like she did that day.

"My dad was irate over the embarrassment I caused him when I failed to report to work on August third. Threatened to fire me, the future CEO of his empire. I couldn't leave. Every one of our memories was made at the cottage. Leaving would have meant leaving you. I couldn't do it."

Kate wipes the tears from her eyes. Her face is covered in black streaks from makeup that couldn't compete with the pain as it flowed from her eyes.

"Somehow, I convinced my dad to let me stay longer. He gave me twelve days to report to work, threatening to fire me if I took one hour longer."

I stare at her, wondering if she's pieced together the punch-line of fate's cruel joke.

"The day I left, I woke before sunrise. Reluctantly packed my bags and loaded the car. Before leaving, I walked to the dock, determined to see our sunrise one more time. I felt like I was walking through quicksand. I think it was my body's physical response to leaving the one place that shared the secret of our whispered dreams." I clear my throat. My recollections have dredged up repressed feelings and sensations.

"I watched the sunrise. By the time the sun had risen over the water, I'd labeled myself a fool, convinced what we had wasn't real. A fabrication of an overactive desire to care for someone, body and soul. I left the cottage, drove to Mitchell

Airport, and boarded a plane. My dad, in a display of anger, assigned me to our Singapore office for the international segment of my training."

I stop talking, raking my eyes over Kate. She's wrapped her arms around her waist, keeping them anchored to her body as she sways listlessly from side to side.

"Kate, I left on August fifteenth."

She raises her hands, covering her mouth in an attempt to trap the moaning sob that trickles from her body.

"You came back the same day I left."

40

KATE

My heart beats like the wings of a hummingbird. Shaw's words hit my ears with the force of an airplane jet, pounding through my head, demanding to be heard.

While my ears heard the words, my brain is still processing all that's been said. My mind is in chaos, and my heart physically hurts.

One phone call and a missing piece of paper stole our forever. The plans we made had been destroyed by a single sheet of paper that created a domino effect and changed the course of our lives.

Grief weighs me down, growing heavier by the minute. I grapple with the realization my own mind betrayed me, tricking me into doubting my feelings for Shaw. I review, with horrifying clarity, the choices I've made because of my doubt.

My mind churns in a sea of thoughts, each one hitting me full-on, sweeping any trace of denial away as it ebbs.

Shaw resumes pacing, no doubt reconciling our conversation with the mechanism he used to move on. I try to push my internal chaos aside as I study him. Searching within this man for the remnants of the young man who was my first, and only, love.

Shaw's outward appearance gives little away concerning his current thoughts. He walks tall, head tilted back. His blue eyes stare ahead, skimming the tree line, the weight of our exposed truths slowing his steps.

I could so easily deny Shaw's claims. Call him a liar, a thief of our fairy tale. But as he paces before me, my heart sees what it knew back then. Shaw never lied.

Shaw holds my heart. No matter how much I deny it, refute it, or attempt to forget, I still feel him within me. His heart and his body are temptations. Inviting me to hold him, taste him, and claim him as mine.

My displaced anger fueled my hate and curbed my hunger for sixteen long years. The fuel now puddles at my feet as its vehicle no longer exists.

I look at him, appreciating his physical perfection. Tingles flare across my neck, my arms, my chest. My mind no longer denies my body its reactions, as my blood heats with want, need, and desire. Desire to forget the past.

I close my eyes and recall tonight's ride. Shaw's body, a canvas of muscle, moving languidly as he steered the bike through the countryside. Pushed up against the warmth of his back, his smell an intoxicating mix of leather and subtle spice had teased my mind.

My thoughts had wandered as I imagined hooking my leg over his knee and sliding around to his front. My face to his chest, my lips to the underside of his jaw.

Lost in the sensations of my fantasy, I startle when I feel his knee gently nudge the back of my legs as his chest pushes against my back. His arms snake through mine and rest around my waist. He is careful and gentle as he squeezes my body, his hug saying more than he can articulate. Without words, Shaw is giving me his body, subtly granting me permission to use his strength until I can stand tall on my own.

I relax, sinking backward against him. His warmth is a weighted blanket to my chaotic mind. We fit together. Pieces in a forgotten puzzle.

I feel his breath, a hot breeze lifting my hair and raising prickles down my neck. I want this. His touch, his strength. Him.

Standing within his embrace, I feel flutters. The flutters of broken dreams. No matter how deep it was buried, my heart always held hope. Hope he didn't leave, hope he would find me, and hope he would still love me.

He didn't leave.

He found me.

But can he still love me?

———

We walk into the restaurant to find our food sitting on our table, ice cold and unappetizing. A shared glance indicates neither of us is hungry.

"I promised I would have you home before dark. In light of what we discussed, I'm not keen on breaking my promise. You cool with leaving?"

I agree and follow him out to the parking lot. I strap on my helmet and wait for Shaw's directions.

Shaw starts the bike, giving me a hand as I throw my leg over the seat. Truth be told, the motorcycle is growing on me. Or maybe it's the fact I have an excuse to touch Shaw.

He reaches back, pulling my arms around his middle. I lean against him, my fingers feeling the breath leave his body as he relaxes into the seat. Giving me no time to question his reaction, he pulls out of the lot and hits the throttle, leaving the shreds of our past behind us.

41

EVIL ONE

Present...

"I see. Are you absolutely sure this information has not been shared with anyone other than me?"

Grant, the private investigator, slides his folder over to his client. It's not in his nature to make speculations outside of what he's paid to do, but this client is cagey and nervous.

Grant's experience reading people, as well as the information he's found, tells him this patron is a snake wrapped in an unassuming shell. Demanding, controlling, obsessive.

He had reservations about taking this job, but his need for money had been the ultimate motivator. Regardless, he's wary and won't be upset when this meeting is finished.

Being around this brand of evil makes his skin crawl, and no amount of money in the world can overcome the feeling.

This had been the first time he'd ever considered concealing information he'd been paid to find. Buried extremely well, it had taken him over a month to exhaust his avenues for information, finally admitting he'd found everything there was to find. Whoever had initially buried it took his job very seriously.

Finished, the client abruptly stands from the table, back ramrod straight and not a hair out of place. Cold eyes barely flicker to Grant, his presence already dismissed. "Thank you. Your services, while helpful, are no longer needed. I will have my lawyer send your final payment within a week."

The Evil One turns and walks briskly to the door. The movements are abrupt yet fluid. Grant shivers in an attempt to rid himself of the chills this individual evokes.

Glad to be done with this assignment, he takes a drink of his coffee as an uneasy feeling pulls at his conscience.

Did he just knowingly give the Huntsman the information to kill Snow White?

42

KATE

LIFE IS AN UNPREDICTABLE SEA. CALM AND SOOTHING ONE DAY, a typhoon the next. Typhoon would be an apt way to label my conversation with Shaw. Sixteen years prepared me for a ripple compared to the tidal wave created when our worlds collided, creating one story from the pieces of our two.

My communication with Shaw has been reduced to three texts. His time has been limited due to a two-week stint of international work travel. He had asked if we could see each other again when he returned, provided I was ready to see him. Code for "the ball is in your court."

He's smart, giving me time to wrap my brain around "Papergate," the term I adopted to describe the demise of our relationship.

Hiding behind volunteering and work deadlines, I'm living in denial. I've pushed all questions from our conversation into a lockbox in the far corner of my brain and focused on completing my final draft. I'm amazed my words are flowing freely, considering my cluttered mind.

I check the time while reviewing the day's writing statistics. One thousand words, time to call it a day. Empty water bottles,

Post-it notes, a pen, and a half dozen different colored high-lighters litter the table around me. My normally organized, tidy workspace has suffered the brunt of the chaos occupying my mind. My singular focus has been my manuscript.

Beacon serves as my home base, allowing me the physical space to work and the mental space to do what I do best—write bestselling novels. I save my work, shut down my laptop, jump up, and carry my empty water bottles to the recycle bin. Arranging the last bottle, I step back and survey my plastic pyramid, chuckling to myself over my strange little quirk.

Once my area is clean and organized, I turn to leave, and I'm greeted by Jon lounging at the door. I hit the overhead lights, slightly embarrassed he may have witnessed my construction ritual.

"What's your record for number of bottles in your pyramid?"

His answer confirms my suspicion. My face grows hot from embarrassment, and I give him a timid smile. "Thirty-one. The last leg of my third book. I was on fire. Wrote for twelve hours straight. Almost resorted to peeing in an empty bottle, so I didn't disrupt my creative flow." His eyebrows shoot toward his hairline, and he gives me a look that says he isn't sure if I'm serious. "Ended up not doing it. Would have thrown off the visual aesthetics of my pyramid in the end."

He stares at me, still trying to figure out the accuracy of my story, so I throw him a bone. We may have become friends, but we aren't at the point of properly judging sarcasm yet. "That tidbit is one hundred percent fact. Think about it, store it in your brain. Feel free to bring it up half past never."

He shakes his head, a deep chuckle wafting down the hall. "You should know, I don't make promises I can't keep. I will never look at another water bottle without thinking of you. That's a promise I can keep."

His stare turns serious, a little predatory. As he looks at me, my body tingles. *Is he flirting with me?* He is very good-looking and considerate. Well-mannered, guy next door material.

No. No. *No.* I already have a jumbo jet of tagged and color-coded mistakes. I do not need to add him to the manifest.

Breaking eye contact, I make a show of pawing through my purse as I look for my keys. It's a nonverbal message I'm on my way out and don't have time to chitchat or whatever else he has in mind.

He raises his hand and massages the back of his neck, and my eyes are immediately drawn to his bicep as it bunches in a tight knot. His skin is tan, even though summer hasn't officially started. *What does Jon do when he isn't running Beacon?* He appears to be an upstanding guy so...build habitats for stray animals? Sidewalk ramps for the elderly? Whatever he does makes his body look like a Roman statue.

Jon would be a dream "catch" for most girls, including me, but I'm not interested. He is perfect, just not for *me.*

It took sixteen years, one night, a motorcycle, and a gut-wrenching conversation to recognize my perfect. He's currently in another country working, doing his boat building thing. Waiting for me to get my shit together and call him.

"I was thinking, maybe you would like to catch dinner together sometime?"

Gentling my voice, I try to say no without sounding like a bitch. "Jon, that's really flattering, but I can't."

As I speak, I watch his head tilt toward the floor. An uncomfortable, tense silence fills the hallway. I stand there, waiting for him to respond, move, or walk away so I can excuse myself from this crappy situation. He finally nods his head in understanding, looking up to catch my eye. A smile I didn't expect, lights his face.

"No big deal. In fact, that's the best news I've heard in years. Thanks." The giddiness in his voice is like a slap in my face. He turns and walks away as a quiet laugh ripples across his shoulders.

What the hell? He'd smiled, and he looked...relieved? Happy? Reassured? *What the hell is going on?*

43

KATE

THREE WEEKS AFTER MY MOTORCYCLE DATE WITH SHAW, I realize it's time to make the call. What started as faint flutters and barely warm embers have grown to full-on, molten desire. I'm primed and ready for action of the Shaw variety.

Honestly, I can't blame my neglected body. The action I've seen over the past few years would match a Jean Claude Van Damme DVD on the rack at Wal-Mart. Touched by only one hand—rough, quickly, and without finesse.

It's Saturday, and I promise myself I'll call him after I slide out of procrastination mode. I clean the kitchen and my bathroom until they sparkle. I can now eat breakfast off my bathroom floor with less fear of getting sick than using a clean plate straight out of the dishwasher.

Physically, I'm exhausted and still recovering from the shock of finding an old moldy cauliflower tree in the back of the fridge. Eating healthy never looked so unappealing.

I let my mind wander as I recline on my bed, head tipped to the ceiling. I'm a woman who needs a plan for everything, including what I'm going to say once I hear Shaw's voice. He has been patient, giving me time to reconcile my thoughts before diving into more questions about us.

I know he's returned because Sarah mentioned it in passing yesterday. Unsure if she meant to pique my interest or provide a topic of conversation, I spent the better part of last night thinking about him.

His last text had been polite, but sterile: *I hope you're doing well. I'll be back in town soon.* I need more in a text so I can reread, analyze, break it down, and read ten different emotions into it until I'm a neurotic mess.

A notification buzzes on my phone, which sits next to my hand that smells like cleaning chemicals. My arms feel like cinder blocks, stiff and unyielding, as I turn my head to look in the direction of the buzzing.

It's probably Amy, sending me her tenth picture of a chicken and kale salad, the kind she's so fond of eating. I have never met someone who can tout the benefits of a kale-balanced lunch, then wash it down with a cream-filled donut. The girl is a different level of strange when it comes to eating, but I still love her, regardless of her love of kale.

I would pay a million dollars for a voice-activated phone right now. My arms and hands are so sore, a newborn baby could beat me in arm wrestling.

After a pep talk, where I promise myself no more aggressive cleaning, I grope my bed until my hand falls on my phone. Bringing it slowly toward my face, I check to see who is subjecting me to such grueling torture.

Shaw: You home? Hungry?

Seems Mr. Patiently Silent is getting a little antsy.

Me: If you mean, does my stomach feel like it's

**ready to eat its own lining? Then yes, I'm
hungry.**

**Shaw: Perfect. Just around the corner. Be there
in five.**

I don't need to lift my head to know I look like a hot mess.
My hair is perched on my head, like a nest waiting for a family
of robins to return to their home. My skin is visible through my
tank top, which is indecently thin from age and repeated wash-
ings. While I'm not positive, I'm pretty sure it's sporting a
mustard stain.

*Will there ever be a time when I don't look like someone who walked
out of a raging fraternity party...the morning after?*

I shoot off my bed, momentarily forgetting my sore
muscles until they scream like banshees in protest to my movement. No time to coddle said muscles if I'm going to open my
front door looking close to normal. My shirt is stripped, and
my jean shorts are halfway down my legs before I hit the ice-
cold bathroom tile. *Note to self: No need for an ice bath later, just lay
down on the bathroom tile. Same effect, less effort.*

Five minutes later, I'm reaping the benefits of Amy's
instructions for quick "morning after" primp and skips. My
face is scrubbed, hair and teeth brushed, and a clean shirt and
jeans in place. I saunter out to the living room, willing my
breathing to return to normal. *Follow-up note to self: Step up the
cardio before I embarrass myself in public.*

The doorbell rings, a dark looming figure throwing a
shadow through the transom next to the door. My entire body
tingles as I take in Shaw's gorgeous beauty. Even his shadow
looks hot. Or maybe my brain is overly imaginative, given its
sexy time hiatus.

I open the door, and a green Mancino's logo monopolizes
my line of sight. The rich aroma of pasta sauce and garlic

bread twists my stomach and hijacks my brain. Shaw is forgotten as my hunger becomes a living, breathing monster clawing the inside of my stomach. My momentary amnesia lifts, and I tilt my head around the bag to smile at a smirking Shaw. He hovers in my doorway, like a teenage vampire waiting for an invitation into my home.

Little does he know, he could be Jack the Ripper, and I'd still let him enter provided I was able to stuff my face before he cut me up into little pieces. I am ravenous, and Mancino's is my food porn. Nothing and no one can come between Mancino's and my mouth.

My left hand brushes the side of Shaw's bicep as I reach to accept the bag. A frisson of electricity shoots through my hand and up my arm. My eyes cut to his, impassive blue orbs stare back at me giving me no indication if our contact affected him the same way it did me. Feigning ignorance of the sexual tension now coursing through my body, I turn toward the kitchen, bag in hand, as I cool down. He closes the door and follows me. *Why do I feel like a lamb to his lion?*

His commanding presence shrinks my gourmet kitchen to the size of a postage stamp. I feel him approach me from behind, his body a match to the embers smoldering at the base of my spine. His nearness sends tingles throughout my body as I fight the urge to touch him.

"I hope this is OK." His voice is a caress on the back of my neck. "I promised myself I'd give you space." The cadence of his voice drops to a low rumble. "Truth is, staying away is killing me. I'm a patient guy, but I'm no saint." I feel his fingers ghost over my hair. His facade of calmness fades away the closer he gets. Raw emotion bleeds from his voice. "I've thought of nothing else but you, for three weeks. What you were doing? Who you were with? What you were thinking?"

I turn and raise my eyes to meet orbs of deep blue. Flames of desire singe me, promising a delicious burn before I turn to ash. Tension sits within his jaw, and his eyes search mine for the smallest flicker of permission.

Throat dry, my body is a sauna, begging me to acquiesce. My tongue darts out to moisten my lips. The compulsion to deny him an answer teeters on my tongue. "I thought you granted me time. Impatience is not like you, Shaw."

"As I said before, I'm not a saint. The tamest of fantasies residing in my head can attest to that."

I move to set the table, the distance offering a meager reprieve from my desire to touch him, hold him...forgive him.

Is forgiveness necessary? The hell we both suffered is a punishment far stronger than withholding a few words of forgiveness. Shaw standing inside my home is a testament to the extent I have already forgiven him.

We lost each other. Lost time that cannot be exchanged or returned. In our situation, fault didn't discriminate. It hurt both of us equally, but differently. It stole dreams and twisted our goals, making the path back to each other nearly invisible.

My brain finally agrees with decisions my heart made weeks ago. My feelings have become a forest fire of want and desire.

"I find saints to be overrated." The playful teasing statement is thrown over my shoulder as I busy myself with preparing the table. "I find some of the best decisions are made by mortals, like yourself."

He cocks an eyebrow and narrows his eyes. His smolder burns through me like warm chocolate. Passion and desire are reflected in his Caribbean blues.

An inhuman growl fills the kitchen, my stomach breaking the intensity of the interaction. I feel the heat of embarrassment crawl across my face as he chuckles.

Two steps and we're toe-to-toe, his hands gripping my elbows.

"Saved once again by your bodily functions. Sounds like a

vicious beast resides in your stomach. Better eat before he convinces your stomach to chew off one of your arms. Or worse, one of mine."

Like a bratty four-year-old, my tongue darts out of my mouth before I can stop it. Quick as a whip, Shaw pulls me in and sucks my tongue into his mouth, grazing it with his teeth.

Surprised by his speed and turned on by his playfulness, I freeze. My body is a statue, as hard as the granite counter to my left.

Too soon, Shaw releases my mouth and pulls back, his grip on my elbows softer than moments before. His eyes bounce between mine. My brain is muddled, and my body buzzes with adrenaline, immediately missing the warmth of his mouth.

"Careful with that tongue. I won't let it get lonely. Ever."

44

SHAW

I LEAN FORWARD, ELBOWS RESTING ON THE TABLE, MY STOMACH full of the best pasta I've ever eaten. My body is drunk on the sights and sounds that have filled my head and jump-started my fantasies for the past hour.

Kate is a gorgeous woman. In looks, temperament, compassion, empathy. She has never trusted her own allure. My heart connects to her compassion and empathy, and my body burns for the gift of her smile.

Laughter lights her from within, and I find myself trying to share every deprecating story about my life just to see and hear her laugh. Her blue eyes dance, and her long, chocolate-colored hair frames her face. Her lips, pale pink, plump, and full. A sculptor's dream sits across from me. She's unaware of her magnetism and my inability to leave.

"True story. I thought he was extending his hand to shake. Instead, he extended his arm to present me to the prime minister. Talk about a professional faux pas."

Her laughter wraps around me, warming me from the outside in. Her eyes sparkle from holding back tears of joy, her cheeks a rosy pink. A combination of laughter and alcohol runs through her blood. She has consumed just enough to relax her, but nowhere near a good buzz.

She looks across the kitchen, and her eyes widen. "Please tell me it's not really one a.m.?"

I chuckle and look to the clock. "It would appear it is. I should probably go before that stomach beast of yours demands breakfast. I'm not sure I'd survive without some form of food peace offering."

Amusement shines from her eyes, letting me know my joke was taken as such. I push my chair back and grab my phone from its place on her counter, where it has been sitting, silenced, since before dinner.

Kate had granted me a dinner. Time alone. A chance to sit across from her. Talk. Laugh. Tease. I'd had no intention of being interrupted by a trivial text or unimportant phone call.

I glance at my phone to see three missed text messages from V.

V: It's Saturday, man. Where are you? Been here thirty minutes. You've got ten more minutes before you owe me one free ticket for an ass kicking.

V: ...nine minutes. My steel toes are itchin' for a little action.

V: I'm out. Call me. It better be good.

Shit. I had Kate on the brain. Determined to see her tonight, I had totally forgotten about our swim.

I exhale, disappointed in myself for forgetting plans with my best friend, but having trouble drumming up any remorse after the night I've spent with Kate.

"Trouble?"

I run my hand down my face. "I forgot a meeting tonight. My best friend and I meet once a month for a grueling, two-person swim meet. Both determined to best the other. The night usually ends at a nearby bar, where we bury each other in trash talk and multiple, verbal replays of the winning lap."

She's quiet. Silence engulfs the room, and I wonder what she's thinking. *Is she questioning the truth in my story? Does she think it was a date with another woman?*

Her face lights with a sudden understanding. "That night I saw you at Beacon. I never really thought about why you'd be there. Swimming by yourself." I'm mesmerized by her thought process as it flies from her mouth. "I didn't really question why you were there. How you got in."

I wait, knowing she's not done.

"You love to swim. You were there by yourself. Not concerned about me calling the cops. Dared me to, in fact." She cocks an eyebrow at me. I want to pull her in and kiss that look off her face. "Sarah spends a lot of time at Beacon. You are outrageously wealthy."

I'm not sure where her tangent is leading.

Her speech stops, her eyes grow huge, and her jaw falls open. It's so abrupt, I search her face for signs of cardiac distress. Shock and realization make her a caricature of cartoon proportions.

"You know Jon Logan. He's your best friend?" Her intense look spurs me to nod, not willing to disrupt her verbal tirade.

"Beacon. *Your hope in a sea of uncertainty.* You own it?" I nod again, not sure if my voice is needed to affirm her angry accusation.

She walks to the island, placing her open palms against its surface. Her head is bowed, and she's completely still. I'm at a loss where this is going. Her body language reflects sadness and defeat.

"How long have you known Jon?"

Expecting her to question my ownership, not my choice of friend, I'm thrown by her question.

"About thirteen years. I trust him with my life. In fact, he's the only one who knows any details about our summer, as well as the hell I've endured." I want to touch her, return to the relaxed conversation preceding this bizarre line of questioning. Not willing to piss her off with unwanted contact, I walk around the island and face her.

She looks at me, eyes wet, fighting unshed tears. Panic bubbles in my chest, my heart picking up speed in the silence of the room.

"I don't know if we can continue whatever this is." Her hand gestures between both of us.

My stomach rolls as nausea climbs up my throat, and I feel the blood drain from my face. *What is happening and how do I stop it?*

I coax myself to form words. "What the hell are you talking about?"

"I have no interest in coming between two friends."

"What? Where's Jon in this picture? Please explain what I'm obviously too stupid to understand."

She looks to the ceiling, trying to stem the flow of tears leaking down her cheeks. "He and I...we've become friends. He's a great listener. We get on well."

I nod my head, wanting to move past this mess of a story so I can fix whatever she thinks is broken. So help me, there is nothing that will tear me away from Kate again.

Her words fall out of her mouth on a single breath of air. "He asked me out the other day."

Not wanting to scare her, I convince my body to appear calm. Inside, however, liquid magma floods my veins until all I see is red.

He. Did. Not. Ask. Her. Out.

As my blood boils, a sick realization fills me. I have to know, but the words stick on my tongue like flypaper. *How did she answer him?*

"I see. What did you say?" Seconds stretch into what seems like years as I wait for her response. I feel like a guilty ass as I internally pray she doesn't want V.

"I said I couldn't."

Her words instantly bring peace to my raging anger.

She stares at me, then swallows before whispering her next words. "I couldn't go out with him because I only want *you*."

Hallelujah, I don't have to kill V. Maybe only maim him. He knows how I feel about her. He knows our history. What the hell?

45

SHAW

My temper knows no bounds as V's office door slams against his wall. I'm barely able to contain my emotions. I cannot remember a time when I have been so pissed.

I know he's here. Tara—who runs the front desk like a well-oiled machine yet has problems articulating words in my presence—told me V was scheduled to work this afternoon.

My anger knew no limits as it simmered during my morning meetings. Meetings couldn't be rescheduled, and the participants paid the price. I recognized my moody impatience well before Karl, my second VP, pointedly mentioned it. It wasn't his fault for stating the obvious, but he still earned himself an assignment that will keep him busy into the better part of next week.

Childish? Absolutely. Am I the CEO of the company? Yep. *Hope your personal life doesn't suffer, Karl.*

V's eyebrows disappear beneath his tousled, wavy hair as his eyes shift to look at me from his seat at his desk. "What crawled up your butt, chief?"

I stalk to his desk. My height towers over him as my eyes bore holes through his face. "Start explaining, asshole."

My intimidation attempts fail to rile my best friend. V stands from his chair and slowly rounds his desk. Casually leaning back against his desk, arms folded across his chest, he splays his feet in front of him. If he intends to piss me off, he's doing a damn fine job.

V levels me with hard eyes. "Come again, Asshole? I believe it's *you* who owes *me* an explanation." His right eyebrow ticks upward as he holds my cold, blue stare. V, for his All-American looks and personality, can drop that persona for one of a menacing bad boy in a heartbeat.

"You. Kate. Start explaining."

He continues to stare at me, silent. His eyes move over my face as he calculates his response. V's lips tick up into a pseudo-smile, challenge radiating from his eyes. "Ah, Kate. Great girl. Sweet as honey, not to mention a total knockout."

His smile widens as he continues to bait me, knowing his words are setting me on edge. My fists itch to connect with his smug face.

"Did. You. Ask. Her. Out?" It takes considerable effort to push the words through my clenched teeth.

V's smile doesn't waver as he looks at me, motionless. My annoyance spikes in response to his casual attitude. "Yep. Last week, in fact."

My fist darts out and connects with his stomach. V doubles over, his smug smile replaced by a coughing fit. We've never resorted to physical violence, outside of an occasional sparring match at the gym, until today. Satisfaction floods my veins, even though I know I'll feel like a complete jerk later. My relationship with Kate is at stake, and I refuse to jeopardize it, even for my best friend.

A small chuckle falls from V's mouth. "Resorting to violence before hearing her answer, huh?"

"She told me she said no."

"She said she *couldn't*." He straightens and walks behind his desk, dropping into his chair. "Let the record show, she said she *couldn't*, not that she wasn't interested. An important difference, I'd say."

His words tighten the band around my chest. He's right.

"I told you she's my *one*, man. Why did you ask her out?"

V does little without a motive, and I'm confused what his angle could be.

"Yeah, you told me she was *your* Kate, but you failed to tell me you were still hung up on her."

Snark drips from my tongue. "Didn't know our friendship had a *feelings swap* requirement."

V's fingers stroke an imaginary goatee. "Way I figure, I did you a favor. Now you know I'm not your competition." His voice reflects an air of sophisticated Southern gentleman, making him sound utterly ridiculous considering his Midwest upbringing.

He drops the accent and runs his eyes over my face. "All kidding aside, I'm not interested in her romantically. But...it was a pretty good way to poke the bear, so to speak. Considering you've confirmed what I already knew."

"Yeah? What's that?"

"You are one hundred percent, certifiably in love with her. I daresay it was worth a gut punch to appease my curiosity."

I run fingers through my hair, annoyed with myself for not figuring out his game. He's one smart bastard. My green-eyed, hairy, jealousy monster had burst from my body, bent on revenge when she told me he had asked her out.

No one could stop me from pursuing Kate or the future I wanted with her.

My biggest obstacle, however...was convincing Kate she wanted a future with *me*.

46

KATE

My eyes scan the letter. It's been years since I've read it. The first time had been a few years after he left. In all honesty, I can't believe I didn't destroy it back then. But I couldn't do it. It was a tether binding me to him.

It was the first and last time I ever saw his handwriting. His hands formed words my eyes feasted upon and cried over.

As I read it again, I hear his voice, prominent and clear. My heart hurts, cracking just as it did back then.

Kate -
This may be a poor substitute for a face-to-face meeting, but I find I need closure and just can't find the time to meet with you. What we had was fun and exciting, a good old-fashioned summer fling. Fling being the operative word. I thought I wanted you, but after our time ended, I realized my feelings were only surface deep. I needed more in a girlfriend and eventually, a wife.
I'm not quite sure how it happened, but I've found my "more." She's smart, beautiful, and, most importantly, a social peer.
Please understand this letter closes the door on our past and is a final goodbye.

Shaw

Since our conversation, my mind keeps circling back to this letter. If what he told me about his final days at the cottage is true, would he have found another woman so quickly? Something isn't adding up.

I need to confront him. Ask him to explain. If we're ever going to be together, we need to be open and honest. This letter will be our first chance. I only hope it isn't going to extinguish the second chance we both deserve.

47

SHAW

I STRUGGLE TO CALM MY NERVES AS I STAND ON KATE'S doorstep. Not willing to run the risk of her avoiding me, I've shown up unannounced. I hear shuffling behind the door as I wait. She's either frantic I've arrived without calling, or she's trying to think of an excuse to get rid of me. I don't dwell on the fact it could be the latter.

As I study the house, I focus on the porch. My brain immediately jumps to thoughts of her and another guy, sharing the swing in a passionate embrace.

Irrational, much? Get it under control, Graham.

I hear a low grunt, and heavy breathing just before a half-naked, sweaty Kate opens the door.

My eyes scan her body. She's wearing tight black pants, a hot pink sports bra, and rainbow-colored athletic shoes. My dick stands up and starts to take notice. Random strands of her ponytail stick to her wet neck. She is truly a hot mess. I may need to fall on the sword and help perfect her look a little more.

Her chest rises and falls as she works to catch her breath

while staring and giving me a nonverbal, "What are you doing on my doorstep?" face.

"Have I caught you at a bad time?"

A wide smile spreads across her face. "I don't know. If you call hot yoga a bad time, then yes. You've caught me."

I relax. I'm unsure what "hot yoga" is, but something tells me it doesn't involve a sweaty male waiting in the wings for me to leave.

"I wanted to—" Both of us speak the same words in unison.

She pauses and fully opens the door for me to enter. I stop in the small entryway, angling my body to face her as she shuts the door and leans against it. Without a word, she holds out her arm and circles her hand, indicating I should speak first.

"I want to apologize for how I left things the other night." I run my hands through my hair, my nerves rising as she looks at me, expressionless.

"I heard you mention Jon, and my eyes only saw red. I was surprised. And, I admit, a little jealous. I was angry, and I shut you out. That's on me, though. I'm sorry, and I'll do my absolute best to never let it happen again."

I swallow and push through my need to throw up walls to hide the feelings swirling through my mind. Embarrassment for having to own my character flaws runs through me. I feel uncomfortable and exposed. But, hell, I'll gladly suffer any discomfort as long as she keeps listening.

"Jon and I talked. Turns out, he's not interested in dating you. He was testing us—mainly me. Said he was measuring the depth of our feelings for each other." A ghost of a smile travels across my lips. "I'm fairly certain my fist went a long way in convincing him just how deep they go."

Her eyes focus on my mouth, her tongue peeking out to run along her top lip. "I wanted to apologize too," she replies, her gaze bouncing between my eyes and mouth. "I felt like a good evening took a turn to horrible and shitty." Her words fall from her lips, like a secret she doesn't want to share.

"Kate, let me tell you something. Nothing, I repeat, nothing could make time spent with you shitty. Vomit-like, maybe, but not shitty."

Catching my intended joke, she smiles. I reach forward, hooking my hand behind her neck and giving a subtle tug, urging her to fall into my chest. I'm hoping she'll accept my reassurance through the embrace I'm offering.

Her forehead hits my chest, her arms snaking around my waist as she lets out a shuddered sigh. Her breath, warm and stilted, slides through the fibers of my shirt, setting my heart on fire.

Kate. My *one*. My *only*. Forever.

I wrap my free hand around her waist, pulling her to me, silently giving her permission to crawl into my life. My soul. My future.

I'm immediately transported to that summer. It feels like a lifetime ago. Chest to chest. Heart to heart. Speaking words only our souls can hear. A peace, I thought no longer existed, flows through my body, cleansing me of the lingering pain of our separation.

Cheated by misunderstandings, we've finally been released from the prison of our misguided pasts.

Her body shudders as she works through the memories invading her thoughts. I stroke my left hand down her spine, gently pulling her closer as I mark her with my touch and my scent. My body begs to open up and make room for her to crawl inside.

My right hand slides up her neck, my fingers splayed through the hair at the base of her skull, enticing me to act on the physical urges her body pulls from mine.

Minutes, maybe hours, later, Kate tilts her head back, looking at me with a grin on her face. "All is forgiven?"

At that moment, I see young Kate. Innocent, guileless, trusting. *How did I survive losing her? How am I still standing?*

No longer able to deny my desire, I bend my head and feather my lips across hers. Searing heat prickles down my spine at the fleeting touch.

Her lips are a haven. Soft, warm, filled with hope as they pull me toward her. They offer light and the promise of redemption.

I pause, hypnotized by a pure blue sea. She has lowered her walls. Her eyes reflect waves of optimism and desire, drowning the pain and sadness floating on the surface.

"Kate, you are my beacon. You're the light that pulls me in, keeping me afloat. Reminding me where I am and where I need to go."

A tear traces a path down her cheek. I lean down, capturing it on my tongue.

Her eyes remain glassy as she smiles. "I want to be the same for you."

"Let me be your light. Always guiding you back to me. Please." My throat is raw and tight with emotion as I wait for her answer.

She raises on her toes and runs her hands up my chest, stopping to cradle my jaw in both hands. "Be my guide."

Her words caress my lips just before her mouth crashes into mine.

48

KATE

I have no time to react as Shaw takes control of the kiss. His lips are a contradiction to my senses. Demanding, yet soft. He presses his lips to mine, pulling me in, consuming me like a parched man deprived of water.

His hands roam, massaging down my spine to the small of my back before retracing the path to the base of my skull. His strong hands pull and manipulate my body until it's perfectly molded to his.

My breasts are prisoners caught against the cage of his chest. My nipples are hard and begging for attention as Shaw continues to devour my mouth.

His tongue pushes against my lips, requesting access, and it's like warm silk as it glides across mine.

Shaw's hands track down my back and up my sides. Firm and strong, his fingers knead my flesh through my pants, sending sparks to my core.

He grabs my ass, lifting me as he turns and pushes me against the wall. I spread my thighs, and he situates himself between my legs before I wrap them around his waist. The roughness of the wall at my back and Shaw's hardness pushing at the apex of my thighs has my panties soaked.

I squeeze my legs, lifting my core just enough to rub against him. I feel Shaw's hands slide under my sports bra, pushing it up to my neck and freeing my breasts. Leaning back, Shaw cups my breasts, watching as he runs his thumbs back and forth across my nipples.

"Beautiful. Always." His words are a reverent whisper captured within my heart.

I watch the ripples in his biceps until the movement of his hands demand my attention as he pushes my breasts toward my neck. We're both mesmerized, staring at my nipples as he continues to glide his thumbs back and forth.

"Please." A whispered plea falls from my mouth as I lift my shoulders, pushing myself closer to his lips.

He leans in, his mouth sucking on my earlobe. "What do you need?"

I squirm, knowing I need the release, but afraid to give him the words.

He watches me, seeing my frustration mount as I continue to fidget while the pressure builds between my legs.

He looks down at my nipple again. My gaze follows his as I focus on the movement of his thumb. I close my eyes and concentrate on the sensations as his skin grazes my nipple. I reach for my orgasm, trying to send myself over the edge without giving him the words.

"Not so fast there." His teasing words make my eyes pop open. His hand freezes, and he lifts his thumb as he stares at me, his lips tipped in a cocky smirk.

"No." I whimper as I drop my head to the side, not willing to acknowledge his blinding smirk. I should have known he wouldn't make this easy.

"Tell me, Kate."

Still refusing to look at him, I bite my lip. If he remembers anything about our time together, he recognizes how difficult it is for me to say what I want.

I need only to ask for the pleasure I know he'll give. He said it always made him hard to hear the words that were so difficult for me to say.

He raises his free hand to my chin, gently pressing down and releasing my lip from between my teeth. He leans in, his mouth nearly touching mine. "Tell me." Reaches my ears on a whispered breath.

The hum of my body has gotten so strong, I can no longer wait him out. I want his mouth on me like I want my next breath.

"I want you to suck my nipples."

Smirk in place, one eyebrow raised like a rogue pirate, he asks, "Is that all, Kate?"

"Maybe...uh...a pinch, or...a bite." My face heats as I push the foreign request from my lungs.

"There's my sassy girl."

He wastes no time as he dips his head, wrapping his tongue around my nipple before sucking it inside his mouth.

I watch as he follows my instructions. Groaning when he lifts his eyes to watch me while he delivers playful bites. He drops his eyelids, pulling my full attention back to his mouth as he alternates sucking and biting.

I lift my shoulders from the wall, desperate for more contact. My pulse pounds between my legs, as I feel my orgasm building. The wetness from my arousal is, no doubt, seeping through the thin fabric of my pants.

I watch him as I cup his jaw while leaning forward and tilting my head and lean forward. I run my tongue along his upper lip, gaze locked on him as I watch for a reaction. His eyes instantly open. Hooded, but aware, they flick up to mine. I see his pleasure as a slight smile appears on his face.

I run my tongue across his lip again, and he opens his

mouth wider. My tongue slips in, grazing his tongue and my nipple at the same time. Any reservations I've had burn away at the pleasure that rips through me.

I want more, and Shaw is willing to give.

My tongue dips in again. Shaw takes charge, guiding and positioning until my nipple is trapped between our two tongues. I'm teetering on the edge of oblivion, whimpering as my body begs for release.

Using his free hand, Shaw pushes two fingers into my mouth, effectively pulling my tongue away from my breast. In the next second, he bites my nipple. White lightning pours through my veins as I explode, stealing my voice as my vision darkens.

As aftershocks wind through me, I'm vaguely aware of being carried. I settle into Shaw's lap as he sits down on the couch. The stress from the previous weeks lift, and my body is instantly tired and lethargic. I grip Shaw's shirt, pulling it toward my face, like a security blanket bringing protection and refuge.

My ear rests against his chest. His heartbeat, the rhythm of a galloping horse, steals my focus and makes my eyes heavy.

Gradually, my world goes black as sleep pulls me under. My mind drifts as a whisper trails across my neck. "Mine. Forever."

49

SHAW

My head tips back, connecting with the wall, seeking comfort, as Kate sleeps cradled in my arms. Her cheeks reflect a rosy glow, a reaction to my body heat mingling with hers. I cinch my arms tighter, not willing to break contact.

As I think about what we just did, I fear Kate's reaction when she wakes. Too fast, too soon, too threatening. I pray my loss of control won't steal the progress we've made since the night at Joe's.

I work to calm my body's natural reaction to having Kate in my lap. My dick, denied and now hungry for release, stands at attention, not willing to relinquish his standby status.

After ten minutes of steel willpower, my body finally gets the message to relax, and I focus on dulling the guilt and pain of our past.

Kate. This woman radiates a light that calls to my soul. She is pure beauty. Her release of pleasure is a perfect reflection of the woman herself. Strong, quiet, and powerful. Her face, as she came, is etched in my memory, and I would gladly drain every bank account I own to see it again.

Kate fidgets in her sleep. Her subconscious is unsettled,

searching for answers to unknown questions. Uncertainty trickles into my consciousness. Kate is insanely private, guarding herself against everyone, either friend or foe. Amy is probably the only friend who holds the secrets Kate has willingly shared.

At one time, I vowed to be her person. Her secret keeper, her truth seeker, her dragon slayer. The one who would love her, protect her, keep her safe. Instead, I vowed in front of God and a church full of so-called friends to love, honor, and cherish Elizabeth. It had been the verbal vow of an unspoken lie.

At the time, I thought I'd lost Kate. Failed contact had fueled a loss of hope. I held no illusions of happily ever after with Elizabeth. I was convinced my one chance was gone, which was the only reason I talked myself into the union.

No longer interested in sharing my heart, I figured Elizabeth would be the best choice. She knew the rigors associated with being the wife of a corporate CEO. She had aspired to be a society wife, born and bred to fill the position, no matter the partner. She was beautiful, ambitious, and driven in a way that would have bothered me had I chosen to look closely.

She saw an opportunity in me, and I allowed it, knowing the shattered pieces of my heart would forever remain locked away after losing Kate.

Elizabeth had grown up alongside me, going to the same social functions, traveling in the same circles. Her parents had been close to my parents, and she'd been a friend of my sister. Or at least, Elizabeth had led me to believe a friendship existed.

My sister confided in me, after our wedding, her uneasiness in a friendly relationship with Elizabeth. She cited her inability to trust Elizabeth because of the way she manipulated situations to gain the upper hand. As I told her then, her astute observations regarding Elizabeth's character would have been more helpful to me *before* the wedding.

Problems between Elizabeth and I truly started when she became obsessed with adding to our family. Elizabeth claimed Sarah needed brothers and sisters. While I wasn't convinced it was a good idea, I agreed we could try. Without immediate success, Elizabeth became distraught and moody and cited my unwillingness to schedule my workday around peak times to have sex as the reason for our failure. To be honest, sex with Elizabeth had become unappealing once I saw the internal ugliness that resided behind her mask of physical beauty.

I stayed with her, hoping to give Sarah a stable home life, not realizing I was probably doing more harm than good. Elizabeth's relationship with Sarah, who was in kindergarten by that time, had already deteriorated.

Elizabeth, when she paid any attention to our daughter, was determined to make Sarah into a replica of herself. Dressing her in "Mommy and me" outfits and taking her on outings to "be seen." What had started as a fissure between mother and daughter only grew throughout the years. Sarah often elected to spend more time with our nanny, whom she loved dearly, than with her mother.

Consumed by guilt for not seeing the toxicity of Elizabeth's treatment toward Sarah, I spent so much time avoiding Elizabeth that I failed Sarah.

Finally recognizing Sarah's need for an attentive, supportive parent, I dove in, shifting my schedule and making time for family outings. Outings Elizabeth continually cried off, claiming a previously scheduled appointment or one of her many fabricated physical ailments.

In reality, Elizabeth gave me a priceless gift—time with Sarah. We went to movies, museums, and parks, often acting like tourists as we explored Chicago. We also spent time on the boat, Sarah's thrill for boating nearly equal to my own.

While my heart knew almost immediately, it took years to realize marrying Elizabeth had been a mistake.

Sarah was my greatest triumph. My daughter was everything perfect in my life of imperfection.

I study Kate as she sleeps.

Elizabeth is vindictive and cunning. When, *not if,* I convince Kate we are meant to be together, I will need to deal with Elizabeth carefully. Even though our marriage and custody battle is finally over, she continues to cling to the irrational belief our family still exists, unchanged.

If she so much as thinks Kate and I are together, she will try to ruin us. Elizabeth has a silver tongue, and I have no doubt she will do everything in her power to destroy our happiness. I fear the strength of my relationship with Kate may falter against Elizabeth's ability to manipulate. What she doesn't know is if she comes near Kate, I will ruin all chances of her showing her face in Chicago, New York, and Los Angeles.

I will stop at nothing to protect the two most important people in my life—Kate and Sarah.

50

KATE

THE LAPTOP SHUTS WITH A SATISFYING *SNAP* AS I PUSH MYSELF away from the desk and stand up to stretch. Today's words dribbled out of me like a leaky faucet. Annoyingly slow, but consistent.

I look at my watch. My stomach knots and my heart stutters. I need to confront him, and I can't be sure this won't end us before we have a chance to begin.

Memories of waking up on the couch, sticky from the bodily fluids that had dried on my skin while I was asleep, fill my mind. Warmth had blanketed me as the grogginess of sleep lifted, and my eyes met orbs as blue as the ocean.

I immediately tried to jump off his lap as the embarrassment of my earlier actions slapped me in the face. Trapped against the wall, the torture of his thumbs, my mind-shattering release...and...falling asleep.

His grip had tightened, and the steel bands of his arms became my sanctuary. The muscles of his abs stretched tight as his whispered words soothed my mind. *"You're safe. I'm never leaving you. Seeing you come was always a gift. Still is."*

He was there, and he wanted to stay.

I was mortified I had allowed my physical needs to overrule my mind. His presence and his words had battered my control, shoving my fantasy straight into my reality. My body had stepped up and took what it craved, a bouquet of endorphins I could still feel bubbling under my skin.

Foreplay that had once been amazing was now electric. Time had heightened my desire. Shaw had become both a want and a need.

I think about the promises that had fallen so easily from his mouth. He vowed never to leave me. Yet, I'd heard it before. A promise of forever, denied in a single moment.

My mind returns to his letter. A punch to my heart, his words had been formal and impersonal and given me tangible proof that his feelings had not matched mine. I remember wanting to hate him, almost wishing we'd never met.

What if someone had compelled him to write it? Did he do it for Sarah? For his parents? Had I trusted a lie born from my mind over an action that was another cruel misunderstanding? My trust in him had been broken, but did I have a hand in fracturing it myself?

My heart, still tethered to his, tells me to move ahead. It begs me to strengthen the bonds that still exist. Start small, dust off the blueprints, and build the dreams that rest within our memories.

But I'd changed the dream, purposely cracking parts of the foundation, thinking it would never be a reality. What started as cracks in the surface have grown to fissures, ones I don't know we'll ever be able to repair.

Shaw wants to mend the bridges that were broken. Repairing the damage means tearing through memories and exposing the secrets flowing beneath them. But I can't guarantee our secrets won't burn the bridge and send it crashing down.

KATE

The whir of the coffee machines distracts my mind as I stare at the door. I arrived early to scope out the seating and have time to throw back a cup of coffee, allowing the caffeine to work through my system.

A warm breeze slides into the cafe as Shaw strides through the door, his designer suit and CEO mask firmly in place while his eyes scan the cozy seating areas.

Blue flames arrest my sight as he strides to my table. A smile on his lips, he leans down and kisses my cheek before pulling out a chair and taking a seat.

The breath I'm not aware I'm holding slides out of my mouth as my eyes feast. His hair, wavy and dark, is finger styled to perfection.

The fingers on his right hand drum a silent melody on the round tabletop, my only indication he's nervous about why I set up this meeting. The two texts he sent since our make out session have gone unanswered, as I debated what I wanted to say.

Butterflies swarm within my stomach as my mind organizes

words. Until he walked in, I had foolishly convinced myself his answers didn't matter. I could walk away without a backward glance, bury my feelings and burn the secrets I keep locked within.

My resolve crumbled when he walked through the door. He is *my one*. Resurrected from broken pieces of my past, he holds my heart. I hope his promised devotion is strong enough to weather the impending storm.

Hoping to avoid a scene, I chose the cafe for its semi-private seating areas and its busy atmosphere.

I offer him a chance to grab a drink. He declines, and I silently suffer through my failed attempt to stall.

My hand clutches the paper in my lap, as it crinkles and reminds me of my purpose. The words I'd gathered scatter, leaving me stranded with no idea where to start.

Shaw smiles and reaches for my hand where it sits near my cup. "I can practically see thoughts burning through your skull. Why don't you let them out before they do damage?"

His open smile and dry humor go a long way in settling my nerves.

"The other day was hard for me."

"Me too. In fact, I can probably guarantee it was *harder* for me." His emphasis on the word reddens my face.

"Walked right into that one, huh?"

He effectively answers my question by tilting his head and raising his eyebrows.

I stare at the table, afraid to say the words that will expose my fears. "I-I-I don't...trust you."

I lift my eyes to see his reaction. He remains silent, his face impassive, except for a subtle flare of his nostrils.

I look down to my lap, quickly piecing my words together before he gets pissed enough to walk out and leave me here alone.

I blow out a frustrated breath. "What I mean is...What I

wanted to say is...I want to trust you, but I'm having a really hard time."

Shaw remains perfectly still, pulling his lower lip between his teeth as he dissects and examines my words. His tone is defensive as I'm pierced with an icy stare. "Can you be more specific? Is there something I can defend, or have you already determined my guilt?"

I raise my hand and place the paper on the table between us. The words—his words—sit heavy and exposed. I hear each one as it screams through my head. Every word burned into my memory the day it was received.

I study Shaw as he glances at the paper, but makes no attempt to examine it. His face and body language give not a hint of recognition for the pain that bleeds from the page.

Confusion settles across his brow as he lifts his eyes to mine. Blue flares seek an explanation, oblivious to the letter's content and purpose. "Kate, please help me out here. What am I looking at?"

I'd been convinced recognition would stream from his body. I had been prepared for denial, not ignorance.

Holding back tears, I tear my gaze from the paper and focus on Shaw. "Your letter. The final nail in the coffin of our dream."

52

SHAW

I JOLT, HER WORDS A PHYSICAL SLAP TO MY ALREADY FRAYED nerves. I'd met her at the café thinking she was feeling skittish following what happened at her house. I was more than happy to meet her, prepared to argue a case for continuing our relationship. Never did I think I'd be staring at a piece of paper determined to set us on a course of destruction.

Fucking piece of paper. We were destined to be ruined by a wisp of a recycled tree. I'm sure there was irony or a moral buried within, but I was too fucking mad to look more closely.

I reach forward and snatch the page off the table, my angry movements nearly ripping the offending piece of trash in two.

What the hell is this thing?

My eyes see words, but I feel like a monkey doing a math problem as I try to decipher them.

It's a letter, written on a plain piece of paper. Short in length, written with a heavy hand.

A hand *that is not mine.*

By the third reading, my brain has caught up to my eyes. The letter had been written by someone posing as me. An impostor, bluntly telling Kate our relationship was no more than a fling, my feelings for her trivial. It even detailed my upcoming wedding, flaunting its existence along with my devotion to my fiancée.

"I didn't write this."

Shock and disbelief cloak Kate's face. Eyes shining, she brings her hand to her mouth, trying to stifle the tortured sounds exiting her body. Her head swings back and forth in denial as tremors wrack her body. "No."

I jump from my seat and kneel before her. I take her face between my hands as my thumbs catch her tears and my fingers cradle her head. "Kate, look at me. I'm getting us out of here." Hauling her against me, I mold her into my body, acting as her armor against the curious stares directed toward us.

Shudders consume her as I guide her out the door and to my Jeep. I've never been more grateful for having driven myself. My confusion and outrage take a back seat to my care of her.

I unlock the door and help her into my Jeep, then reach across and buckle the seatbelt, securing her body as her mind careens out of control. Knowing I shouldn't, her distress a danger to my own anger, I chance a look at her.

Her eyes are a thunderstorm of grays and blues, red and wet from her tears. Her face is like a newly cleaned whiteboard, stark and blank of any information.

My blood boils as I will myself to calm. Releasing my rage for this situation will only prove to scare Kate and diminish my ability to think rationally.

After making her as comfortable as possible, I circle to the driver's door and jump in. My mind switches to autopilot, starting the car and fastening my seat belt at the same time. I put the car in gear and head to my condo. I'll be able to think more clearly as I puzzle through this situation while taking care of Kate and her needs.

As I drive, I recall the words of the poisonous letter currently stuffed in my pocket. Somehow, I had the presence of mind to grab it from the table and shove it in my pocket before we left the cafe. It wasn't written by me, but someone had gone to considerable trouble to make Kate think it was. *Didn't she recognize it wasn't my writing? More importantly, someone had found her.*

I think back to that summer, quickly running through how we spent our time. Biking, hiking, the boat, lazy days spent in my bed. Memories that occupy my thoughts more than I need at the moment. Re-focusing, I realize she never saw my writing. *First question answered.*

Why didn't I write notes giving her tangible evidence as to how I felt? I'd relied solely on spoken promises to convince her of my sincerity. Looking at it, years later, I see my stupidity and failure. Without my written words, she had only had faded, aging memories to validate my heart's true intentions and chase away her doubts.

The letter had to have been sent more than a year after we separated, considering I was buried in work on the other side of the world for the better part of the first twelve months. Plus, no one knew about Kate, or so I thought. I had elected to wallow privately in my grief. My sister, Grace, was the only person in whom I chose to confide. My mom and dad would have told me to "grow up," if they had any idea of my mental state at the time.

Who else had known? Who would have known I was engaged? News flash, anyone who read the society pages in Chicago or New York would have known. Elizabeth's family had insisted an engagement announcement run in both *The New York Times* and *Chicago Tribune*, considering the magnitude of the union between Elizabeth Ashcroft and Shaw Graham. I'd kept my head down, consumed by work. I hadn't cared, but someone apparently did.

I would give my left nut to talk to my sister, but she was gone and could no longer be bothered with her brother's problems. My parents, so lost in their own lives, would have thought my problems too trivial to address.

Considering the dead ends I was throwing up in my own mind, solving this mess could prove impossible. The thought spikes my ebbing anger as I drive through the busy Chicago streets.

Occupied by my own thoughts, I had forgotten Kate sitting next to me until her fingers brush my right thigh. My leg involuntarily twitches as it reacts to the contact.

A shy smile appears on her face, and I'm reminded I'm one lucky bastard as she looks at me like I'm her protector.

I capture her hand as I lean toward her. "I'd say 'penny for your thoughts,' but I'm afraid I don't have nearly enough pennies." Her reaction to my humor reaches through her eyes and lights them from within.

Her casual shrug ripples across her shoulders as she squeezes my fingers. "Honestly, my mind hasn't stopped on any single thought. It's like I'm on a merry-go-round, unable to focus and unable to stop."

I lift her hand and place a chaste kiss on her knuckles. "Perfect description."

I feel her arm relax slowly as she releases her death grip.

Thankful my car seems to know its way home, I hang a left and hit a button, opening the access door to my building's underground parking.

"Where are we going?" Kate's voice is elevated and panicked as I ease into my parking spot. Her anxiety has me mentally considering the placement of all exit doors, in case she decides to bolt.

I bring her hand to my mouth and wait until she looks at

me. My eyes never leave her face as I kiss each of her fingers, while her eyes concentrate on the movement of my mouth. Kate's anxiety over her whereabouts is no longer an issue.

"This is my condo. I thought you could use a more private environment to decompress than the busy café, and my place was closer than yours."

"Ohhh-kay." An aura of shyness covers Kate, her eyes bouncing around the Jeep's interior like popcorn.

Her reaction awakens a desire to pull her to my chest and settle her on my lap. Instead, I reach out and grab her chin, tilting her face toward mine so I know she's listening.

"That fucking fake letter. Seeing your reaction. Knowing the pain it caused, and still causes. It was like a bomb exploded in my chest." I release her chin as my palm climbs up her jaw to rest against her cheek. "You hold my heart. Have for a long time. I want you to be happy. And I will do anything in my power to make that happen. Understand?"

She stares at me, and my heart picks up speed in the silence between us. I have no idea how she's going to react to the information I thrust upon her.

She nods once, followed by a whispered, "Yes."

I sense she has more to say, so I wait, giving her time to continue.

"My heart believes you. It protected the hope that the letter was somehow a fraud. But while my heart protected my hope, it couldn't protect me from the devastation of abandonment. The pain from our history has been debilitating. I need to move forward and take a break from the hurt. I need you to help me forget."

My heart beats a tattoo against my ribs. I want nothing more than to be the man who helps her forget. It may be stupid, but I can't convince myself to deny her. "Let's head upstairs. Maybe we can have a drink or something to eat? That paper isn't going anywhere, and I don't think I have it in me to look at it, again, so soon."

Deep blue pools of calm water mesmerize me. "OK."

I exit my door and round the car. She stands next to the passenger side, smirking at me as I shake my head. Her quick exit strips me of my gentleman's status.

"How long was I supposed to wait? I sprouted gray hair in the time it took you to round the car, old man. You need to be quick if you want to romance an independent woman. Better luck next time?"

There she is. *Feisty Kate.* Throwing sparks and barbs when I least expect it.

I stretch my arm out, indicating she walk in front of me toward the elevator bay. "By all means, baby. After you."

The little minx gives me a wink, attitude radiating from her hips as she sashays toward the elevator. Her earlier meltdown is momentarily forgotten.

My eyes eat up her show like a superfan at a Bears game. She's going to be the death of me. But it'll be one pleasurable way to go.

She stops in front of the elevator, then cocks her head and twirls a strand of hair around her finger. "Going up, sir?"

Her ability to switch gears from stressed to playful is almost scary. Just a half an hour ago, she had an emotional meltdown.

As for me, my body is on the verge of going into overdrive. My cock hardens, subtly reminding me of its shutout the last time Kate and I were together.

She pushes the button to call the elevator as she eyes me up and down, slowly reeling me in.

I step up, crowding her, so she has to tilt her head all the way back to make eye contact. "Up. Definitely going up."

Her eyes go wide, and her cheeks turn pink as my answer highlights the double meaning behind her words.

The chime of the elevator breaks the moment as the doors slide open.

"Ladies first."

Kate steps in and turns to wait for me as my feet stay rooted to the safe haven of concrete. Not willing to reveal my fear by asking her to climb twenty-two floors, I drag my feet forward, stopping next to her as I scan my key.

I watch the doors slide shut, and my heart takes off like a shot. A full-blown panic attack threatens as my brain returns to the three hours I spent trapped in the pitch-black metal car suspended between the fifty-first and fifty-second floor of Singapore's Guoco Tower.

The air gets heavier and thicker as we ascend, restricting my oxygen and burning my lungs. Twenty-two floors separate me from a full breath.

I should have taken the stairs.

Kate eyes me, reading my anxiety and stepping closer. Thick waves of brown ripple over her shoulders with the movement. My heart pulses with desire as it reacts to her nearness. She gently places her hands on my shoulders, steadying herself while leaning up on her toes.

"Anything I can do to take your mind off the ride?" Her voice is a seductive balm.

My eyes bore into hers as I weigh the advantages and disadvantages of answering her question. Nerves pulled tight, my body eagerly responds. I drop my eyes to her high, firm chest, covered by a V-neck T-shirt. Mouth parched, blood burning through my veins, I stand frozen as Kate slides her hands down my chest to the button on my trousers.

I try to take a deep breath as I close my eyes, afraid movement will break the fantasy.

Kate unbuttons my pants and dips her hand beneath the waistband of my boxers. Wrapping her hand around my hardness, she squeezes the base.

As soon as she touches my cock, control is no longer possible. I cover her hand with mine, squeezing tight while moving from base to tip.

Tactile instructions are my only option. The ability to talk is a luxury I no longer possess.

I remove my hand as Kate continues the rhythm. Base, squeeze, pull. Base, squeeze, pull. Our eyes focus on her hand as it disappears under my boxers on the down stroke. A secret pleasure. Hot and erotic.

"Yes...Kate...more."

She changes the rhythm, stopping to rub her thumb across the head. My precum makes her thumb slick as it slides back and forth.

I hear a buzz, quiet and faint. Not my concern, as I focus on the tingling in my abdomen and the fullness of my balls as they draw up tight. I feel my orgasm building as I skate toward the finish.

"Ummm, Dad? Everything OK?" A familiar voice slashes through my pleasure fog like a hatchet.

Kate stills, secretly trying to pull her hand from my boxers as I jump back like she's made of molten lava. "Shi—"

Luckily, I remember to grab my pants, lest they expose me to the juvenile eyes staring into the elevator.

"Sarah." Her name is like a drill sergeant's command as it bursts from my lungs. "This isn't what it looks like!" Kate's eyes bug out of her head as she keeps her back to Sarah.

Sarah spins around, giving us her back, but not before I glimpsed the canvas of red splashed across her face.

Kill me now. I am the worst father in the world.

53

KATE

Shaw looks to me for help as he tries to button his pants with one hand. Excuses pour from his mouth while he tries to downplay the situation. If I wasn't so mortified, I could help plead our case. As it is, my emotions are all over the place.

You know when you're overstressed and your body fires inappropriate emotional responses to a situation? Laughing at a funeral. Smiling when someone is crying. Or giggling when you get caught halfway to orgasm by an innocent teenager. A few rogue giggles manage to escape, earning me a death glare from Shaw.

Luckily, we had been fully clothed when Sarah caught us. The worst she saw was the position of my hand and the obvious action of said hand. Visually, we barely qualified for a PG-13 rating.

"Sarah, I'm sorry if we embarrassed you." No doubt, the visual of us will be permanently burned into her brain. At times like this, I'm glad I'm not the one raising a teenager.

Before I can reconcile the thoughts in my brain to the movements of my mouth, I toss a totally inappropriate comment on the fire. "Sarah, what you thought you saw was exactly what you saw. Your dad and I have a chemistry that never died."

What is wrong with me?

Not an hour ago, I was bawling and hysterical, trying to maintain sixteen years of convictions against one verbal denial. Now, I'm talking about hand jobs with Shaw's daughter. My sanity is most definitely in question.

My physical needs and sexual desires have crushed sixteen years of repressed pain. I berate myself for my lack of self-control. Had Sarah not caught us, my guilt would have buried my euphoria before the last drops of cum left Shaw's cock. My actions are solid proof my body can't be trusted around Shaw.

Sarah's face flushes red with embarrassment, as she rubs the back of her neck and looks at the ground. "I think I'll just head to my room. If you need me, I'll be the one with blinders taped to my eyes and headphones glued to my ears."

As she walks back into the condo, Shaw's biting remark hits me full-force. "Aren't you progressive? When I walk in on Sarah and her future boyfriend, I'll be sure to give you a call so you can smooth things over while I scrub my eyes with bleach."

Having not left the confines of the elevator, Shaw gives my lower back a firm nudge, spurring my feet forward. An anxious awareness hums through my body.

As Shaw opens the door to his condo, I stop, a breath catching in my throat, as I see whitecaps skim across the surface of Lake Michigan. The entire living room wall is glass. The grandeur is spectacular. Shaw steps around me, heading to the gourmet kitchen tucked into a corner on the other side of the living room.

"I think I understand why you're willing to live here, regardless of your fear of elevators. Your view is breathtaking."

"No matter what kind of day I've had, this is the first sight I see when I get home. It goes a long way to draining my stress." He fills a glass with water and takes a long drink. His attention is focused solely on me as I look around the room.

"I never thought I'd see you walk through my door again." His eyes are playful, yet his face is a mask of stone. *What else is going through his mind?* "I'm going to change. Have a look around. I'll be back in five, then we're going to talk."

The letter. The reason we're here. It's like my mind shut down at the cafe and rebooted, wiping out all earlier events. It's Shaw's presence—I feel safe with him, but he also makes me lose my mind.

I wander over to the windows. Staring at the water clears my mind, and a calm settles over my body.

He said he didn't write it. No recognition crossed his face. Who sent it, and why? My mind circles, discarding theories while getting no closer to an answer.

As Shaw saunters down the hallway wearing a pair of faded jeans and a gray T-shirt with "FBI" emblazoned across his chest, I see the twenty-two-year-old boy ready to conquer the world. I raise my chin, indicating his choice of T-shirt. He shrugs and smiles. "I figured the situation called for it."

I move from the windows and take a seat on the couch. It's huge and comfortable, molding around my body with a soft leather hug. Shaw waits for me to sit, then settles into the couch next to me. *Right* next to me. A sheet of paper would be too wide to slip between us. I turn my head and look at him.

"Would you rather sit on my lap?" I push his arm with both of my hands, trying to gain personal space. His body is stone, not moving even a centimeter. "Give a girl some room, Romeo."

He smiles but makes no effort to move. "I'm good right where I am. Thanks."

Good. Because you smell incredible and your body heat is sublime.

I shoot him a quick side glance to check for his reaction,

afraid I may have said that aloud. He continues to smile at me, neither a positive or negative confirmation. *Great.*

He places his hand on my knee as he starts to talk, his words a monologue of bulleted thoughts. "I'm thinking you must have received the letter when? Two? Three years after we were together?"

Two years and two months, to be exact.

"Yeah, two years or so." I stare at the opposite wall, our bodies positioned where I can't see his face, and he can't see mine. My mind's version of the childhood game, "If I can't see him, he can't see me."

As much as I dread this conversation, the pain I've harbored has already started to disperse. I know now, Shaw's hand would never betray his heart in such a way.

"Where did it come from? Postmark? Return address? Does anything stick out in your mind?"

Let me see...Amy finding me passed out on my living room floor the morning after. Eyes practically swollen shut from hours of crying.

"Postmark, Milwaukee. Return address, some law firm. Whitehall, Crause, and something or other."

The minutes stretch as we sit in silence, both of us working through the revelations of today. I watch his hand as it slides over my knee. I'm mesmerized by his tapered fingers and blunt nails. His touch is my salvation, soothing pain and providing protection.

He didn't write the letter. What was done will never be explained, the perpetrator never apprehended.

I'm tired of fighting.

My desires.

My heart.

My mind.

I want Shaw with a force sixteen years in the making. Strong, mindless desire consumes me.

Shaw's hand stills as I cover it with my own. An electric

current rushes through my fingers, up my arm, and spreads throughout my body. My core heats as sensations pulse and build.

I lift my eyes and meet intense blue orbs silently questioning what I want. What I need. What I crave.

I lean in, my lips ghosting just below his ear. "Help me forget the pain...the past...the loneliness. I believe you didn't write it. Show me. Show me what you would have said. What our hearts have always known."

My tongue traces his neck, his heart beating a song on the tip of my tongue.

Hands grasp my hips, placing me on his lap, as fingers tunnel into my hair, clutching my head.

His eyes are like a rehabilitated animal released back into the wild. Tentative, curious, and hungry for a second chance.

I provoke his hunger and call him forward. He searches my face, looking for the girl he once knew in the woman I have become.

"Beautiful." A prayer dances across my skin as his fingers sift and tighten in my hair.

"Forget with me."

His lips press against mine with a fierce urgency. I grip his shoulders, snaking my hands around to the back of his neck, pulling at his hair as his hands grip my breasts through my shirt.

Our mouths duel, tongues intertwined, sliding back and forth as we explore. We swallow each other's pain as it leaves our bodies. He tugs at my shirt, the threads tearing and separating under his rough movements.

A moan catches in my throat as his teeth sink into the sensitive flesh of my lip. His tongue soothes the sting as it traces the marks left by his teeth.

An inferno rages below my skin as blood gathers between my legs, the pulse of my core matching the beat in my chest.

My hands move down his chest, and I hate the fabric denying me the hard, warmth of his skin. My fingertips explore the ridges of muscles hidden from sight. Finding the hem of his shirt, I slowly push it up as my palms gather the heat from his skin.

Shaw's body is a sculptor's dream. Sharp lines and defined edges, covered in silky, smooth skin. My fingers, my tongue, my heart had known every inch of his body when he was a boy.

The man beneath my fingers is a honed and hardened stranger. A work of art. My fingers and tongue are ready to paint every piece of his magnificent canvas.

I pull back, my eyes roaming his chest as I memorize each inch. A small, faded tattoo above his heart pierces my consciousness. As I stare, Shaw goes still. His hands freeze and eyes close like he's waiting for something. I lean in, my fingers caressing his skin as my eyes study the ink he keeps close to his heart. My mind shoots back to the night at Beacon, when he stood before me, gloriously naked. While my brain can't recall the tattoo, I know it had been there, waiting to be noticed. The once vibrant colors have faded with age. It's a puzzle piece, small and intricate. Shaped like a letter "K."

Kate.

It's mine. He did it for me.

I trace his cheek with the back of my hand. His eyes flutter open, burning a path straight to my heart. His voice answers the question before I can ask. "The last day I saw you. Before fate stole our path. You were the piece my heart needed. Forever with me and in my heart."

Tears sting the back of my eyes. So much has been stolen from us. Time. Happiness. A family. I hate the irreversible. Silently vowing to repair every piece of filth that has tainted our lives, I lean in and brush my lips against the tattoo. It's a whispered confession of promise, warming the skin above his heart. "Even in the most painful of my days, you have been a part of my heart. Forever was a promise. Tarnished, bent, and damaged, but never broken. Love me like yesterday is our tomorrow."

His hands pull my lips to his. "Today is ours and tomorrow is our forever." I move my legs to encircle his waist and guide my arms behind his head. "Hold on, baby."

He stands and carries me down the hall. His eyes are blue flames, our gaze held hostage by love as it burns this moment into the forever of tomorrow. My heart is ready, my body is hopeful, but my mind is scared.

"Please be careful with me. I'm scared." I confess my fear. My plea is a prayer only he can answer.

"I will never be anything but careful with you, my heart."

Kate's legs squeeze my waist as I enter my room. Without seeing her face, I imagine Kate's reaction to the room I've never shared with another woman. This sanctuary holds the memories I release to the anonymity of darkness. Kate's ghost is the only woman whose body has touched my sheets. Her name, the only one ripped from my lips as her memory milked my self-induced releases.

The *click* of the closing door is loud in the silence of the room. Kate's head rests on my shoulder as her warm breath prickles my skin. My cock is primed and begs me to sink into the slick heat between her legs. Failure to control my body is not an option.

Thoughts of Sarah flit through my mind as I think of her just down the hall. *Will this be embarrassing for her? Am I a bad parent? How do other single parents do this with a kid in the same house?*

The warmth of Kate's tongue pushes all thoughts of Sarah from my mind. I walk to the bed, placing Kate in the middle. I skim her pants and lace thong down her legs and step back, allowing my eyes to feast on the sight before me. The collar of her shirt hangs over her shoulder, ripped, the fault of my hands as they pulled the fabric to expose the beauty of her breasts.

Her eyes shine in the dim light as they roam over my body. She rises to her knees, lifting her shirt over her head. Her breasts are barely contained by a black lace bra. Her nipples, dark and pink, are puckered and tight. She smiles, her tongue darting out to wet her bottom lip as her body is poised and waiting for me.

"Kate." My mouth goes dry as she moves her hands and kneads her breasts. She tilts her head, her mouth falling open as she rubs her thumbs across her hardened nipples. Responding to her invitation, my dick strains against my zipper. I step to my nightstand and grab a strip of condoms from the box I bought the day after I collected her panties on the street. Her eyes grow wide as she watches me toss the strip to the bed near her knees.

Sexual exhaustion is my desired cure for erasing years of separation.

I watch her hands as she plays with her nipples, then reach behind my neck and pull off my shirt. Her eyes flare as she studies me, her gaze roaming my body. I pause allowing her to replace the memory of the twenty-two-year-old body she had intimately known with the man who stands before her. No longer willing, nor able, to wait, I move my hands to my zipper. On all fours, Kate crawls across the bed, stopping just in front of where I stand. Her eyes arrest mine as I push my pants to the floor. Kate's position puts her mouth directly in line with my cock.

Her tongue darts out to graze my dick as she leans forward, my boxers the only cover between my cock and her lips. My knees threaten to buckle as she inhales and licks from base to tip. The heat of her breath mixes with the dampness of my boxers, pulling a moan from my lungs.

"Kate, keep this up, and I'm going to blow before my boxers hit the floor."

Her grunt, as she continues to lick the fabric, indicates she has no plans to stop. Her tongue swirls through the drop of cum glistening at the tip of my dick as it protrudes beyond the waistband of my boxers. Her blue eyes, beneath dark lashes, rise to meet mine as she continues her game.

Her body, her mouth, her eyes. My control snaps. "Fuck."

Sending up a silent prayer that I don't scare her, I push her shoulders back and pull her legs from beneath her, spreading them wide. I grind against her core as I push her arms above her head. "Don't move."

The dominance of my voice earns an affirmative nod. I stand and push my underwear to the floor. My dick springs free, engorged and ready as I watch her eyes grow wide.

I reach for a condom, and tear it open with my teeth, my gaze never leaving the heat of her stare. Her eyes blaze with desire as she watches me roll the condom down my length, and her chest rises and falls. Her body trembles, waiting for permission to move.

"Shaw, please. Touch me. I need to feel you."

Her words are the match that ignites me. The muscles in my arms bunch as I hold myself above her, my hands bracketing her head. "Don't move. I've got you."

I work to control my urge to take her like the animal writhing within me. I dip my arms, my dick rubbing her clit as her whimpers turn to moans. I quicken the pace, spreading her wetness pooled between her legs.

Four long thrusts across her clit and my balls are already drawing tight. My orgasm builds, and I fight for coherent words as I bend forward and lick her nipple. "First time. Not going to last. Make it up to you. Need. Inside. You."

Kate's back bows, lifting her nipple to my mouth. "I'm nearly there. Harder."

I grind against her. Her wet warmth is my reward.

I balance on an outstretched hand, using my other to grab my cock. I stroke it once as I line up with her entrance. Her hips rise, her thrust sucking my tip into her body. I plant my hands on either side of her head as I capture her eyes.

"Always us." I freeze, pinning her hips to the bed with my own, as I wait for her to acknowledge our truth.

"Forever." That one beautiful word floats to my ears on a thready breath just before I lean back and push forward in one quick thrust. Her loud cry is pleasure tipped with pain.

"Shit, Kate. So tight."

I watch as she shifts, working through the sting as her body stretches around mine. I want to slam into her. Claim her. Possess her.

A smile graces her face as she lifts her hips. "You going to move or do I need to do this myself?"

"No, ma'am." I pull out almost to the tip and push in, rotating my hips and grinding my pelvic bone into her clit as I work to send her over the edge.

"More, faster. So good." She bucks, lifting her back from the bed as she continues to keep her arms positioned above her head. *My girl, the rule follower.*

She lifts her legs, clasping them around my waist and squeezing me like a vice. Black spots dance across my vision as I pump into her, the force moving the bed and slamming it against the wall.

I feel the walls of her pussy contract as she screams my name. Her voice is my trigger as my cock explodes. The pulses from her pussy milk my cock through the aftershocks of our shared orgasm.

My arms tremble as I roll to Kate's side. I lie on my back, my eyes focused on the white of my ceiling. My heart races like I've just run the Chicago marathon. Minutes pass before I turn my head, where I see Kate's profile mirrors mine as she stares at the ceiling. Her chest rises and falls in a rapid rhythm as she works to calm her breathing. I reach out, my pinkie sliding across the creamy velvet of her thigh.

She turns her head, her eyes locking on mine as her lips curve in a smile. Wrecked and panting for breath. "This night just breached my top five of all time."

I take the words as a compliment, yet they sit in my stomach like a rock. *What times reside in her top five? More importantly, who does?*

The bitter pill of jealousy nearly chokes me. *Who am I to condemn her choices?* I'd been married to another woman for nearly a decade. She owes me nothing, yet I wanted to punish every single person who has stolen every minute of my happiness with her. *Irrational? Yes. Did I feel like a bastard? Yes. Could I stop myself from wanting to obliterate any memory we didn't share? Not a chance.*

I push my thoughts away and roll to my side, propping my head on my hand as I smile at her. My other hand reflexively reaches out to trace the lines of her ribs. Kate releases her hands still clasped above her head, lowering one to my fingers as they trace her skin.

"I never thought we'd ever be here again. So much has changed, yet the way your body makes me feel is as familiar as the skin that covers my own."

Her words speak a truth my mind yearned to articulate. She is my yesterday colliding with my today. I still cannot fathom how we got here, but I will never wonder how we get to tomorrow.

I tuck her hair behind her ear. "I feel the same. You have been in my blood since the first day I saw you waiting tables."

I sit up and walk to the bathroom to dispose of the condom, then quickly turn to head back to the woman I left sprawled across my bed. A scream worthy of a horror flick actress leaves my mouth. Not my best moment, but who wouldn't jump when the buck-naked woman you think is waiting in your bed is standing behind you, lit only by the eerie blue light of a cell phone charger. Her approach is that of a professional ninja.

A full-body laugh fills the air as she doubles over in front of me. Her hand whips out to hold the doorjamb lest she lose her balance and crash to the floor. I clutch my chest, choking, my heart—currently lodged in my throat—obstructs my airway. My actions fuel Kate's reaction as she continues to laugh.

As I work to calm my senses, I watch her. Her face reflects freedom from the pain she harbored earlier. *Was the café just today?* I feel like our relationship has traveled a thousand miles, barefoot across the desert, since I walked in and saw her across the café.

I reach out, pulling a startled Kate to my chest. My chin rests on her head as I smooth a hand over the silky strands. "Think it's funny, do you? You won't be laughing when a hot female paramedic has to give me mouth-to-mouth during the heart attack *you* caused."

Her face falls, her laughter dying on her lips. "Almost as funny as the studly male paramedic who'll need to restrain my naked body as I gouge out the eyes of your mouth-breathing hussy."

"There she is. Feisty Kate is my favorite." I turn her around and point her toward the bed, giving her ass a firm tap. It's a subtle reminder the night is young, and I'm in charge.

KATE

My phone chimes, and I can't contain the chuckle when I see A.S.S. aka 'Abs' olutely Sinful Shaw pop up on my screen. *My man and his off-color humor.*

I scan his text, reminding me to dress warm and bring extra clothes. His way of telling me he has no intention of letting me sleep anywhere but in his bed. It's been six weeks, and we haven't spent one night apart. I've practically moved into the condo, much to Shaw's pleasure.

Our relationship has been stuck on fast forward since the day I shared the "breakup" letter with him. Shaw insists there's no label of "too fast" when we've spent years apart. *Who am I to question his logic?*

My only concern has been how Sarah feels about her dad and me. Sharing the breakfast table the morning after she caught us in the elevator was a bit stilted and awkward. Shaw in low slung pajama pants and nothing else. Me, in a pair of Shaw's sweatpants and his FBI T-shirt. My original shirt had looked like the Incredible Hulk ripped through the neck and shoulder. Compliments of Shaw, who smirked when I showed him the next morning.

A few minutes of discomfort faded away quickly after Sarah admitted she hoped we'd find the happiness we'd lost. Shaw informed me he'd spoken with Sarah shortly after our initial dinner. He'd explained we had been victims of a huge misunderstanding and lack of communication.

To a girl who had never known a life without the Internet and slept with her cell phone under her pillow, she'd been horrified to learn we lost contact because we didn't have a way to reach each other. No cell phones, no email.

In truth, she'd accepted our relationship easier than me. I still had days where doubts wormed inside my head, but I was determined to shut them down as soon as they surfaced, not willing to fall into a dark hole of mistrust.

Each day, I see Shaw's love. In his actions, his words, and in the plans he's making for our future. He has now recruited Sarah to convince me to move in with them. I can feel myself weakening. The feeling of living as a family is a temptation I won't resist for long.

Amy's encouragement to pursue a future with Shaw has also spurred my own acceptance. Her approval had been a welcome surprise. Between her increased workload and the time I was spending away from the house, we had resorted to random texts and two-minute phone calls made while one of us used the porcelain throne. Gross to admit, but a fact in the relationship of Kate and Amy.

I check the time and shut down the computers in the lab, hoping to catch Amy at home before she leaves for her exercise class. I do a quick check for forgotten cell phones and backpacks, then hit the lights before walking out Beacon's back door. My head is nearly buried in my purse as I look for my keys.

A squeal of tires grabs my attention. A white car with darkened windows speeds past and turns left out of the lot before disappearing down the street. The car was so close I could have knocked on the window as it sped past. *What idiot drives like that through a parking lot?*

I want to punch the driver for throwing my heart into my throat. I need to mention this to Jon tomorrow. Maybe he can come up with a way to safeguard students and volunteers from the stupidity of bad drivers.

As I approach, I unlock my driver's door and hit the remote start. I climb in and lock the doors, then take a few minutes to steady my nerves before heading to my house. I won't be any better than that idiot if I try to drive with my hands shaking as they are. I hit the call button on the steering wheel, and a moment later, Shaw's sultry voice seeps through the speakers, surrounding me on all sides. The sound calms my nerves and makes me smile.

"Hello, gorgeous. Everything OK?"

"Of course. Can't a girl call her man when she misses him?" I inject a bit of humor into my voice to cover the tremor.

"Absolutely. You home yet?"

"Just getting ready to leave Beacon. Keep me company on the drive?"

"How much company are we talking?" His voice drops low. If sex had a voice, it would be his. Low and deep, with an edge of dominance.

"Save it for tonight, Casanova."

He's done what I need, and my nerves have calmed. I pull out of the lot and head toward my house, as we share the events of our day.

Dressed in a sports bra and thong, Amy saunters through the kitchen. She's a woman totally comfortable in her skin, and not the least embarrassed I've walked through the door. She opens the fridge, purposely leaning forward farther than necessary. Before I look away, I catch a glimpse of her lady bits, freshly waxed, if my eyes are correct. *This girl, all sass and no class.*

"Please tell me it's not 'show your assets' night at the gym?"

Totally unfazed by my sarcasm, she stands and walks to the counter, dropping an armful of raw vegetables across the empty surface. "Don't hate what men like to date."

"Speaking of date, Shaw will be here in about thirty minutes. I was hoping we could chat for a bit before you hightail it to the gym."

"Absolutely. It's a rare treat to see you at the house."

Guilt crawls up my throat and coats my tongue. I know Amy is one hundred percent supportive of my relationship with Shaw, but I think my absence has been difficult for her, even though she won't admit it.

"How was your date on Friday? Entrepreneur, right? Please tell me that isn't code for unemployed and selling his plasma to make rent."

She's silent as she arranges vegetables on a plate, keeping her head down as I continue to throw questions at her back.

"Was he hot? An ax murderer? A stage five clinger?" Before my mind runs further off course, she turns to me with a huge smile.

"He's awesome. A gentleman who totally has his shit together. Smart, courteous, and smoking hot. In fact, we're going out again tonight."

"Ooooh, do tell? And by tell, I mean, *all*." I'm ecstatic for my friend. The woman, who is pickier than a forty-year-old virgin, is seeing the same man more than once. The. Same. Man.

In Amy's dating repertoire, more than one date is equivalent to getting a nun to have a threesome.

It's no secret I call her the "One Date Wonder." I'm convinced she suffers through online dating, blind dates, and mediocre one-night stands because no one measures up to her perfect man. I give her props for continuing to look. Maybe she's found her unicorn in this one.

Amy arranges her food, making neat, even lines of carrots, celery, and red peppers. "It's the first time in over two years that I've seen the same guy more than once. It's a big thing for me." Her eyes peek up at me. "I'm almost afraid to talk about him for fear of jinxing it, you know?"

I sympathize with her nerves. I'm not one to talk or even give advice in this area. When it comes to guys, she may be picky, but her experience is off the charts in comparison to mine. "I get it. Makes sense. Do I at least get to put a name to this magical unicorn?"

A snort laugh escapes her mouth, making us both laugh. After a few seconds, Amy turns serious and grabs my hand. "Don't get mad, but you already know his name."

My face grows overheated and hot. I know my reaction is highly irrational, but I panic. I only know one man, and he is *mine.* My mind takes off at a sprint. *Can Amy run fast enough to get away?*

Amy laughs hysterically when she sees my face. *Probably trying to throw me off my current thoughts of murder.* "Y-y-you thought I was talking a-about Shaw?" Her words come out stilted and breathless between bouts of laughter.

Of course, she didn't mean Shaw.

"Noooo. Absolutely not." The over-exaggerating head shake nearly knocks me from my chair.

"Oh yes, you d-d-did. If I could b-b-breathe right n-now, I'd kick your a-a-ass for thinking th-that."

"Seriously, who else would it be if it isn't Shaw? You know he's the only man I know."

Amy wipes tears from her eyes as her laughter dies. "Thanks for that. Best laugh I've had since you got your period and accidentally put your pad on inside out, then pulled half your pubes out when you pulled your underwear down."

"And there's the answer to why I have a plethora of tampons." Her reminder of my blunder sends a zing to my nether regions. *Worst pain ever.*

"All kidding aside, you do know him. And it'll give him a great chuckle when he finds out he doesn't even fall into your 'man' category."

"Cut the suspense already. I believe we've already established I have no idea who it could be."

"Jon Logan."

56

EVIL ONE

Present...

I unlock Box 755 and carry it to the designated private viewing area. Its size is small, the gray metal construction cheap and flimsy in comparison to the priceless value of the contents nestled inside.

In the eleven years I've had this box, I have opened it once a year, trusting only myself to verify its contents and give me the addictive jolt of power I feel each time my eyes lay claim.

Today is no different. I smile as I lift the lid. Butterflies dance in my stomach, my heartbeat increasing until I confirm three items still rest inside.

Today, I'm adding the final piece to my puzzle. Today is the day my collection grows from three to four.

The excitement in seeing my pieces makes my body heat, as my eyes move over the contents like an addict seeing endless lines of coke. Shifting, calculating, craving the promise of euphoria.

To an untrained eye, this box holds nothing more than a few worthless pieces of paper and a photograph. All three are beginning to show age by the presence of yellowed edges.

These items hold more beauty than the untrained eye can grasp. Each of them has the ability to inflict an emotional punch full of pain, agony, and despair.

Grouping these pieces together? That is where the glory of my plan resides. Delivering all items simultaneously will deliver a fatal knockout, Vegas heavyweight-style, creating utter chaos and devastation, and effectively ruining all chance of recovery.

I can ruin lives.

It's simple, really. I must do nothing more than make the information available and sit back and feel the rush like a run of falling dominoes. My heart races at such a satisfying prospect.

I fidget with the box's key, still in my hand. I press it into the skin of my palm and relish the ability to draw blood, should I squeeze it too tightly.

I crave the feeling I get from holding this key, from holding the power to destroy lives. It's been my slice of heaven, but it has also been difficult. Waiting for the perfect moment, I've been biding my time, an eleven-year seduction of patience.

The day my Pandora's box will be revealed draws near. I can feel it inching closer, and my anticipation is building.

The day of destruction is uncertain, but three things are not.

Lives will change.

Trust will be broken.

Dreams will burn.

And I'll have a front row seat to the beginning of the end.

57

KATE

I LOOK AT SHAW AS HE NAVIGATES THROUGH CHICAGO TRAFFIC. Our relationship continues to grow. For a woman who has barely dated, the transition to girlfriend has been incredibly easy.

Communication has been key. Shaw is open and honest with what he wants in his future. I admit it's taken me longer to arrive at the same comfort level, after being on my own and guarding my privacy so closely. While we do talk about everything in the present and future, we have subconsciously avoided delving into the past. The past brings turmoil we've tried to leave behind us.

The problem with trying to leave secrets in the past is they resurface at a time one least expects. My mind drifts to the phone call I received at Beacon today. It left me an emotional mess. Jon did his best to comfort me in silence, even though I could sense questions lingering in his eyes.

I was paged to the front desk for a phone call. Confused who would be calling me at Beacon, I blindly answered.

"I know what you did, and I'm going to share it with those you care about

the most. You can choose to walk away whole or leave in pieces. The choice is yours."

My hand had trembled so badly, I'd dropped the phone before the call ended. The voice, plain and unmemorable, tricked my brain as I tried to reconcile if it belonged to a man or a woman, young or old. Those words, coupled with the message, "I KNOW" written on my SUV window last week, were enough to send me into a full-blown panic attack.

Witnessing my distress, Tara had immediately gone to find Jon. By the time he arrived at my side, I had pulled myself together, but tremors had continued to shake my body.

I told him it was nothing. Just a prank caller with a sadistic sense of humor. My explanation seemed to appease him, but he still insisted on calling Shaw, who arrived way faster than Chicago traffic should have allowed.

Shaw had immediately taken charge, asking Jon and Tara to see if the number could be retrieved from the phone system. He also asked Tara to write down everything she could remember about the caller. Male or female. Voice characteristics. Everything.

From Beacon, Shaw and I had driven to the police station. My urging to forget about the incident fell on deaf ears. Shaw was like a dog with a bone, not willing to leave it be.

The police station had been dank and stuffy. A solemn, male officer had taken our information but told us there was little to be done since there was no evidence of a formal threat.

I thought Shaw would put his fist through the officer's face, but he held his temper and practically dragged me to the car, fuming the entire way. Once inside, my thoughts had wandered, catching snippets of his angry tirade. Bodyguard. Personal driver. Moving in. His protective nature reaching an all-time high.

As I look at him now, I see a controlled Shaw. Appearing

calm, he navigates through the streets, heading to his condo. One hand is on the wheel, the other clasping mine. He insisted I stay with him, so we stopped at my house to get enough clothes for the "unforeseeable future." His words, not mine.

While I won't admit it, my mind is in total chaos. The police's suggestion the phone call was a prank is not possible. What I can't figure out is how the caller knew my secret. I can't fool myself into believing it's just a massive coincidence.

My past harbors a secret, one I haven't shared with Shaw. I've been waiting for the right time, yet that moment hasn't presented itself. Maybe it had, and I'd ignored it, in favor of staying in my bubble of happiness.

I need to tell him. I know this, but it doesn't make it any easier.

Shaw is a passionate, intelligent, and perceptive man. While he's been understanding about the situation that pulled us apart, I can't help but wonder if his forgiveness will extend to the secret I still hold.

I've given myself over a decade to accept it, and I still have days when I have to force myself out of my dark thoughts.

Shaw turns into his underground garage, the door lifting as he hits the transponder. I think we've shared less than ten words since leaving the police station, both of us dealing with the thoughts swimming through our heads.

He parks and comes around to my side of the car, opening the door and helping me out. Shaw holds my hand in a strong grip, his anxiety for the situation seeping through his calm facade.

"Wait here while I grab your stuff from the back seat."

Feeling the darkness of the mood blanketing us, I try infusing a little levity. "Well damn, there goes an impromptu five-mile jog."

My attempt at humor falls flat as he looks at me with a

furrowed brow and narrowed eyes. He slams the door, rocking the car in the process. I've never seen this side of him. I've seen him upset, but not like this. His feelings of helplessness feed his anger.

He places his hand to my lower back and leans close to my ear, his breath tickling the side of my neck. "I'm sorry, Kate. If something ever happened to you, I wouldn't survive. No amount of time could repair my broken pieces if you went away again."

I turn and look over my shoulder. The pain he describes bleeds from his eyes as mine lock with his. I realize I haven't allowed myself to accept the depth of his feelings for me. I've succeeded in withholding a small piece of myself, allowing a feeling of impending disaster to linger in the corner of my mind. I know I won't survive if Shaw's response to my next curveball is ill-received. Fate can be a heartless umpire.

I am overcome with emotion, and Shaw's hand comes up to cup my face and brush away a tear. I lean into his touch, bringing my own hand up to cover his as I turn and place a kiss on his palm.

I love this man. He has held my heart for nearly half my lifetime. His light calls to me as I inch closer to his promise of forever.

"Let's get upstairs. I have no desire to keep you huddled in the corner of my parking garage when a person has their sights set on you."

We step up to the elevator. I tip my head to him, silently asking if he's OK with the ride, considering his elevated stress level. He answers my question by stepping inside and, seconds later, he's pulling me close, wrapping his arms around me from behind. As the doors slide closed, Shaw places a kiss on the top of my head. The tension of his body ebbs the longer he holds me.

"My fear of elevators doesn't hold a candle to today's scare.

I don't know who this person is, what they want, or if they'll strike again. It's like I'm fighting a damn ghost."

The tension Shaw has held on to over the last few hours slowly seeps from his body. My body, in sync with his, releases the tight feeling around my chest.

"I want nothing more than to wash this day, the fear, and the uncertainty away from us."

I turn to him, fingering the contours of his face. "You read my mind."

The elevator gives its familiar dip to announce its arrival at his floor. Shaw holds the doors and steps behind me, placing his palm against my lower back as he guides me into his condo.

I hear his briefcase hit the floor a second before my hips are pushed into the side table where it rests against the far wall. The heat of Shaw's chest covers my back as his thighs pin mine against the table. He grips my hips, holding me in place as he grinds into me. I feel his delicious warmth as it filters between the heavy fabric of his dress pants and the flimsy cotton of my own.

He slams one hand against the wall above my head to steady us, while his other glides around to squeeze a breast through my shirt. Goose flesh raises across my skin as the tips of his fingers find slivers of exposed skin between the buttons of my shirt. He slowly flexes his hips, his hardness sliding against my backside and releasing a dam of wetness between my legs.

His lips find my ear as he continues to move against me. "You feel like home." His words fuel my need as I try to move my hips against him. I feel his responding groan as vibrations ripple through his chest across my back. His hips create a rhythm my body recognizes.

My breathing starts to race as I feel the tingles of my impending orgasm. My breasts sit heavy against my chest, my nipples forming sharp peaks beneath my lace bra.

"Where's Sarah?"

Shaw slows his actions, controlling his movements and withholding my pleasure. His response is stilted as he slides a finger down my spine while thrusting against my ass. A whimper of frustration slips past my lips as I try to speed up the pace by pushing against him, searching for a much-needed release.

"Texted earlier. Going to movies. Staying at Julie's."

His teeth find my ear, giving it a bite and reminding me that he holds the control. "I decide when."

The gravel in his voice is gasoline to the fire building within me. My body bucks, craving release only he can give.

"Please." My skin is on fire as I bring one hand up to massage my other breast.

"Please what?" The cunning lilt in Shaw's voice tells me the devil has come out to play.

Emboldened by my own haze of pleasure and the dominate timbre of Shaw's voice, I look over my shoulder and wait for our eyes to connect. "Your cock. My pussy. I need it hard and fast. Don't stop until my legs give out and I'm hoarse from screaming your name."

A predatory smile lights up Shaw's face. He releases the button on his pants, roughly pushing them down to expose his hard cock.

My eyes widen. "Commando?"

His grin is sly as he pushes his hips forward, the bite of the table cutting through my lust.

Both of his palms move up my sides, kneading my skin. His thumbs ghost the underside of my breasts and his fingertips land just above my waistband.

In a single move, he slides his hands down my body, catching my pants and thong on the downward pull. Cool air hits my exposed flesh as it's warmed by his heated gaze. I give a frustrated scream as he massages the roundness of my ass, his eyes burning with lust.

His right hand slides up my spine, pushing down on my back until my chest is flush against the surface of the table. The muscles of his thighs flex against the back of my own. This is Shaw, the man. Spontaneous, animalistic, hard, commanding.

"Warm up your lungs, baby." The melted caramel of his voice floats over us before he slams into me, and my screams of pleasure fill his condo.

58

SHAW

Shadows from lights outside the window dance across the ceiling as I recline on my back. Sleep eludes me, the events of the past few months leaving a stain on my mind.

The prank call Kate received has my protective instincts working overtime. I bring my hand up and run my fingers through Kate's hair as she sleeps against my chest, cradled at my side.

Awake, she is mesmerizing. Strong, independent, and beautiful. Asleep, she is captivating. The innocence she hides peeks through the cloak of independence she normally wears. She stirs, her breathing changing, but not enough to rouse her from much-needed sleep. The stress of the day and the force of our foyer sexcapades have stolen the energy from her body.

My mind circles back to the letter. Someone wanted Kate to move on, forget our time together, and erase me from her thoughts. Only a select few knew of our relationship. *Could one of them have done it?*

My sister was an absolute no. She was the only one who cared and supported me through my depression. My dad had been more pissed from the embarrassment of me missing work than me being hung up on a girl. Hell, he probably didn't realize a girl was the reason for my absence.

I don't know if I talked to my mom more than twice that summer? If I did, I know I wouldn't have mentioned Kate. Hell, I loved Kate and was making plans for a future, but there was no way I mentioned her to the woman who would have demanded proof of pure bloodlines, a financial statement, and a doctor's report of fertility.

My brain drifts to Kate. Who, in her life, knew about our relationship? Amy, of course. However, Amy seems more protective of Kate than me, which nixes her as the letter sender. Kate's dad passed away before I met her. Her mom's death unknowingly triggered the demise of our relationship. I question if it could have been a boyfriend? Maybe she had one who felt threatened? My stomach turns at the possibility of Kate with anyone other than me.

I'm missing something, but what? The letter served its purpose in keeping us apart. *Hell, how did the letter find her?* My own private investigators hadn't found her. The situation didn't make sense.

Then, there was today's phone call. Thinking back, Kate was shaken and upset, more than a simple prank call would incite. A sliver of suspicion twists my gut, telling me the call wasn't random. It seems Kate may know more than she's letting on. Something spooked her. Either she isn't going to tell me, or she's waiting for the right time. Both options piss me off. It means she still lacks trust for me and our relationship.

Over the last month, we talked about us, our goals, our plans, our future. Not once had we broached lack of trust. *Am I naïve in thinking we're moving forward in planning a future?*

As my thoughts continue to circle, my lack of answers fuels my anger. I slip out of bed and pad to my closet to grab a pair of sweats and a T-shirt, before heading to my office. I need space before I fall farther down a rabbit hole for the woman sleeping in my bed.

As I walk into my office, my eyes fall on the picture frame in the corner. An identical one rests on the desk in Sarah's bedroom. I walk over and pick it up, sadness clenching my stomach. Two smiling faces, happy and carefree, look out at me. What I wouldn't give to go back to that time. But fate had chosen a different path, and there isn't one thing I could have done to stop it. I glance at the picture once more before placing it on the bookshelf.

I walk to my desk and turn on my computer. Work has always been a welcome escape from my heavy thoughts and hopefully, tonight isn't any different.

59

KATE

I ROLL OVER, LETTING MY ARM SKIM THE SHEETS AS I REACH for the warmth of Shaw's body. My brain jolts me awake as my hand comes away empty. Using the sheet to hide my naked-ness, I sit up and scan the floor for something to preserve my modesty as I venture outside Shaw's bedroom.

I reach out and snag the crumpled Oxford shirt I vaguely remember peeling off Shaw's shoulders. As I shuffle down the hall, careful not to stub a toe or run into any protruding walls in the darkness, I listen for sounds indicating Shaw's location. His absence concerns me as I've yet to wake up without his body draped across my own. Knowing the way his mind works, the phone call and visit with the police has stolen his ability to sleep.

As I step into the living room, I see him. Pajama pants slung low, torso bare, he stares out the window, lost in thought and oblivious to my presence. The early morning light has brightened the sky to a medium blue. Glancing at the clock above the mantle, I see it's just after five a.m., a little early for Shaw's normal daily alarm. I approach, careful not to startle him lest he screams—again—and wake the entire building.

I stop behind him and lean my cheek against his back, absorbing the warmth of his skin. My hands snake around his middle, resting on his lower abdomen. The steadiness of his breath and ease of his muscles indicates he heard my approach. His hands wrap around mine, fingers intertwining and holding tight.

"I woke up in a cold bed. What happened to my heater?"

A chuckle rumbles through his chest as he lifts one of my hands and presses his lips to my palm. His whiskers tickle my hand as he mumbles between kisses, "I'll be happy to warm you up. On the couch? The kitchen counter? Against this window?"

I scoot around in front of him and lean my head back to see his face. Somber, electric blue eyes stare back at me, completely void of the playfulness just seconds before. "What's wrong?"

His eyes track my face as he imperceptibly shakes his head. Sensing the turmoil locked within him, I try again. "What pulled you from me and our warm sheets?"

His silence is cold, and his stare is frigid as I stand there, waiting for him to speak. Still, he says nothing, and I watch a battle rage across his face. His desire to speak his mind wars with an unknown force keeping his jaw locked tight. After another moment of tense quiet, he backs up and heads for the door of his office.

"Shaw you're scaring me. Talk to me." My words rise in intensity as they pelt his retreating back. His office door closes, and I'm stuck wondering what's happening and why he's not talking. My confusion turns to anger as my feet fly across the floor. The force of my momentum throws his office door into the wall as I enter.

He looks at me, surprise painted across his face. "Something is bothering you, and instead of talking it out, you walked away from me. This is us. We don't walk away. You promised."

His eyes narrow, and I steel myself for whatever words he's held back. "You want to talk? Want to know what's bothering me?" His voice grows to an angry shout as he stabs his chest with his finger. "*You*. You're what's bothering me. I know you're not telling me something. I can't protect you from what I *don't* know."

His temper hits me like a battering ram. I'm stunned into silence as his anger blankets the room, leaching into every crevice. Tears threaten to fall as I look at him. I hear him sigh, and the pain he's feeling reaches out and grips my body. My heart jumps into my throat. He knows. Maybe not the full story, but he knows I'm keeping something from him. It's tearing him up, feeding his fear that he can't protect me.

I take a deep breath and release it as I grasp for words. "You're right."

His gaze, which had dropped to the floor, cuts to mine. I walk over and sit on the couch, knowing I won't be standing by the end of this story.

"It happened a long time ago, but I still have problems accepting the choice I made." He walks to the couch and kneels before me, his face directly in line with mine.

"Please, tell me, Kate. Whatever this is, we'll work through it. Together."

The earnestness of his voice spurs me on, knowing I can't prepare him for my next words. "I think I may have figured out why that letter was sent. Considering I thought you sent it, I never had a reason to consider alternatives. Until now."

He waits as I collect my words.

"When we met, I had no plans to get married or have a family. I'd seen, firsthand, the devastating effects of a person losing their soul mate. When my dad died, his death stripped my mom of every happiness. She became a shell, no longer concerned with herself, nor the life of her daughter. I never wanted to experience such a loss. My dad said, 'A soul truly isn't whole until it finds its mate, and when it does, the two parts create one.'"

Shaw's eyes shine with unshed tears as he listens, squeezing my hand as unspoken encouragement to continue.

"The summer I met you was the happiest, and the scariest, of my life because I felt whole. I finally understood what my dad had said. You were the mate to my soul. I tried to fight it. Refusing to go on a date, but your soul felt the pull and wouldn't give up. Meeting you opened my heart to dreams I hadn't dared to wish for. You were my *one*." My eyes stay glued to my hands, unable to process the emotion pouring from Shaw's eyes. I force myself to meet his stare, my voice sticking in my throat. "You are still my one."

A shaky smile splits my face as tears fall, unchecked, down my cheeks. Shaw raises my hands to his mouth, brushing his lips across my knuckles. The action gives me the strength to continue.

"After meeting you, I knew I wanted children with you someday. I know we never talked about it, but I wanted at least four."

He leans in and kisses my forehead. "Kate, we're still young. We can still live that dream." The earnestness in his voice comforts my heart, even as it splinters. The stark pain of the truth momentarily steals my ability to speak, and my head shakes before my lips form the words.

"We can't."

He looks at me, confused, not grasping the meaning of the words trapped within me. "Baby, we *can*. We can start trying right away."

My tears fall faster as I look at his face, full of hope and excitement. "What I mean is, I can't. I c-c-can't have children."

I watch my admission reach his ears. The hope on his face

dies as he looks at me. I've stolen the words from his mouth, and his plan for the future, with one sentence. "Oh, honey. I'm so sorry."

He reaches out and pulls me into a hug, giving me a physical comfort only he can provide. I never thought I would tell him. I'd altered my plan the day my dream died, but for him, the dream still lives. I never imagined the dream I buried long ago would rise from the ashes of my past and threaten the happiness of my future.

Until he walked back into my life.

I pull back and release myself from his embrace. The remainder of the story rests on my tongue, waiting for my voice like a death row inmate waits for the flip of the switch. I use my shirt—*Shaw's* shirt—to dry my tear-stained cheeks. Up to this point, I've been peeling back the edges of the Band-Aid, too fearful of ripping it off.

Shaw's voice, halting and unsure, startles me from my haze of fear. "Me. Sarah. We'll be your family. You need a family, and we need you. Having you in our life is the only *need* we can't live without. We don't need a biological child between us to have a family."

My muscles contract as I listen to his words. His love for us pours from his heart as it fills the cracks in my own battered and bruised heart.

"But we—" My voice withers, the words dying like a rose cut and left without water. I breathe deeply, harnessing my resolve as I push the words from my soul. "Our dream was born fifteen years ago."

Unable to share the pain I've inflicted, I look to the floor, avoiding his eyes while willing him to understand the words suspended between us.

"What?" The word is a razor blade to the bond between our hearts.

"I...we have a child."

I hear his butt hit the floor as shock strikes him down. I raise my eyes to his and feel the fissures in my heart expand as cold, blue shutters block me from reading the pain radiating from his soul.

His head drops forward, and I see the first of his emotions hit the carpet, creating a circle of wetness. His strong, broad shoulders silently shudder as the dream we created exits his body on the tears of his pain.

I watch as the other half of my whole shatters in front of me. My anger at his abandonment shielded me from experiencing the guilt of my secret. My walls have been destroyed, and guilt coats me like hot tar with its burning, suffocating stench. Impotent in my ability to offer comfort, I simply sit and watch him break. Tears stream, unhindered, down my face, pooling in my lap and soaking my shirt.

I have no idea if minutes or hours pass as we silently, and independently, mourn for the loss of our dream—raising our child, living as a family. As the pain ebbs, I feel his questions mounting like bricks of a castle fortress. He stands behind them, the judge and jury of our future.

Sensing his need for space, I stand and make my way to the door, intending to grab my bag still packed from my arrival the night before. His voice, hoarse and raw, stops me at the threshold.

"Do I...do we have a son or a daughter?"

My mind springs back to the day she was born. The tension in the room, the sharp orders from the doctor, the quick movements of the nurses. My energy waning as my eyelids drooped. Fighting to see the small, round face, the head of dark hair. To hear the lungs of a fighter. I was granted one brief look at her perfect face. She was my greatest accomplishment wrapped in my biggest failure.

"You have a daughter." Defeat turns my tone monotonous. The need to explain the decisions of my twenty-year-old self, scared and alone, spurs me to face him, answering the one question burning through his gaze. "You were gone. I was...not well. I gave her the only thing I had left—our dream, the promise of a family."

60

SHAW

THE *CLICK* OF THE OFFICE DOOR AS SHE WALKS AWAY SHAKES ME from my stupor.

"Shit. Fuck. Shit."

The booming anger in my voice bounces off the walls and slams into my chest. Cramps in my leg muscles spur me to action as I get up and start pacing. I pull at my hair, making the pounding in my head even worse.

What the hell just happened? Kate tells me we have a child, and I let her walk out the door. Questions circle my mind as I try to harness my anger and guilt, packing it away until after I find Kate. My feet move me across my office, unsure of their destination.

My head pounds, carrying the weight of the truth smoldering in my gut. I have no idea what to do, my brain lacks direction and purpose. *How did I not know? Did she not trust me to help her?* I feel like I've been cast into a sea, set adrift, with no shore in sight.

The pain of her words courses through my veins as I work through the devastation. I have a daughter. Sarah has a sister.

I walk into my bathroom, stripping off my sweats and

boxers as soon as my feet hit the marble floor. The desire to purge the damage of the past pushes me toward the shower. I turn the water to the hottest setting and step in. The scalding temperature burns away my anger to expose a suit of guilt.

My mind returns to the early days of Sarah. The debilitating fear I felt in caring for her and second-guessing every decision I made. Her arrival had been the one true blessing from a tragic situation. She was the one who helped me breathe again. As thoughts of Sarah flash through my mind, I realize I lived the dream. The dream Kate and I imagined. I had Sarah. I had a family. I had it all while Kate had nothing. No child, no family, no dream.

Kate had willingly given away the promise of those experiences. *Because of hate for the child we created? No.* She loved our daughter with such passion; she gave her our dream. The last remaining tie to each other—the dream of a family.

A hole bores through my heart as I think of the times I've had with Sarah. Trips to museums, the park, the movies, a stop for her favorite ice cream.

Our conversation about Sarah that day on the boat comes back to me. Kate's silence and sudden withdrawal from our animated conversation.

Stories of my life with Sarah must have decimated her. I shared them, wanting her to know about my life. The life that happened between our past and our present. My words must have held the prick of a needle, sharp and unforgiving.

Words had failed me as Kate's silence grew that day. A story, long overdue, sat within me, begging to be released. I allowed her silence to scare me, fear ruling my conscience and quieting my words. I chose to hold back pieces of my life that she had every right to know.

Nothing other than shame fills me. The full story could have bound us together instead of driving us apart.

A sob climbs, unbidden, from my chest. The pain and

desolation Kate must have felt sends a chill straight to my bones. This woman, for whom I searched, is the definition of love. She is strong, independent, selfless. I love her. I need her. She is the other half of my whole.

I shut off the water, the scalding heat reduced to a trickle of warmth. An urgency fills me as water drips from my chilled body. The devastation I saw in Kate's eyes, before she walked out the door, is like sandpaper rubbing across my skin, exposing the rawness underneath.

I am an insensitive ass. I had been focused on what Kate seemed to be holding back, never once realizing the importance of what I have yet to tell her. We can have a family. Not the one from our dream, but one infinitely better because it lives in reality.

Relief hits me when I see Kate's car parked in her driveway as I pull up two hours later until I remember we dropped Kate's car off yesterday on the way to the police station. My heart jumps into my throat as I realize I have no idea how she left my condo. My faith in protecting her falls to an all-time low.

Sarah had called me to ask if she could sleep at a friend's house again tonight. Hopefully, my immediate permission doesn't disqualify me for any father of the year awards. With Sarah occupied at a friend's house, I'll be able to focus on Kate.

I park behind Kate's car, studying the house for signs of life. In my rush, I never considered she may not have returned here.

My hand feels like a fifty-pound weight as it knocks on the door. I hear yelling, angry and pissed, filtering through the foyer. My hope for someone to be home is quickly replaced by my fear of the feisty woman belonging to that voice—Amy.

Not knowing which head to protect, north or south, I step back and clasp my hands in front of me.

I hear a rattle and click before the door is thrown open.

Fiery red curls dance around her head, matching the sparks shooting from Amy's eyes. Her chest heaves and her nostrils flare. A brittle smile, reminding me of the Joker, curves her lips. "Here to claim the remaining piece of her cracked heart?"

Not having planned to plead my case to Amy, the gate-keeper, my confidence scatters like fall leaves in the wind.

"What? No bakery treats this time, asshole?"

I clear my throat and open my mouth, but I'm cut off by another round of Amy's venom as it's pushed through clenched teeth.

"You must have balls of steel. I told you I'd ruin you if you hurt her. And what did you do? Let her walk—literally, *walk*—away from your condo after telling you why she nearly *died*! Get off my property before I call the cops."

My mouth drops, my body frozen, as I make sense of Amy's words. Her body turns to slam the door. Snapping to action, I extend my hand and lock my knee against the door, catching it just before it slams.

"Wait a damn minute. What do you mean, almost died?" My voice cracks as my mind shifts through Kate's admission. *You were gone. I was...not well.*

Amy's surprise is plastered across her face. Her hand covers her mouth like she's trying to capture the words that already hit my ears. "You didn't know? She didn't tell you?" Her voice is pleading like she didn't just drop an emotional bomb.

"Get your phone, if you must, but I'm coming in, whether you call the cops or not."

Amy stands mute while I shoulder past her, determined to find Kate. Knowing Amy's anger is aimed at protecting Kate, I turn and offer the only words I can string together. "Thanks for being here."

My body hums, its reaction to Kate's nearness. As I walk into the living room, I see Kate, her small form wrapped in a blanket and huddled in the corner of the massive couch. Her eyes are red and puffy like she spent time sparring at the gym. As I approach, she lifts her gaze, and I'm brought to my knees before her.

Her energy and spirit are lifeless in the desolation of her pale face.

I bow my head and rest it against her chest. Submitting. Silently asking her heart to forgive sixteen years of my failure.

Her body gives no reaction. The electricity that flows between us has been reduced to a flicker of recognition.

I splay my hands, running them up her neck, my thumbs rubbing across her cheeks before my fingers meet at the base of her skull. "Please talk to me. Forgive me. I'm so sorry."

I lift my head and pull her face to mine. Brushing my lips across her mouth, I encourage her to feel the bond between us.

I lean back and study her. Her vacant stare hits the wall across the room. I'm decimated. She has retreated, shut herself behind a door for which I don't have the key.

Her lips open, but her words are foreign. "Shaw, I can't do this right now. Leave, please."

I stare at her, my hands itching to catch her words and shove them back into her mouth. Time is a commodity my body refuses to trade. I need to know we'll get through this.

Amy pushes off from her position against the wall. "Shaw. I'm sorry, she wants you to go."

I stand, defeated, my head hanging between my shoulders. I bend down and kiss the top of Kate's head. "I love you. Always."

I turn and walk to the door. My feet drag like the floor is made of quicksand. Amy watches me. Her anger replaced with empathy for the scene she just witnessed.

"Give her time. She loves you."

I simply nod, refusing eye contact, so I don't fall apart in her foyer. "Please watch over her."

"Always."

As the door shuts behind me, I release the dam on my emotions. My heart screams its anguish all the way to my car.

61

EVIL ONE

Present...

My eyes scan his body as he leaves her house. His nearly immediate departure has my body sizzling with questions.

Following her has been terribly boring until I finally spied the chink in her armor today. Leaving his place, walking aimlessly, before hailing a cab a mile from his condo.

Not too smart, after the phone call she received yesterday. Then again, she's never been smart. Believing the letter came from him, the man with whom she had a child.

Stupid bitch, if you ask me.

Something has happened for her to send him away.

I watch as he steps to his car, his face a mask of utter devastation. Agitation makes my skin hot, not knowing what rift has churned the waters.

Panic grips me with the possibility my years of patience could be ruined.

I need to step up my timeline, pounce while emotions are high and trust is floundering.

I think of my box of treasures.

Tomorrow has always been a thorn in my side.
Excitement lights within me.
Tomorrow it is.
Tomorrow, I take back what's always been mine.

62

KATE

THE BUZZ OF MY PHONE, DANCING ACROSS MY NIGHTSTAND, seeps through my haze of sleep. Rolling to my back, I compel my phone to stop ringing as my brain awakens. My throat is raw and parched from hours of crying.

The brightness hits my eyelids, alerting me to the cheerfulness of the day just beyond my window. Knowing all chance of further sleep has fled, I attempt to open my eyes. My eyelids feel like sandpaper as they flutter across my eyeballs.

The silence of my room is interrupted by the vibration of my phone. Again. I turn my head, watching my phone dance while debating the merits of using my energy reserves to reach out and pick it up.

If his three unanswered calls last night are any indication, I will bet my favorite Tori Burch purse A.S.S. is the one currently blowing up my phone, his impatience ignoring my request for space.

As I argue the pros and cons of engaging in a verbal conversation, my phone stops, only to start vibrating a minute later. I reach out, slapping a hand over the screen and pull it to my face. The name on the screen immediately surprises and worries me.

"Sarah? Are you OK?"

The silence filtering across the line has me sitting upright, my heart racing.

"K-K-Kate, I woke you. I'm sorry. I'll just call lat—"

"I'm up. What's wrong?" My panic rises after hearing her broken words.

"Today. Today is a day my dad and I always spend together, but he's not here."

"Where's here?"

"Our c-c-condo. I spent the night at a friend's house. Her mom just dr-dr-dropped me off, but dad's not h-here. Is he w-w-with you?"

Calm, easygoing Sarah has been replaced by a girl filled with distress and panic, and I cannot come up with a reason why. My heart soars with her choice to call me, while at the same time, it breaks because I can't give her the information she seeks.

"I don't know where your dad is, but stay where you are. I'll be there in twenty minutes."

I hang up and jump off the bed, my phone getting lost in the mess of bedsheets. A pair of jeans in the corner catches my eye, and I grab them. I pull them on while hopping over to my dresser for a bra and a shirt.

Five minutes later, I'm backing out of my driveway after sending a text to Amy letting her know where I'm going. Getting to Sarah is my number one concern as I fly down side streets, hoping to avoid the time drain a speeding ticket would cause.

Questions bombard my mind as I wonder what's going on. Sarah's distress was so strong, I could feel it through the line. My attempt to reach Shaw on my way is met with voicemail. After leaving a short voicemail asking him to contact me as soon as he gets the message, I hang up and pull into the parking garage of Shaw's building, mentally thanking him for giving me full building access.

I park and walk to the elevator, pulling out the electronic key that takes me to their floor. My anxiety rises as the elevator ascends. A few minutes later, a slight bump alerts me of my arrival to Shaw's floor. The elevator doors open, and I hurry to enter his condo. My feeling of dread is greeted by silence as I walk through the foyer. I call out to Sarah as I make my way to her room. Gut-wrenching sobs meet my ears as I knock on her door, and I barely catch the whisper of her broken voice beckoning me inside.

As I cross the threshold, I'm surrounded by soothing gray walls covered in abstract art, reminding me of the vivacious girl I've come to know. Her desk, a mirror to her thoughts, is covered with an assortment of pens, papers, and water bottles. A doorway to the right opens into an en suite bathroom, a luxury I wish I'd had when I was her age.

My eyes are drawn to the young woman buried within the voluminous white covers of an enormous bed. Sarah's face is hidden, but her pain is not. Her shoulders, bunched and tight, echo her quiet sobs. Her pain engulfs me, cutting off oxygen like a burlap bag pulled taut across my face. I alert her to my presence by calling her name quietly as I approach the bed.

As I reach out and touch her shoulder, she turns her head, revealing a tear-streaked, puffy face. An urge to wrap her in my arms and absorb her pain hits me as I sit on the edge of her bed. My hand slides up and down her back in an attempt to transfer strength and comfort through her body.

Minutes pass in silence, her sobs quieting as my hand continues stroking in a soothing rhythm. I love this young woman more than I thought possible. She's intelligent, headstrong, sensitive, and so much like her dad. Yet, I recognize a vulnerability fed by her mom's shallow desire to shape her instead of love her. Sarah hides it well, but I see it. Like recognizes like.

As I sit, waiting for her to speak, I vow to dedicate myself to loving her like she deserves to be loved. Circumstances may have caused me to give up the right to comfort my own daughter, but I will never give up the right to comfort Sarah. Never will she have to question who she can call for help. She will always have me. It's a promise I will never break.

Sarah's voice cracks as she speaks. "Do you know what today is?"

I sift through random family details Shaw has shared with me and fail to come up with an answer. "Other than August fifteenth, I'm afraid I don't."

She pulls herself to a sitting position and leans against her headboard. "Has Dad shared anything with you about his sister?" Her eyes reflect a pain deeper and darker than the depths of Lake Michigan.

I wet my lips, choosing my words carefully, unsure where this conversation is going. "I know your dad had a sister. They were close in age."

"Anything else?" The earnestness of her voice begs me to guess what she doesn't want to share.

"I know your dad's parents had a falling out with her. They didn't approve of her fiancé, I think."

Sarah nods, encouraging me to continue talking, yet my knowledge ends here. Shaw and I haven't spoken about his sister. In fact, I'm a little surprised I haven't met her, considering the affection that infuses his voice whenever he speaks of her.

Sarah takes a deep breath, and her face contorts, telling me the information she's about to share will not be said easily.

She starts, then stops. Looking at the ceiling, she starts again. "My dad's sister and her husband died in a car accident twelve years ago. On August fifteenth."

August fifteenth. A day laced with heartache, and now, death. It should really just be removed from the calendar.

Tears slide down her face, and my own face is a mirror of hers. I stretch my arms toward her. She doesn't hesitate as she leans in and wraps her arms around me. Her body shudders as her sobs grow louder.

Shaw's sister. The first person he ever loved. The person, who meant more to him than anyone in the world, had died. My own body feels the razor-sharp loss as if it were my own. Her death must have been a devastating blow. Feelings from my dad's death resurface, reminding me of the pain and anguish Shaw must have felt.

I rub her back, whispering words of comfort and encouragement into her hair. I promise to help her find Shaw so she can be with him today, then ask what I can do to help.

Still clutching my body, she leans back and looks at me. "Can you take me to the cemetery? Maybe he forgot me, or maybe he needed to go without me this time."

"I have no idea what your dad may be thinking." I give her a smile, hoping to offer comfort, while internally I'm drowning in uncertainty and confusion.

"You'll take me?"

"Do what you have to do to get ready. I'll call your dad again. Maybe I can take you to meet him."

She wipes her face with the sleeve of her shirt and drops her feet to the floor. "I know I haven't said this before, but I'm so thankful for you and happy that your path collided with my dad's, again. I wish I had—" She stops abruptly, slicing off the end of her sentence. Her eyes bounce around her room, and embarrassment brings a pink hue to her cheeks.

Not knowing what stopped her sentence, I smile, but I don't push her to continue, knowing she'll tell me if, and when, she's ready. I watch as she walks to the door of her bathroom.

Longing, heavy and cumbersome, settles on my shoulders. I

find myself wishing beyond anything she was part of the dream from my past.

Her quiet voice, shy and unsure, drags me from my wishful yearnings. "I wish I had a mom like you."

Her words, so close to my own musings, squeeze my heart and suck the air from my lungs.

I wish I had you.

KATE

As I DRIVE ALONG THE EXPRESSWAY TOWARD THE CEMETERY, Sarah plays with my car's audio system. Pairing her phone, her music filters from the speakers and fills the cabin. I see her tactic for what it is, a welcome distraction from the confusion and the difficulty of the day.

I glance at her as she watches the Chicago skyline in the distance. She's quiet, stuck in her own world of swirling thoughts. Unsure what to say, I stay silent and let my own thoughts wander.

Shaw's lack of response to Sarah's texts and my own phone calls has me worried. He checks his phone religiously, and he's never without it. It's both a positive and negative effect of running his company, as there isn't a day where his phone doesn't interrupt his life. Somehow, he doesn't seem to mind its intrusions, until they interrupt his time with Sarah or me.

Over the past few months, I've seen a subtle change in his demeanor toward the demands of his company. He's more willing to assign tasks to employees instead of feeling he has to do everything himself. It's been a nice change, but one that doesn't bode well for our current search for him.

Considering the way we left things, I'm worried about his state of mind. I told him he has another daughter. One he's never known. His absence and silence is my doing. I refused to talk with him when he needed me, but at the time, my emotions had been too raw for the questions I knew he would ask. So, I sent him away. It explains his refusal to return my calls, but it doesn't explain his lack of response to Sarah's attempts to reach him.

Sarah and I are on our way to visit his sister's grave, whom I've never met, on the anniversary of her death. Will he be angry Sarah called me or that I took her to the cemetery? If he's there when we arrive, will he want me to stay? Or will he send me away, like I did to him? As we near the exit ramp for the street the cemetery is on, my palms start to sweat, and I feel clammy.

Sensing my trepidation or needing reassurance herself, Sarah looks at me and smiles. "Kate, thank you for doing this with me."

The sincerity in her voice helps calm my nerves, even though my heart continues to race. I follow her directions as I pull through the cemetery gates, following signs and pulling into the designated visitor parking lot. Quickly scanning the small lot, I find the chances of seeing Shaw are dismal, considering neither his Jeep nor his motorcycle is here.

I turn to Sarah, unsure of the appropriate words to utter before visiting the graves of Shaw's sister and brother-in-law. "Are you ready?"

She nods as she pulls the handle to open the door.

"Just remember, I will be with you the whole way. Take as much time as you need."

"Thank you, Kate."

Sarah steps from the door and walks toward a copse of large oak trees in the back corner of the lot near the wrought iron fence outlining the cemetery grounds. I follow, hanging back slightly to give Sarah time with her thoughts.

Looking around, I see a newly-covered plot. There is a statue of a sleeping infant resting on top of a small headstone. It's so lifelike and serene, and my heart hurts for the parents whose pain is as fresh as the soil covering the plot. How devastating to know your child will never learn to ride a bike, graduate from high school, get married, or have children of their own. The loss of my daughter is nothing compared to the loss of knowing this child will never know this world.

I continue on, willing myself to embrace the knowledge that I gave my daughter a life she would never have experienced. Looking ahead, I find Sarah seated, facing me, in front of a large headstone. As I approach, I note the shine of the smooth gray marble and how it reflects the sunlight. It is a beautiful reminder of a horrific tragedy.

Sarah's voice draws me to a stop. Not wanting to interrupt the conversation she is having with her aunt and uncle, I hang back and to the side of the headstone. Sarah's head lifts and her eyes meet mine as she smiles and continues to talk.

As I watch her, I see an animation I didn't think possible after finding her earlier in such a distraught emotional state. Her hands lift and drop as she speaks. The smile on her face is breathtaking and magnetic, and my feet bring me nearer before I realize I've moved.

"...she's perfect for him. I've never seen Dad so happy."

Sarah's words warm me with embarrassment. She is talking to her aunt about me and her dad. She's sharing her happiness like she's talking to a silent friend. A smile tips my lips as Sarah's eyes lock on mine. She flicks her hand, indicating I should come to her.

I follow her directive, debating if I should say something or stay silent once I reach her side. As my hand connects with her warm palm, it feels like an electrical shock burns up my arm and across my chest. The widening of Sarah's eyes indicates she feels something too.

I smile and turn to face the headstone.

In memory of
Charles & Grace Lawson
Loving parents of Sarah
And loving sister and brother of Shaw

I gasp and drop to my knees. My heart drops to the ground and splits wide open on the grass in front of me.

Sarah startles and looks at me, her smile slipping from her face, replaced by fear and confusion for my reaction. "Kate, what's wrong? Are you OK?"

I can't breathe, can't think. I can't talk as I stare at the headstone in front of me. A picture of Grace and Charles is imprinted above the inscription. *How?*

I feel lightheaded and nauseous as my hands start to shake. I fall to my butt as Sarah's voice grows louder, her worry mounting the longer I stay silent.

Sarah squeezes my hand and uses her other one to grip my shoulder. "Kate, *what's wrong? Please.*"

Her eyes are wild as I struggle to fill my lungs with air. I pull her to me, embracing her in a hug I hope will soothe her panic until I can recover my words.

Gulping air like a fish, I try to pull myself together. I'm in shock, and I'm scaring Sarah. Sheer force of will helps me steady my breathing enough to speak, even though my stomach threatens to release its contents at the slightest provocation.

"Tel— Wh-when is your birthday?" Even though I know, my brain still needs confirmation before it races ahead.

She pulls back and looks at me, confused by a question having no bearing on my reaction to seeing the headstone. "March fifteenth. Why?"

Her eyes tell me her brain is working overtime, as she tries to figure out the relevance of a seemingly innocuous question.

I close my eyes and bow my head as the significance of her answer tears through me. Controlling my breathing, I lift my head and look at the picture of the two people I hadn't seen in over fifteen years.

Grace and Charles Lawson, the people I had chosen to raise my daughter as their own. Their love for each other, so deep and unconditional, had drawn me to them the moment we were introduced.

I turn and look at Sarah as tears run down my cheeks. I stare at the face of my daughter. She is the living, breathing product of the love shared by her father and me.

Fate has stepped in to add another twist.

All at once, I am a sponge and Sarah is my water. I want to know everything about her—her life, her dreams. Knowing it may be difficult to discuss, I cautiously ask about her parents. "If you feel comfortable, can you tell me what happened to your parents?"

She looks at me, confusion marring her face, as she wonders why I reacted the way I did, and why I'm suddenly asking questions about her parents. She takes a breath and releases it from her lips.

"Well, I don't know a lot. Only what Dad has told me. We were on the way to the park. I was in the car too." I feel a tear escape down my face, as I nod to encourage her to continue. "Witnesses said two cars were messing around, racing or something. One of them swerved, hitting our car and pushing us into a tree."

My hand covers my mouth in an attempt to stifle a sob. "Mom and Dad didn't make it. I was in the hospital for a while. I lost a lot of blood. Luckily, I don't remember any of it. Not the accident and not the hospital. Dad said that's probably for the best, considering what happened."

We lapse into silence as I digest what she's told me. Shaw must have been the guardian they named in the event of their death. He would have been done with his training and just starting out, working alongside his dad. *How did he manage the company and a toddler at the same time? Was Elizabeth already in the picture?*

The fractures in my heart grow deeper as I picture him dealing with his sister's death, receiving guardianship, and building the company.

I had given our daughter the dream, and he had fulfilled it.

Sarah squeezes my hand, my brain forgetting she still holds it clasped within her own. "I think I'm ready to go. Are you?" Her eyes, cornflower blue, issue questions for which I don't have answers.

I stand and hold out my hand, pulling her from the ground, and we walk to the car in silence. My eyes feast on my daughter's profile as my brain rejoices at the magnificent young woman Shaw raised.

We need to find Shaw. I need him to look at me and tell me we'll get through this—the three of us. The family we wished for so long ago, finally together.

64

SHAW

STRONG HANDS SHAKE ME HARD ENOUGH TO RIP MY ARMS FROM their sockets. I roll to my front, shoving off the annoying appendages currently working to pull me out of my dream.

Kate and I sit on a beach, my hand resting possessively on her swollen stomach. Clear, blue water fills my vision as birds squawk overhead.

Even though I work to push him away, V's voice penetrates my dream, pulling me from the first peace I've felt in forty-eight hours.

"Shaw. Wake up *now*."

I lift an arm, punching the air as I attempt to connect with the voice stealing my happiness.

Stinging heat blooms across my cheek and I open my eyes. V pulls his hand back, after slapping my face with a force strong enough to loosen a tooth. "Go to hell. Leave me alone."

"Listen to me. Sarah and Kate *need* you."

Hearing both names, I'm instantly awake. The alcohol haze swimming through my veins is gone with a single sentence. "What?"

"Amy called me an hour ago. There was a car accident.

She said she's tried calling you. She told me to find you and meet her at Rush University Hospital."

Bullets couldn't have done more damage than his words. My body stills, forgetting to breathe.

My girls—Sarah and Kate.

I jump from the bed, the floor meeting my chin as my leg tangles in my bedsheets. Shock has stripped me of remembering how to walk and how to breathe.

"You're in no condition to drive. Throw on some clothes. We'll leave in four minutes."

His order sends me into action. "I'll be in the car in two."

The ride to the hospital is agony, not knowing what happened. I can't focus. I can't breathe. I feel like a thousand rubber bands surround my chest.

"They'll be OK, man."

V's words ring hollow without knowing the news we'll receive at the hospital. I look at my phone and stifle a moan of frustration as I will the car charger to charge faster. My dead phone, the victim of my drunken stupor, sits on the seat next to me. A blinking red battery icon mocks me for my stupidity.

"Sarah and Kate were together? Why?"

"I don't know, man, but I promise we'll find out."

He rolls into the parking lot, and I jump from the vehicle before V pulls into a space. I run, my legs threatening to give out the closer I get to the hospital door. I sprint straight to the information desk and an older woman, who looks like she just sucked a lemon, raises her eyes to mine.

"May I help you?"

"Sarah Graham and Kate Bra— Uh...Waters were brought in earlier. I need their room numbers...please."

"And you are?" Her dry voice matches her sour expression.

"Shaw Graham. Sarah's dad."

"I'll need to see your ID. I'll also need you to verify your daughter's date of birth." I retrieve my driver's license and hand it to the woman, thanking God my wallet is still in the pocket of the jeans I'd worn yesterday.

"Just a minute, Mr. Graham." I issue a silent apology for my earlier judgmental thoughts as I'm immensely grateful her arthritic hands move faster than I would have thought possible. Efficient is this woman's middle name.

She looks at the screen and writes something on the notepad next to her keyboard. She presses a button on her headset, her voice low as she asks if a nurse can meet me at the door of the fourth floor. Ms. Fire Fingers studies me as she listens to the voice on the other end, yet she gives me no indication of the news awaiting me. She utters "thank you" and hits a button on her keyboard.

"Hang a right at the fountain, take the hallway all the way to the first bank of elevators, take one to the fourth floor. Take an immediate left when you step off the elevator, then a right at the end of that corridor which will take you to a set of locked double doors. A nurse from the floor will meet you there."

Right, left, right. Got it.

"Everything OK?" I jump as V claps me on the back.

In my rush to find Sarah and Kate, I forgot he drove me to the hospital. V gives my shoulder a squeeze and hands me my phone and a charger.

"Let's go find your girls."

65

SHAW

My nerves are frayed, and my stress level is off the charts after getting lost and forced to ask directions, twice, in this maze of a hospital. Approaching entry to the fourth floor, I catch the eye of a nurse standing on the other side of the locked double doors. She smiles and pushes a button to open them as V and I approach.

"Mr. Graham?" Lauren, a registered nurse according to the badge around her neck, has a kind, yet cautious voice.

"Yes. I'm here to see Sarah Graham and Kate Waters. How are they doing? Could you point me in the direction of their rooms?" I fire questions like a tennis ball machine.

Instead of immediately answering, Lauren leads me to a room off the main hallway. The room, barely bigger than a coat closet, with a few uncomfortable plastic chairs and low lighting, has me on edge. These walls do not hold the secrets of good news. This is a room where doctors usher family members to deliver bad news, away from prying eyes. I'm standing in one of those rooms, and the way Lauren seems to be ignoring my questions has me ready to leapfrog over her and take off down the hall in search of my girls.

Lauren perches on the edge of a plastic chair, her back straight, eyes sharp like she's calculating the number of seconds before she can flee the room. V, sensing I'm seconds away from yelling at this poor woman, squeezes my shoulder and forces me into a nearby chair.

"Mr. Graham, I'm sorry. I cannot release any information about Ms. Waters without her consent. I can, however, offer you an update on your daughter, Sarah."

I jump to my feet, looming over her as she stares up at me. The deep sympathy on her face makes me reconsider my attempted intimidation. She may be scared witless right now, but her body gives no indication of fear.

She takes a breath before releasing her words in an efficient, but empathetic manner. After her first sentence, my brain shuts down, ignoring her words and focusing on the nuances of her voice. The tone, the pitch, the resonance.

"Mr. Graham, do you have any questions?" She reaches out her hand to touch mine. My tongue is paralyzed by my brain, which is running the hundred-yard dash.

The ability to string words together eludes me as V jumps in with questions my brain is too discombobulated to ask. "Sarah's been in surgery for an hour? How much longer? Can we see her as soon as she gets out?"

Lauren looks to me, nonverbally asking for permission to answer the questions of the man sitting next to me. I nod, needing to know the answers to these questions as well.

"Like I said before, all we know is she was brought in about two hours ago. She and Ms. Waters were together in a vehicle that was involved in an accident. Sarah suffered a broken arm and leg. Her arm was a simple fracture. Surgery was required to set the compound fracture to her leg—the hospital was hoping to reach you before she was taken to surgery. She had lost a lot of blood from her injuries. Luckily, we were able to get in touch with your wife, who gave consent. Sarah's surgeon will come to speak with you as soon as he's done. You may stay here, or I can get you a pager that works anywhere in the hospital."

Her words release my tongue from its silence. "*Who* gave consent?"

She looks at me like I sprouted two heads. "Mrs. Graham."

I see red. I wouldn't hesitate to wring Elizabeth's neck if she were standing in front of me. "She's. Not. My. *Wife*." The words burst from my clenched teeth one at a time.

Her face registers confusion. "I don't understand. Is she not Sarah's mother? I was told the police retrieved emergency contact numbers from Sarah's cell phone, which led the hospital to contact Mrs. Elizabeth Graham."

"Yes, she is Sarah's mother, but she's *not* my wife." My anger rises as I envision Elizabeth breezing in, high on her heels with thoughts of saving the day. She may be Sarah's mother on paper, but she hasn't been Sarah's mother for a very long time.

Lauren rises and places her hand on my forearm. "I'm sorry for your daughter's accident. I need to get back to my station. Please have someone page me if you have any questions."

She turns to leave, but V's voice stops her at the door. "Ms. Waters. Where or how can we find out about her?"

"She has a friend who arrived a little bit ago. I can send her out here if that would help."

"Yes. Thank you." V's manners help smooth over the poor impressions lingering in the room.

After she leaves, he looks at me, unsure what to say. "I'll call Amy. She's here somewhere."

I nod my head. A headache, from last night's alcohol and today's stress, throbs throughout my temples.

Emotion hits me as I turn to him. "Thanks, man. I feel like those words aren't enough, but it's all I've got right now."

"They are both fighters, Shaw. They're going to make it."

The nurse's references to Elizabeth hit me. I'm not sure what game she's playing, but I need to find out. However, Elizabeth is a problem for a different day. Sarah and Kate are my number one priority. While Sarah is in surgery, I need to find Kate.

I pace the small room while V contacts Amy. Fear of the unknown has burned away all traces of my hangover. Not being able to see Kate, nor receive updates about her condition, is gut-wrenching.

I pull my half-charged phone from my pocket, randomly scrolling through missed calls and reminders. Three texts and a phone call from Sarah, and a phone call and voicemail from Kate, all before nine a.m. this morning, over five hours ago.

I open my messaging app. Kate's pleading words are like a hammer to my heart.

August 15 jumps off the home screen of my phone. *How could I forget and leave Sarah alone today?* Today has always been our day. Every year, we use this day to visit the past in a positive way. I tell stories, filling in details Sarah's young memory has no way of remembering.

Our annual trip into the suburbs. A quick visit to our favorite bakery before visiting the two people who created and shaped our lives with a bitter tragedy.

I take Sarah to the cemetery every year on this day as a reminder. The first year, she toddled around, stacking sticks she found in the grass into a pile at the base of her mom and dad's headstone. At three, she had no idea death had cheated her of the immense love showered upon her by Grace and Charles.

She had thrived in their love.

I miss my sister every day. She was my rock. A woman who loved me unconditionally and without preamble. She had acknowledged my need for love, and she'd done a damn fine job filling the gaps left by our absent mother and father.

It was her love that flowed from me into Sarah as I strove to be the present, involved, loving parent my sister and her husband were meant to be. I wanted to make them proud of the brother they trusted to raise their only daughter.

Twelve years ago, a hit-and-run driver had stolen a mother and father, a sister and brother, forever altering lives. Twelve years to the day of her parents' passing, a hit-and-run driver had attempted to steal my daughter and my heart.

I'm overcome with an extreme feeling of helplessness. I slump down in a chair, my elbows resting on my knees, my head in my hands. They have to pull through. They have to be OK.

V drops his phone to his lap. I can see his face in my periphery as it studies mine. "Don't waste my time, what did you find out?"

V's eyes jump around the room, his face a screen of poorly-disguised anxiety. "I just talked to Amy."

His quiet voice fans my own unease as I wait for him to drop the ax I sense teetering over my head.

"They won't tell her anything about Sarah, but she told me what she knows about Kate."

I give him an icy stare, telling him he has exactly two seconds to start talking.

"Happened about eleven this morning. Kate was driving, Sarah was with her. Other driver ran a red light. Hit Kate's car, pushed her through the intersection, and drove off. According to what the paramedics told Amy, both Kate and Sarah were conscious when the ambulance arrived. Kate lost consciousness on the way to the hospital and remains unconscious."

"No. Kate. No." Her name explodes from my lips, my anguish too strong to hold within my chest. My heart cracks as questions flood my head. *What kind of sick bastard nearly kills my girls and drives away?*

"She suffered a couple broken ribs, a concussion, a broken wrist, a broken tibia, a bruised pelvis, and a ruptured spleen. She's out of surgery, but she hasn't woken yet."

I look at V as tears cloud my vision, embarrassed at my inability to control my emotions, but so damn thankful he's here to protect my sanity. V opens his mouth, then closes it. He presses his lips together, clearly avoiding the words festering behind his lips.

"There's more, yeah?"

The way his eyes shift across the room tell me the worst still hasn't hit my ears.

"There were complications. She lost a lot of blood. Some existing medical condition. Do you know what the hell she's talking about?"

I remain silent, my stomach crawling up my throat. My mind races over the past few months. Sifting through every word Kate has uttered, every nuance I may have missed.

Damn. The day she told me about our daughter. *You were gone. I was…not well.* Shit. She had tried to tell me, but I'd been too blindsided to listen. Stunned, I hadn't let myself revisit the specific details of her words.

I failed her. My heart was lying in a hospital bed scared, confused, and alone. If I had refused to leave her house yesterday, I would have been with her. She would know what today meant for Sarah and me. I could have told her everything. We would have made it through today together. Now, I'm helpless, and my girls are alone.

"Amy said she would be out as soon as she talked to the doctor about getting you cleared to see Kate."

I hear his words, but I'm numb.

One damn decision had changed our lives…again.

Amy stands in front of me as I pace the waiting room. "Isn't there anything you can do to get me in there?" The desperation bleeds through my voice.

"I'm her emergency contact. While I have access, I don't have the authority to grant visitation."

"I haven't seen her since she threw me out of your house. There has to be another way. I'm creeping closer to insanity by the hour."

My body feels like it's going through physical withdrawals without her. I went sixteen years without contact, and now I can't go a few days without losing my shit by not seeing her.

It's been a week since the accident and Kate hasn't woken from her coma. I'm not sure my nerves can take much more.

Amy looks tired and stretched to her limit. Between juggling the demands of her P.R. firm and coordinating Kate's care, Amy deserves a superwoman cape. She has kept me updated through texts, calls, and face-to-face meetings, like the one we are currently having in the closet—or, family conference room, according to the plaque on the wall.

Kate has come through two surgeries, but she's closely monitored due to a disease in her blood that had been diagnosed about a year after we parted ways.

According to Amy, Kate is diligent in keeping up with her checkups because of a severe health scare she had back in college. Amy didn't offer any additional information and encouraged me to wait and speak with Kate when she finally woke up.

The doctors have assured Amy the length of Kate's coma is not a concern, considering she tolerated being taken off of the ventilator and is breathing on her own. I nearly suffered a heart attack when Amy told me this, considering she'd neglected to tell me Kate had been on one. I'm pretty sure my reaction has scarred Amy for the rest of her life, but we reached an agreement. I will be told everything in the future.

As far as I know, Amy has been forthcoming in her updates since we reached our little understanding.

I don't just want to see Kate, I *need* to see her. Like an addict, I've gone through withdrawal over the past week, barely sleeping when I crash on the cot in Sarah's room each night. I've eaten just enough to keep my body functional, and my shoes have worn a horizontal line in the hospital's linoleum as a result of my agitated pacing. The nurses love me, but their pity stares are starting to wear me down. I need to see Kate, and I'm determined to find a way.

I dig my phone from my pocket, the ring indicating an incoming FaceTime call from Sarah. I swipe the screen and come face-to-face with my beautiful daughter, albeit a horrible patient. She claims her doctor, who says she'll be released next week, is ruining her social life.

"Hey, Dad." Her smile stretches across my screen, and I give her one in return.

"Hey, you. Did your girlfriends come to visit today?"

"Yeah, they just left. There's some kind of free concert at Navy Pier tonight they kept droning on about. Seriously, what is wrong with them? Hello. See me? Girl in the hospital. Stuck here. Can't go. Quit reminding me."

I find it annoying, yet oddly fascinating, my intelligent daughter reverts to two and three-word sentences as soon as a cell phone is placed in front of her face. I blame it on texting. The texts of a teenager are crazy. I need a damn urban translation app just to figure out she's going to the library after school. I question my return on investment for the tuition I pay to her school.

"Dad? Earth calling, Dad. I'm bored. Are you coming to see me today?"

I smile. It isn't every day I field a call from my daughter, asking me to hang with her. Yeah, she may be confined to a bed, with no friends in sight, but I'm honored. I take what I can get.

"Absolutely, honey. I wanted to make sure you had some time with your friends without your old dad crashing the party."

"Dad, you're awesome and in better shape than half the guys my age." My daughter, the ego booster. "In fact, Stephanie thinks you're hot. She even asked if you were going to be stopping by while she was here."

And... now I feel violated by a teenage girl. Remind me never to allow a slumber party in my home. I don't need to get cornered by one of my daughter's friends.

"I'll be there in a little bit, honey. Love you."

"Love you too."

I end the call, slipping my phone in my pocket. I turn to leave, surprised to see Amy still standing next to me.

"I can't believe I didn't think of it sooner."

"What?"

"*I* may not be able to get you in to see Kate, but maybe we could do the next best thing."

I raise my eyebrows and wait for Amy to share her idea. I'm willing to try anything short of kidnapping.

"I'll FaceTime you from her room. You can see her and talk to her, just like you were sitting next to her."

"It doesn't compare to being able to sit with her and hold her hand, but I'll take it."

She smiles, her eyes twinkling, obviously proud of herself for coming up with an idea a kindergartner probably would have suggested a week ago.

"Why aren't you in her room already? I need to see my girl."

66

KATE

Awareness rushes through me, instantly putting my body on alert. It feels like I have a brick sitting on my eyelids, the effort to lift them too much for my battered body. Anxiety spikes my heartbeat as my eyes dart back and forth behind my eyelids. Grasping for clues, I try to focus, letting my ears and nose take in my surroundings.

I am alone.

Something is stuck in my mouth, my jaw sore and open at an awkward angle. Cold rushes past my teeth, hitting the back of my parched throat. My chest rises in sync with a repetitive hiss, like a bicycle pump, filling the silence of the space.

I'm reclined, and a soft yet firm platform supports my weight. I try to wiggle my fingers, but I can't tell if the movement I feel is real or in my mind.

I know the smell. Memories, unbidden, assault my mind. Frustration mixes with anxiety.

Why am I in the hospital?

I try, in vain, to open my eyes, banishing the memories of a past too painful to visit. Exhaustion overpowers my frustration, and I slip back into the escape of unconsciousness.

Bright overhead light hits my eyelids, waking my senses. Warmth covers my body. My mouth is no longer propped open, but my throat is raw like it's been scraped by a vegetable peeler.

My eyes flutter open, and I scan a room that's bright and out of focus. A single window, a silent TV, a vinyl chair, a bed, and a door to what I presume is the bathroom.

Normal, plain, and empty.

A flash of a smile. Blue eyes, twinkling in the sunshine.

Sarah? Where is she? She was with me. I cringe as her screams fill my head.

Kate, Kate, don't leave me!

I need to find her. I try to sit up, but excruciating pain lances through my chest and abdomen, pulling me back to the bed.

I. Need. To. Know. *Now*. I try to hit the call button, my fingers clumsy, as I pray that Sarah is OK.

Nurse Bridget bustles around the bed. She's feisty and doesn't take any shit. She's a straight shooter, and I like her. She's been my night nurse since I woke up, scared out of my mind and demanding answers.

I'd been in a coma for over a week, and no one had been cleared to see me, outside of my listed emergency contact, Amy. Nurse Bridget is the employee who broke hospital protocol when I resorted to pulling tubes from my arm, saying I would find Sarah myself if she didn't give me some type of update on her injuries.

Bridget told me Sarah had suffered a broken arm and a compound fracture to her leg, which surgery had been successful in setting, and she was resting comfortably just down the hall.

She hands me the TV remote, even though I don't request it. Television has no chance of occupying my mind. She smirks as I stare at her. "Not one of those 'binge' watchers, huh? Don't blame you. I sit down to watch a one-hour program and before I know it, four hours have passed, and I'm questioning where the hell my day went. That Netflix is as addictive as heroin. I can't seem to get through one week without a binge. Embarrassing."

Not willing to speak and endure the burn in my throat, I nod. Thoughts bounce around my mind, my stomach fluttering with nerves. *Will he come? Does he even care?*

Bridget fills my water, humming to herself as she works. "Now that you've been cleared by your doctor, as you requested, I've updated your visitor profile in the computer. Your approved visitors are listed and shouldn't have a problem getting in to see you." She makes a final adjustment to my I.V. bag and leaves my room, giving me strict instructions to stay in bed.

She'll get no complaint from me. Earlier, I had tried to push my body up the bed with my arms, and I nearly passed out from pain.

Silence fills my room, and I curse my ability to do nothing but wait. I stare at the ceiling, my mind is unwilling to give me the sanctuary of sleep.

Thirty, thirty-one, thirty-two. Thirty-two yellowed ceiling tiles hang over my stark, uninviting mattress. My bed is both a refuge and a prison for my bruised and broken body. Sharp arrows of long-buried memories flash across the invisible thread connecting my bruised heart to my confused mind.

Haunting blue eyes.

An encouraging smile.

The cloying scent of industrial cleaner unsuccessfully

covers the stench of urine and sickness. It invades my nose with an aroma that coats my tongue, threatening my gag reflex.

Cold.

Sad.

An innocent life.

My soul breaking.

Memories bombard my mind like scenery outside the window of a moving train.

Sunshine.

Happiness.

A look.

His smile.

My heart.

A soul-piercing cry.

This scene isn't new. I've been here before.

Crippled by my unreasonable hope.

Waiting.

Waiting for him.

Hope has made me her fool.

A fool who knows he'll come.

But it won't be for me.

He'll come for the truth.

And I'll be left in pieces.

Utterly broken.

Again.

My body stiffens, sloughing off the dregs of sleep, as I feel a presence in my room. The curtains Nurse Bridget closed earlier cast shadows across the floor. My eyes move across the room, connecting with the other half of my heart.

A light beard covers his face, a rumpled dark T-shirt stretches across his chest, and worn jeans hang loose on his hips. A dark knight keeping watch over his princess. I raise my hand, calling him to me, my throat too raw to give power to my voice.

He steps to the bed and drops to his knees, grabbing my hand and holding it against his cheek. His blue eyes hide behind red rims. He moves my hand to his lips, pressing a kiss to my palm before returning it to his cheek. A single tear traverses his handsome face as he stares at me.

I wait, my hand not the only piece of me he holds.

"Kate."

I move my thumb and catch his tear before it falls to my bed.

"I thought I lost you...again. I thought my heart broke the first time, but I was wrong. I can *never* live without you again." The intensity of his whisper triggers my own tears.

"I'm sorry. I don't remember many details of the accident. How's Sarah? Is she in pain?"

He leans toward me, reaching to push hair behind my ear. "She's a fighter, and she's going to be fine. She's been begging me to find a wheelchair so she can come to see you."

She's my daughter.

The cemetery.

He doesn't know.

I avert my eyes, unsure how to tell him, and scared of pushing him away.

"Kate, I was so scared. Amy said something about a medical condition. Are you sick?"

His stare is unrelenting and demanding, leaving no room for avoidance.

I release his hand and pick at the bedsheets, hiding my eyes from his probing stare. "I told you I can't have more children." His pinkie wraps around mine, tethering me to him as he continues to listen. "When I gave birth, I started bleeding. Not just a little, but a massive hemorrhage. Our daughter was removed from the room, and I was prepped for surgery."

The chaos of the day grips my heart. "I had an emergency hysterectomy to stop the bleeding. Tests confirmed I have a disease called Von Willebrand. It's like hemophilia, but not as severe. It can cause tiredness, fatigue, and uncontrolled bleeding. It's treatable. But, undiagnosed, it nearly ended my life."

I look up at him through wet lashes. "When I woke after surgery, the couple I'd chosen to adopt our daughter was there. I was lost and didn't know what to do. I was a college student, with a part-time job barely supporting my needs, let alone the needs of a newborn. I didn't have health insurance. I had nothing, so I signed the papers, giving them the legal right to adopt her. They were so supportive and kind. They helped me with my medical bills and incidentals until I could go back to school. They loved her at first sight. Just like I did. Shaw, she was perfect. I'm so sorry you weren't there to meet the daughter our love created."

I lift my head and watch his impassive face, looking for signs of unforgivable anger. Anger at the situation, anger at the couple, anger at me. His mouth opens, and words I never expected tumble out.

"Kate, I'm sorry I wasn't there. I'm *so fucking* sorry." His voice breaks as he squeezes my hand. "You were totally alone, but you loved our daughter enough to give her our dream—a loving family."

He stands up and reaches out, framing my face with his hands. "Thank you. I love you."

Shaw's lips brush across mine, the naked emotion bleeding from his body, directly into me. He presses our foreheads together as we sit in silence, absorbing the pain and guilt that has plagued each of us for over a decade. He pulls his head away and looks into my eyes. "What were their names? Can we contact them? How does that work?"

My eyes plead with him to release me from answering. I rub my lips together, tasting the saltiness of my tears. "Please, don't let me go. I love you."

His brows crinkle, my words painting confusion across his face. "Never. I'll never let you go."

I drop my head. I can't form the words.

Shaw's fingers lift my chin until my eyes meet his. His smile is gentle and encouraging. "To whom do I owe my gratitude for loving our daughter?"

I close my eyes, imprinting his love on my soul. The truth is a broken whisper as it falls from my lips.

"Grace and Charles Lawson."

67

SHAW

Grace and Charles Lawson.

The stress of the past week closes in on me as her words pierce my skin, a double-edged sword obliterating my truths.

I push away from the bed and pace to the wall, putting distance between me and the strike of her poisonous words. Pain pricks my scalp as I pull at my hair. I stop, refusing to look at her, and I hurl words of disbelief into the air. "What the hell are you telling me?"

Her angry words stab the air, drawing blood, as I continue to pace her room. "You know what I'm telling you. I refuse to repeat myself until you calm down."

"Calm down? That's rich, Kate. Is this some elaborate joke?"

"Go. To. Hell. Our daughter will never be a joke." Her anger is so thick, I could scrape it from the walls with a knife.

I stop and look at her. "Damn. I'm sorry. That's not what I meant."

I walk over and sit down in the lone chair, the vinyl squeaking under my weight. I drop my elbows to my knees, then take a deep breath as I run my hands through my hair. The coincidence of this story is too ludicrous to believe.

Kate's voice cuts through my musings. "Contrary to your accusations, I didn't know until the day of the accident. Sarah called me, upset and nearly hysterical as she tried to find you. I found her at your condo, sobbing through her emotional pain. She told me it was the anniversary of your sister's death and asked if I could take her the cemetery. She was so broken, I wanted to ease her pain."

Guilt seeps through the fractures in my heart. Kate must have felt powerless to help Sarah. The fact Sarah called Kate instead of Elizabeth speaks volumes to Sarah's feelings for Kate.

"I hung back at the cemetery, hoping to give Sarah privacy. I didn't want to intrude. She explained you and she make sure to visit every year on August fifteenth."

I listen, wanting to hear the point at which Kate realized she was standing next to our daughter.

"I overheard her talking about us, and how happy you were since we met." She peeks at me, a tentative smile on her lips. "She called me over, intending to introduce me to your sister. My eyes slid over the inscription before landing on the photo of Grace and Charles on the headstone."

The emotion of the encounter flickers across her face. Disbelief, guilt, elation. Kate's chest rises and falls as her mind returns to the cemetery, and her face twists in agony as she recalls her shock.

"I think my heart stopped beating. I know I quit breathing. It was like I was floating in space, trying to make sense of what I was seeing." Her eyes find mine. "I'm sorry for your loss."

Her simple words break my composure, lancing open the wound of my sister's death. I miss her every day. I miss her sarcasm, her wit, her encouragement, her love.

"Sarah is beautiful, inside and out. You have done what I couldn't do. Thank you."

My blood runs through her veins. I'm Sarah's dad, and she is my daughter, just like it's always been.

Realization hits me. I have raised Sarah, kissed her goodnight, taken her to school, and seen her grow. Kate has missed every one of those days. She's been cheated from knowing our daughter.

Shit. Another woman, one Kate didn't choose, helped raise her daughter. Fate has certainly twisted the path of our lives.

I look at Kate and note her exhaustion. This conversation has drained every bit of energy from her body.

"You need your rest. I should go."

"Will you stay until I fall asleep?" She picks at the blanket covering her legs, looking anywhere but at me. "And will you be here when I wake up?" Trepidation and uncertainty lace her words.

My heart squeezes. The fact she questions my feelings kills me. "Forever. I'll be wherever you are forever."

She rests her head against her pillows. "Tell me about your first night with Sarah. I want to know everything."

I take a drink, my throat dry and my voice hoarse. Kate and I have been talking nearly nonstop for the past two days. She is relentless in her quest for information about my life, my company and, most importantly, Sarah. Kate's body may be physically bruised, but her mind is sharp, and her memory is amazing. No wonder she is such a renowned author. Everything she hears, no matter how inconsequential, is filed in her mind, in case it's needed later.

"Tell me about Sarah's first day of school. Was she excited? Nervous?"

I sit back and wrack my brain, trying to recall her first day. As it comes to me, I'm embarrassed to tell her I wasn't there. How do I tell her a business trip to a supplier in China kept me away? My memories of Sarah's first day come from the pictures our nanny took as Sarah walked into school.

I look up and see her eyes on me. Assessing, but not judging. "I'm sorry, Kate. I wasn't there." Her unspoken disappointment suffocates me. "I have always tried to do right by her, but I haven't always been successful."

Distance fills her eyes, her mind miles from this room. "Don't ever apologize for providing for her. I've seen you with her. You were born to be her father." Her answer is in opposition to the defeat written on her face. "You may not feel like you've always been successful, but at least you were there to try. I will never be able to recall memories from her childhood because I wasn't there."

I'm on my feet and at her bedside in two paces. "You're here now. You'll be the keeper of her present and future memories, just as I'm the keeper of her past ones."

She pulls me to her, resting her head against my chest. "I love you, Shaw Graham. Always have, always will."

Our relationship may not be perfect, and we definitely have some hurdles in our future, but this woman will always own my heart.

68

SHAW

I slip out of Kate's room, checking in with the nursing station to let them know I'm leaving and to call me if Kate needs me before I return.

While my thoughts have been in complete chaos since the accident, one thought remains constant—I love Kate.

We have spoken at length about Sarah and what we should tell her. We both agree Sarah is an intelligent girl. She witnessed Kate's near breakdown at the cemetery, and we know she'll start asking questions.

There is no doubt she cares deeply for Kate. Her phone call on the anniversary of Grace and Charles's death is a testament to her already deep feelings; however, we have no way of knowing how she'll respond to learning Kate and I are her biological parents. Truth be told, I'm still coming to terms with the news.

One thing is certain, the story of our lives is too bizarre to be anything but true.

I pull my cell from my pocket and dial V's number. He answers before I hear it ring.

"News?" His anxiousness is a sign of his love for Sarah and his feelings toward Kate.

"More than you could ever imagine. No time to explain. I need a favor."

"Anything for you. Hit me with it."

"Can you come to the hospital? Sit with Kate. I need to see Sarah and run an errand while Kate's sleeping. If I don't make it back in time, I want someone to be here when she wakes up."

"Give me thirty minutes. I need to finish something, then I'll head over to the hospital. Work for you?"

"That works. Thanks."

"How are your girls?"

I wipe my hand over my face. "Kate's a fighter. The doctor thinks she'll be out sometime in the next two weeks. Sarah's going stir-crazy at home. Complaining daily about the nurse I hired to be with her when I'm gone."

"Great news, man. Be there soon."

As I disconnect the call, I picture the woman who stole my heart sixteen years ago. She is a fighter. Now, I just have to convince her I'll forever be in her corner.

I work to keep my anger in check as I drive to Elizabeth's apartment. Thinking about the file, I received yesterday from the police, burns through me like acid. Elizabeth's visit to the hospital the day of the accident and her introduction as my wife had been odd and suspect. I'd called in more than a handful of favors to get a handle on the crazy brewing in Elizabeth's brain.

The information had devastated me. I knew Elizabeth was an egomaniac and a manipulative, control freak, but the details the police unearthed were enough to chill my blood. My ex-wife is insane, and I have the information to prove it.

I walk to the door of her brownstone, inspecting the outside facade with distaste. The peeling paint, shabby stoop, and overall poor lack of attention indicate the monthly stipend for maintenance on the building I own is not being used for its specified purpose. I let it go with barely a thought, considering the conversation we'll be having momentarily.

I check behind me and see the shadow of two occupants in the unmarked police car across the street. Friends in high places have granted me a narrow window of opportunity to confront her before they pick her up and take her to the station.

I ring the bell and listen for her footfalls on the other side of the door. Dressed in a thin, silk robe, Elizabeth cracks the door, her face registering pleasurable surprise for my unannounced visit.

Elizabeth leans against the doorframe, eying me up and down like a pair of shoes she can't decide if she wants to slide on her feet or throw to the back of her closet. She fully opens the door, using the motion to straighten her back and stick out her chest.

"Well, if it isn't my husband. To what do I owe this pleasure? Need a little pick-me-up to brighten your day?"

I reach down and pick up an imaginary box from the floor. "I believe this bottle of 'In Your Dreams' belongs to you, *ex-wife*."

She huffs in annoyance, turning to walk into her living room while leaving the door open for me to enter. She takes a seat on the twelve thousand dollar couch I paid for, but am seeing for the first time today.

The room is cluttered with overpriced possessions and feels as cold as the woman who holds court at its center. I wonder if she'll miss this room and the opulence surrounding her, considering her place of residence and cash flow will be sorely lacking after today. A fact I'm happy to keep secret—no point in ruining the surprise.

I walk around the room, eying the novelties designed to show off my ex-wife's wealth. Or mine, if I'm being accurate. My anger simmers like a dormant volcano.

"Why haven't you dropped by the condo to check on Sarah?" I refrain from looking at her as I take a deep breath to control my rising anger. "She's been through hell, and you can't even be bothered to pick up the phone to find out how she's doing? How's the award for 'Mother of the Year' working out for you?"

Her eyes grow wide with barely contained rage as she clutches her robe and jumps to her feet. Her emotion is Oscar-worthy, both in timing and execution.

"Oh, jump off that high horse you rode in on. It was *me* who signed her surgery consent. *Me* who answered the hospital's call. *Me* who was there when she needed her parents. Not you—*me*."

Her face is a grotesque mask of shocked concern. This woman is certifiable.

Silence fills the air as I stare at her. Her hair is matted, darkness evident at her roots. Her face, normally a cosmetic masterpiece, is devoid of product. The small lines around her eyes and lips are recognizable. This is the first time in years I have seen her without her mask of beauty. The ugliness residing within her can no longer be contained as it seeps out and taints her external appearance.

"Don't even try to pin this on me. You had every opportunity to call me when you heard from the hospital. Our daughter could have *died*. Would that have been a good enough reason to call me?" My teeth are clenched so firmly together, I feel a muscle twitch in my jaw.

Her mask instantly drops. The look she shoots me is cold

and calculating. Her brand of evil winks at me beneath her cracked facade.

She walks to the liquor cart and removes the stopper from a brandy bottle, her back to me as she pours. I hear liquid hit the bottom of two glasses before she turns and walks back, handing me a glass before raising the other to her lips.

"You're right. I should have called. I was so distraught, I just forgot. The hospital called, and I panicked. I drove like a maniac to get there. As soon as I arrived, they shoved paper-work under my nose, and Sarah was whisked into surgery. They said her surgery could take hours, so I returned home. A nurse called later and told me Sarah was in recovery, but by then, visiting hours were over. I figured I'd give her some time to recover before bombarding her. Since the accident, my time hasn't been my own. I've been buried under work for the Paws for Vets gala, and I haven't had a chance to slip away."

"Sarah's your fifteen-year-old daughter. *Fifteen*. And you left her *alone* to deal with her pain." My heart hurts for my daughter as my mind returns to that day. "She *needs* a mother. *Deserves* a mother. But you've done everything to strip her of that pleasure."

"Cry me a river. Sarah doesn't care about having me around. Her conversation with the family court judge screamed it loud and clear."

I fist my hands at my sides, never wanting to do someone physical harm more than I do now. "As much as this pains me to say, you have been her mother since she was almost four years old. It's your *duty* to be there. There is no excuse."

Elizabeth approaches me, standing toe-to-toe as she prepares her attack. "Must I say it again? When she was in pain and needed surgery, *I* was there. Not *you*. Don't place your shortcomings as a father at my doorstep."

She knows her words hit their mark. Sarah has always been

my priority, and the fact Elizabeth was at the hospital before I knew about the accident is like lead in my gut.

Feeling she's established dominance in this situation, Elizabeth takes her seat again and looks up at me. "Tell me, where were you when our daughter was scared and in pain? Do you feel guilty you weren't there? Angry? Ashamed? Maybe the same way you felt when you found out that whore, Kate, gave away your child?"

Elizabeth gives me a satisfied smile as she waits for my reaction to the bomb she casually dropped. I taste blood from biting my tongue to keep from lashing Elizabeth with my anger.

Elizabeth has one hell of a poker face, but her jealousy just revealed her hand.

The anonymous envelope with its blackmail demands delivered to my lawyer, just days after the accident, was now in the possession of the Chicago police. A tear-streaked note written by Kate to an infant Sarah, a picture of the two of us, a copy of the birth certificate with Kate's name and my daughter's birthdate, and the copy of the adoption papers I never thought to check.

Like breadcrumbs leading me to the scene of the crime, the evidence pointed directly to Elizabeth. Elizabeth's meticulously crafted blackmail plan demanded I agree to pay her off or face media exposure as the man who, in a rare twist of fate, unknowingly raised his biological daughter from infancy. It was the exact type of story that would stir entertainment news outlets into a frenzy of epic proportions. No one could have predicted Elizabeth's planning would be unraveled by a single phone number written across a random piece of paper stuck, unintentionally, to the back of another sheet.

A single piece of paper had sealed her fate. *Well played irony, well played.*

That phone number led police to a cash-poor private investigator whom Elizabeth hired to follow Kate and learn her routine. The investigator had gone with his gut and kept tabs on Elizabeth after concluding his business with her. His pro bono work, which he willingly handed over to the police, produced evidence linking Elizabeth to Rick Stimas, a man rumored to have ties with an organized crime syndicate, who was hired to scare Kate into leaving Chicago.

As luck would have it, Stimas had been picked up for drunk driving three hours after the accident involving Kate and Sarah. He'd become a little overzealous in his desire to please my ex-wife, resorting to a hit-and-run, for which he was now being charged. Hoping for leniency, he offered Elizabeth's name in exchange for a plea deal from the district attorney.

The case broke wide open following Stimas's statement, coupled with the additional envelope of information my lawyer provided after checking its legal validity. Never have I been so thankful to my lawyer for acting on my behalf before bringing information to me.

At my lawyer's request, the police and the district attorney contacted me yesterday to describe the bizarre tale. I leaned on every available contact at my disposal to secure this meeting with Elizabeth.

I would continue to use my influence and contacts to make sure she and Stimas spend time behind bars for trying to hurt my family. I didn't feel one ounce of remorse for the bastard who nearly killed my girls, nor the viper who hired him to do it.

A good lawyer would get misdemeanor charges of tampering with a birth certificate and stalking dismissed, but no one could get extortion and an attempted murder-for-hire charge dismissed. No one Elizabeth would have the money to hire that is.

My lawyer had earned his annual six-figure retainer all at once, in this single situation. First, with his handling of the anonymous envelope, and second, with the completed paperwork he was waiting for my authorization to file. The paper-work would freeze all of Elizabeth's financial accounts, pending a forensic audit as a result of the criminal charges that would soon be filed against her.

"Let me guess. Kate isn't as shiny as you thought? Holds a few secrets you didn't know?"

Elizabeth waits expectantly for my response as poison spews from her mouth. Her vile words will be the only posses-sions she'll retain after the courts are through with her. I will spare no expense in making sure she can't hurt Kate or Sarah ever again.

I walk to the door, Elizabeth already confirming informa-tion I knew to be true. My purpose in confronting her about the atrocities she's committed has been fulfilled and satisfied.

I open the door and pause, my hand on the handle, knowing the devil is at my back, waiting to witness the carnage her barbs have caused.

"How does it feel to be a failure? Kate made me a father. Gave me a child. Sarah loves her and so do I. Tell me, how does that make *you* feel?"

I hear something shatter as I walk out the door, nodding to the two detectives loitering near the bottom of the stoop. "She's all yours, gentlemen."

As I walk to my Jeep, I think about Elizabeth's lies. They had slithered through my life, fracturing every promise I made to Kate. Elizabeth's pathological deception had stolen our dream and robbed me of time.

Time can't be recovered nor rewound, but it can grant me my forever.

69

KATE

My hand flutters nervously across my lap. This wheelchair is my mode of transportation, for the foreseeable future, until I can kick ass in physical therapy and kick *it* to the curb.

It's been four weeks since the accident, and a little over a week since Elizabeth was arrested, for blackmail with the intent to extort money and attempted murder-for-hire, as well as a handful of additional charges.

Learning she withheld the information about Sarah and wrote the letter that sent me into a dark depression was difficult to swallow. The reason Elizabeth did what she did is a twisted mystery, one we may never solve.

She stole time that cannot be replenished, but I need to make peace with the path of my life and move forward. If I dwell on the time she stole, I won't have room to gather memories the future will offer.

Today's the day. I've finally been cleared for release. Shaw has been here every day. He spent so much time with me, I'm not sure how he has a viable company. Every time I ask, he waves me off and says he's got it covered.

Amy has been a professional rockstar, spinning my story into a passionate public service announcement to eliminate drunk driving. Readers have been sympathetic and under-standing, sending me words of encouragement and support through my social media account, while momentarily forget-ting their demands for the release date of my next book. Janet even granted me an eight-week extension on the deadline for my manuscript, a huge concession that had me *almost* forgiving her for the interview request a few months ago. With Sarah's help, while I've been stuck in the hospital recovering, we've nearly finished my second draft, and I should have no problem meeting the extended deadline.

After much debate, it was decided I'll be moving into Shaw's condo. It was an argument I lost since the condo has better wheelchair access than Amy's house.

Through the stress of this whole ordeal, Amy and Shaw have formed some type of sibling bond. They love to gang up on me, treating me like I'm a toddler, whose only decision-making ability is to decide if I want milk with my grilled cheese sandwich.

I hardly register the knock on the door before Shaw breezes in, a duffel bag slung over his T-shirt clad shoulder. His hair is mussed like he just got out of bed, but I know darn well he's been up since six a.m. His texts about my clothing preferences have been frequent and comical. For a man who prides himself in knowing all aspects of running a successful, multi-billion-dollar company, he is clueless when it comes to picking out women's clothing.

I asked him to pick up something I could wear home from the hospital, considering I wasn't too keen on exposing my backside to the world when I walked—scratch that, *rolled*—out of the hospital.

He bends down and brushes a featherlight kiss across my cheek. "I stopped and picked up your clothes. Amy said she'd bring over dinner tonight after you were settled. Need me to help you get dressed?"

I pride myself in being an independent woman, but I know my injury-induced limitations. Getting dressed is one of my most dreaded tasks, considering the condition of my ribs and pelvis, as well as the cast on my leg. All are healing nicely, but unnecessary movement sends me to my knees, figuratively speaking. "Yeah. I could use your help if you wouldn't mind."

Shaw's instant scowl makes me laugh. "When would I ever pass up a chance to see Naked Kate? I may be many things, but stupid isn't one of them."

He wheels my chair to the side of the bed and leans over to engage the brake. As he places the duffel bag on the bed and removes his chosen outfit, it's my turn to scowl at him.

"Really? Seriously?" My eyes bore into a sparkling sea of blue.

"What's wrong?"

I stare at the outfit as it mocks me from its place on the bed. "What's *wrong*?" I tone down my elevated volume and pull him down to my face, annoyance rolling off my body. "When have you ever seen me wear a leopard print thong, a sequined skirt, or a tube top? Much less, at the same time?"

"Don't knock it till you try it, baby." A wink punctuates his obnoxious delivery.

Don't get me wrong, every piece of clothing had come from my house. I just don't have any idea how he managed to unearth them. If I'm not mistaken, they came from the Goodwill donation box I'd been too lazy to drop off. *Curse you, Goodwill, for making me wear an outfit of regrettable clothing choices.*

"Are you saying you'd rather wear your hospital gown home?" He smiles and raises an eyebrow. "As long as I get the 'behind the scenes' view, you won't get any complaints from me."

A laugh escapes my mouth before I can contain it. It's been

so long since I've seen the playful side of Shaw. *Who am I to condemn him for his help?*

"Fine. Help me get dressed, and let's get out of here."

I use my arms to push into a standing position and place my hands on his shoulders for balance as he bends down, holding out the scrap of leopard material. After I've carefully gotten my foot and my cast through each leg hole, he slides the material slowly up my legs, his thumbs skimming from my outer ankle up to my hip bones. My breath catches as his eyes devour every inch of my exposed skin.

He follows the same steps with the skirt, tugging ever so gently as the tighter material slides over my butt. He leans in, and his breath tickles my ear. "If I'd known you were hiding these gems in your closet, I would have thrown away every other piece of clothing you own."

He flutters his fingers across my throat, stopping to massage the flicker of my pulse as it drums against my skin. "Your body deserves to be covered...in my kisses."

My eyes drift shut, and I feel him lean in to pick up the remaining piece of clothing from the bed. I open my eyes and watch as he bunches my top like a sock. His fingertips graze my shoulders as he carefully pulls it over my head and down to my lower stomach. "Lift your arms just a bit, beautiful."

My body responds on autopilot as he gently pulls the top into place. I have to admit, bringing this top was a stroke of genius. No bra and minimal body movement on my part. Genius or not, I won't be uttering that nugget of information aloud any time soon.

He hooks my hair behind my ear as he places a soft kiss on my lips. The care he uses melts my heart. I look at this man and marvel at our story. We have been stripped of our dreams, robbed of promises, and deprived of time, yet our love has held strong.

He makes a final adjustment to my top, a wolf-like smile tipping his lips.

"What's with the smile?"

"Just committing you and this outfit to memory. No doubt, the visual will come in handy during my next business trip." His overt suggestion has my ears heating, and he chuckles. "Are you ready to bust out of this joint?"

"Absolutely."

I try to hide my wince as he helps me settle back into the wheelchair. Every day gets a little easier, but it will still be a few weeks before I'm pain free.

The nurses huddle around their station as Shaw wheels me toward the elevator. We both wave goodbye as a few catcalls and wolf whistles pierce the air, a definitive confirmation they all see Shaw's awful clothing sense currently displayed on my body.

Embarrassment colors my cheeks as I drop my head and hiss, "Could you go any slower? I think the janitor at the end of the hallway may have missed my outfit."

A chuckle rumbles from his chest as he leans down to my ear. His voice dips low. "I suppose now isn't a good time to tell you I also brought you a cotton sundress as a clothing option?"

"I hate you." I shoot him a death stare over my shoulder, biting back the pain the movement causes. If looks could kill, I'd be needing another driver to take me home.

"You love me."

I glare one more time for good measure. Turning forward, I hide my ghost of a smile. No matter what life chooses to throw at us after we leave this hospital, it will always be filled with humor, happiness, and love.

EPILOGUE

Two months later...

I walk through the sliding glass door, spying Kate, a stocking cap pulled low on her head, wrapped in a thick blanket and snuggled into an Adirondack. I inhale, letting the bite of the night air fill my lungs.

Our honeymoon has been priceless.

The past two weeks have been pure heaven.

Door County had been our immediate choice. We wanted to bask in our memories of two and create new memories with our family of three. The cottage was the place where we could do that, and it was perfect.

Returning to here was like coming home to an old friend. It bombarded us with memories, encouraged our smiles, and willingly absorbed our tears.

Initially, it had been difficult for Kate and me to revisit the finality the cottage represented. But it also harbored the conception of our most precious secret—Sarah. Our daughter, who ultimately brought us back together and was quick to point out her instrumental role in our current happiness.

As I walk across the deck, I recall teaching Kate how to

sail. Kate showing me how to make scrambled eggs. Late night swim contests. Hiking through the woods. Nights wrapped in each other's arms. This place held our memories, keeping them safe until we were ready to revisit the past.

I stop behind Kate, placing my hands on her shoulders while inhaling the fresh scent of her coconut shampoo. Flashbacks flicker to life.

This deck.

Kate wrapped in a blanket.

Head thrown back in ecstasy.

Kate's quiet voice forces me back to the present. "Italian crisis averted?"

"I told Jim if he plans to continue collecting his hefty paycheck, he'll get it sorted on his own and not interrupt my honeymoon again."

I squeeze her shoulders, pushing the blanket and her hair out of the way as I lean down and kiss her neck. Her moan lights a fire within me. I love this woman with every piece of my heart. While it's far from fixed, her love has begun to patch my heart, repairing sixteen years of painful fissures.

I move around the chair and offer her my hand, then pull her to her feet and into my chest. She pushes up on her toes, molding her body to mine, as she brushes a kiss across my lips. Desire snakes through my body as the heat of her core burns through her jeans and mine.

"Unless you're ready to have Sarah walk in on us, again, I suggest you tame this beast." Her hand cups my crotch, giving it a firm squeeze before she backs away. Her eyes trace the outline of my rock-hard cock, and I groan.

"Feisty minx. You would back away from a guy in need?"

She throws her head back and laughs. Her exposed neck begs for an imprint of my teeth. "Considering said guy satisfied his need not once, but twice, this morning, I'd say I'm within my right to back away."

"Speaking of Sarah. Shouldn't she be back by now?"

Kate scoffs and walks to edge of the deck, placing her hands on the railing. "You do realize she's just next door playing cards, right? I think she has a crush on Jason."

Jason. The son of the neighbors next door, who apparently spend Thanksgiving at their cottage every year. *Lucky us and our intended privacy.*

Kate sees a harmless, polite sixteen-year-old rugby player. I see a horny, high school jock who sneaks right under the parent radar with his 'yes, ma'ams' and 'yes, sirs.' *I'm on to you, Rugby Jason.*

"I don't like him for Sarah."

The steam from her breath curls around her head as she looks across the water. "Not really our choice. She's young. There will be others. Some better, some worse. Best we can do is give her support and let her know she can always come to us for anything." I step behind her, caging her body with my own as she peeks over her shoulder. "Luckily, she's only here for the last three days of our honeymoon. Not much can happen in just a few days."

My stare begs her to remember the trouble we managed to get into in as many days when we were young. *Very little can happen if I camp by the cottage door and put bells on the exits.*

Kate is a natural when it comes to being a mother. She's calm, understanding, and loving. I never thought I'd have someone with whom I could truly share parenting. She's my rock, having talked me off more than one ledge this fall.

Fall. We both stepped off the ledge sixteen years ago, and, miraculously, we finally managed to catch each other. I cannot recall a time in my life that surpasses my current happiness.

Following Kate's accident and the news of Sarah's paternity, I wasted no time making Kate my wife. Knowing there was an expiration date on the medical excuse I used to convince her to live with me, I dropped to one knee outside the doctor's office the day she was cleared to drive. She looked at me like I was crazy, not believing me until I pulled out the ring, the thirty thousand dollar lint collector I'd carried in my pocket since Kate's release from the hospital. Tears pooled in her eyes as she whispered "Yes" against my lips.

Unwilling to waste more time, we married a week later in Judge Langdon's chambers. Sarah, Amy, and Jon served as our witnesses, as we legally promised each other forever.

The evening of our wedding, we sat down with Sarah and explained how the events of our past shaped our future. Kate pointed out how Sarah's invitation to dinner was the event that closed the circle and brought us back to each other.

Sarah listened to our story as tears streamed down her cheeks. After we were done, she clasped Kate's hand and spoke with conviction.

"I have no words to explain it, but from the moment I met you, I felt this pull to have you in my life. I used to wish my dad was married to you so you could be my step-mom. Finding out you're actually my mom is the best gift I will ever receive."

Kate had embraced Sarah in a tight hug as I wiped my own tears from my cheeks. Our daughter was an amazing young woman.

One week ago, Elizabeth was found guilty of falsifying government documents for changing Sarah's birth certificate to reflect a birth mother other than Kate. Elizabeth claimed she had sought to protect Sarah, but the judge saw through her tearful statement, sentencing her to three months in a mini-mum-security prison. She will serve her time while awaiting trial for attempted extortion and solicitation of murder-for-hire.

It had taken a few weeks, but the district attorney's office had found two withdrawals from Elizabeth's personal checking account matching the exact amounts Stimas claimed she paid him to get rid of Kate. That information, along with the additional evidence, provide a strong case against Elizabeth. If convicted, she could face a minimum of fifteen years in prison. The district attorney, up for re-election in the spring, has vowed to try Elizabeth's case to the maximum extent of the law.

As far as I am concerned, Elizabeth doesn't deserve one drop of our time or sympathy. She'd been living alimony check to alimony check. Her parents wrote her off in an attempt to save their own high-class social standing. Her life, as she'd known it, is over. I doubt we'll ever hear from her, but my security team has been prepped to eliminate the possibility of any future threats.

I nuzzle Kate's neck as I snake my arms around her, pulling her back tight to my body.

"I remember this. You wrapped in a blanket, the stars above us, Green Bay in front of us, a solid foundation below us." I squeeze her waist and place a kiss on top of her head. "We have so much time to make up for on our way to forever. Are you willing?"

"Without a doubt in my heart. I'm with you today, tomorrow, and always."

ACKNOWLEDGMENTS

First, and foremost, thank you for choosing Kate and Shaw's story. Whether it's the only book you'll read this month or one of five this week, your enthusiasm and support are what encourages me to continue sharing characters and stories offering that temporary escape from reality. Thank you readers!

Sarah Hansen at *Okay Creations*, thank you for your fabulous artistic talents in taking my random ideas and turning them into the perfect cover. You read my mind when I didn't even know what I was thinking!

Jenn Wood, I was lucky to find you. You took my unpolished gem of a story and transformed it into a sparkling diamond. Your editing made Kate and Shaw jump from the page, not just flirt with it.

Karen Gill, my best friend and ALPHA reader, thank you for not blocking my numerous phone calls, texts, and emails! Never did you ever complain when "girls' nights" were spent finding plot holes, re-working scenes or writing a catchy blurb. Not once did you ignore my neurotic questions nor tell me you didn't have time (even though I know you didn't always have it to spare.) Your faith in me is a priceless gift, and your excitement for this book rivals my own. You are my person —my Amy.

My fabulous BETA readers—Norm Jannisch, Kim Norton, Lucy Frieders—thank you for giving up your Thanksgiving weekend to meet Kate and Shaw when their story was still rough and evolving. Your suggestions and comments helped steer me in the right direction.

A shout of thanks to my family. Mom, you recognized my drive and desire to write a book before I realized it within myself. (This is the best version, you have my permission to read it now.) Dad, despite never reading a romance in your life, you were always there to give your opinion and support. My sisters, Andrea, Alyssa, and Ashley, thanks for your help and talking your sissy up to all of your friends.

Lastly, Scott and the 3Ps, I couldn't have gotten to the finish line without you. Your smiles and kisses are the only incentives I need. Big P—I'm counting on you reaching the finish line before I do the next time.

ABOUT THE AUTHOR

Ali Pierce's romance debut, *Fractured Promises*, has been rattling around in her brain, along with a plethora of other stories and colorful characters, for a number of years. Ali makes her home in Northern Illinois with her husband and three children. When not writing, Ali can be found shuttling children to and from school, trying to figure out the formula for a perfect Instagram feed or buried face first in an angsty romance novel. Ali loves to hear from readers. Connect with her on social media or through her website, www.alipierce.com.

facebook.com/alipierceauthor

twitter.com/alipierceauthor

instagram.com/alipierceauthor

goodreads.com/alipierce

CPSIA information can be obtained
at www.ICGtesting.com
Printed in the USA
LVHW091015210519
618356LV00001BA/1/P